CALLISTO

THE AN'EO CHRONICLES
BOOK 1

MYRANDA RAE

Publisher: MyrandaRae.com

Publication date: September 2024

ISBN: 978-1-961031-25-8

Author: Myranda Rae

Email: connect@myrandarae.com

Website: myrandarae.com

Please direct all enquiries to the author.

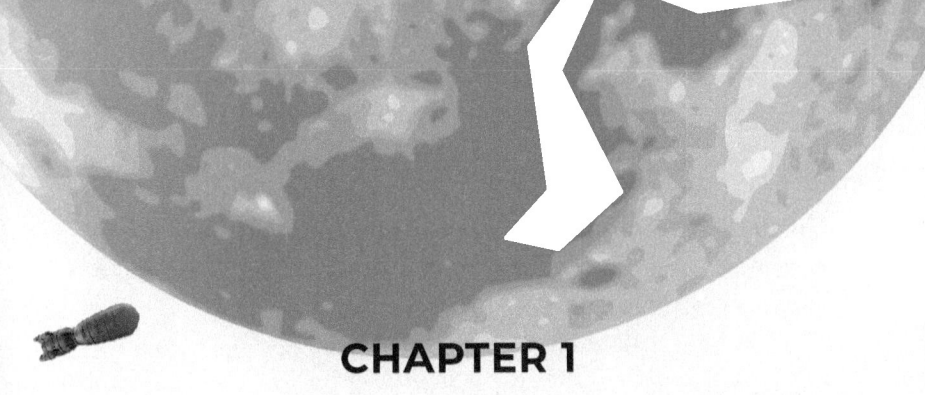

CHAPTER 1

"These dedicated scientists and researchers will usher humanity into a new era. It is with the highest respect and appreciation that we send them forward into the future. Your sacrifices are not lost on anyone here…" The head of LevenCorp speaks. Her words are translated into English through a large, clunky headset, but I'm still having trouble focusing.

This is my last day awake for the next hundred years. I know that we have to attend these celebrations and ceremonies, but I'm antsy to get out of here.

Everyone around me stands and I jump up, just half a beat behind.

"Dr. Abdul Sayyid, Afghanistan - Cytologist, Dr. Alma Perez, Argentina - Geneticist…" She reads through the list, each doctor walking across the stage to thunderous applause. This was cool the first time we did it, the ninth time? Not as much.

"Dr. Nicole Isbel, United States - Anatomist," she reads my name and I walk the length of the circular platform and down the main aisle toward the door. Passing the cameras that are broadcasting this ceremony around the world, I beg silently to the universe, "Please, don't let me trip."

"I wish we could drink tonight, I could use one," I overhear a group talking on my way toward the back door.

I've overheard many similar conversations over the last six months. The extensive process for preparing ourselves to be frozen included a year of no drinking, drugs of any kind, and a very particular alkaline diet.

Most of us would kill for a cheeseburger and fries before we deep freeze.

As I slip through the crowd, I try to keep my head down. I have one last task to complete before tomorrow.

Just as I reach the door, I hear my name.

"Dr. Isbel?"

Turning, I'm met with a microphone shoved in my face by a perky reporter.

"Veronica Salter, channel four," she holds her hand out, "would you mind speaking to me for a moment?"

Plastering on a fake smile, I nod, "of course."

Damn, I was so close to freedom.

"I'm here with Dr. Nicole Isbel, one of the fifty scientists being frozen tomorrow in LevenCorps groundbreaking research experiment aimed at learning more about the preservation of life." She smiles at the camera. "Dr. Isbel, what made you decide to volunteer for this unprecedented project?"

"This is a once-in-a-lifetime opportunity. Science, research, and the human body, that is my life. LevenCorp is giving me the chance to be a part of something bigger than myself, something that will change so many lives for the better."

"Are you nervous? Being put into cryosleep for one hundred years has to be frightening, plunging into the unknown like that…" she probes.

I get the feeling she's hoping that I break down crying to boost her ratings.

"Of course I'm nervous. I turned twenty-seven this year. I only graduated last year, so I'm stopping my life before I've even started it. We're prepared for this, though. The trial groups of one year, three years, and seven years had all positive outcomes. We're learning from those experiences and doing more each time. There always has to be a first group for everything. We're honored to be that group."

"Your parents both passed away. Did that factor into your decision to volunteer for this? Do you think that played a part in why you were chosen?" She smiles like she didn't just ask that.

Weeks of media training and script memorization have equipped me for these potentially awkward moments. Reporters keep trying to throw us off, to make us emotional. They've been digging around in our pasts to uncover any skeletons that might be hiding out in closets. Internationally, this is the biggest news story of the year. We're being almost hunted by eager reporters hoping to have something new to break.

"Well, Veronica," I hope my fake smile is convincing, "The criteria for eligibility to participate was extensive. Physical, psychological, and genetic factors, as well as credentials and health, were all factored into the approval process. There were over seventy-five thousand applicants. LevenCorp was very selective in their process of accepting applicants."

I smile, blatantly ignoring her other, deeply personal questions.

Quickly wrapping up the interview, I all but run to my car before someone else can stop me. Sliding into my backseat, I quickly change from my professional television-appropriate clothes to jeans and a t-shirt.

Letting the top down on my '76 Trans Am, I dart out of the parking lot and onto the open road. Blasting music for the three-hour drive makes me feel relaxed. I set my sights on the palm trees swaying in the breeze.

Leaving Lake City, I can breathe a bit easier. Passing the state line into Georgia, the weight in my chest dissolves. As I drive into tiny Spain, Georgia's city limits, the comfortable familiarity of home washes over me.

Pulling off the quiet two-lane highway, I park in the tree-lined gravel lot.

My body moves on its own, muscle memory leading me to my little spot.

"Hey, Mom and Dad," sitting cross-legged on the grass, I stare at the etched headstones for a moment.

"This is it. Tomorrow is the day, so I won't be around for a while. I promise I'll come to visit as soon as I'm able, after they wake me. I'm nervous." I rub my hands over my dark jeans. "I wish you were here. I could really use some of that Jim and Nancy Isbel positivity right now."

Picking at the tiny clovers that grow in patches in the grass, I just sit in silence until the sun goes down.

"I love you and I miss you both," I blink a tear from my eye. "Next time I see you, I'll be one hundred and twenty-seven years old, technically." I chuckle. Staring at the headstones for an extra minute before I leave. I commit every crack in the stone to memory.

"See you on the other side," I press a quick kiss to my hand before touching each of their names.

Settling back into my car, I drive. Letting myself follow the road, I just wander, no destination in mind, letting the wind blow through my hair.

CHAPTER 2

A pit of churning, twisting nausea rolls around in my stomach. I didn't sleep for one second last night. I figured I'd be getting plenty of rest starting today. I should spend my last hours doing anything else.

From the looks of it, the rest of the crew had the same idea. Everyone looks tired and slightly green.

"Doctors," Mr. Fischer calls all of us. "If we can have everyone move to the holding bunker to begin."

My hands tremble as I fall in line with everyone else. We're herded down the hall and into the underground holding locker. An uncomfortable chuckle slips past my lips as I realize, for the first time, that we're being stored underground. Buried.

Wow, a bit slow on the uptake there Nicole…

We've been briefed repeatedly on each step of the freezing process. I know exactly what's coming, but I'm still nervous.

The next three hours are filled with every embarrassing bodily fluid that they could think of. Blood is drawn, and we have decontamination showers and supplements to prepare our organs for freezing. Evacuations of the bowels and bladders…

Stepping toward my pod, I reach into the large tub of skin protective cream and start to slather it over my body.

"Are you ready for your suit, Dr. Isbel?" One of the lab technicians steps forward to help me when I'm sufficiently greased.

"Yes, thank you."

She pulls my wetsuit-like cryo-suit out and helps me slide my gooey body into it.

"Doctors," Mr. Fischer addresses the crew again, "if you would be so kind as to lie down in your pods, we will be administering the last round of muscle fortification shots. Please stow any personal items in your pod lockers now."

I know we're supposed to put personal items safely away, but I sneak a picture of my mom and dad into a small pocket on the sleeve of my suit. I want them right beside me, watching over me for the next hundred years.

As I crawl into my cryo-pod I am filled with the sudden urge to run. What kind of stupid idiot am I? Who volunteers for something like this?

With frantic eyes, I scan the room. I'm met with the frightened faces of the rest of the crew. Everyone looks like they are working through similar feelings of panic.

"Oh my god, what the fuck am I doing?"

"Freaking out?" The man in the pod next to me attempts to smile, but I can see that he's shaking.

"Why are we doing this? I feel like I'm about to throw up and then pass out."

It's like dominos falling over. Unease spreads through the room, gripping everyone's necks at once.

"Scheiße!" Dr. Schneider jumps out of her pod beside mine to retch into the trash can. We're empty. There isn't anything left to throw up.

The room is suddenly filled with the sound of sobbing, heaving, and labored breathing. Everyone is panicking. Everyone has lost it at once. My mind drifts back to the day, months ago, when we all sat in a room full of LevenCrop lawyers and signed our lives away.

"Under the terms of this agreement, upon defrost, if the

signing party does not reawaken, LevenCorp is released from any and all legal liability..."

The point is to be unfrozen in one hundred years, but the legal discussion had to happen. It's enough to make even the most excited applicants nervous to even think about it. One hundred years is a long time. So many things can go wrong. Each pod has backup generators and solar panels attached to keep them operational under any conditions, but that suddenly doesn't feel like enough.

"Science is your life. You are a part of something bigger than yourself. This is something that could save thousands of people every year... people like mom and dad." I whisper quietly to myself with my eye pinched tightly closed. Trying to ignore the panic swirling in the air around me, I cup my hands over my ears and repeat that sentiment over and over again.

I'm so panic-stricken that I almost notice the nurse poking the gigantic needle into my thigh. Almost.

"We will release Nitrous Oxide into the pods now, for your comfort."

I jump into my pod and try to take deep breaths. I need as much laughing gas in my system as I can get, quickly.

The slight hissing sound of the gas being released swirls around me as the weight in my chest starts to lift. Calming gas is...lovely.

"The doors to your pods will now be sealed. Please film your final video logs." The voice sounds hazy and far away.

A whooshing sound, then a click. I'm locked into my pod. I know that's what's happening but it doesn't make me feel anything. Calming gas really is the best. When my screen lights up, I press record and try to think of something profound to say in my final log for one hundred years. These will be my last words for one hundred years. I want to make them count.

"Today is April third, 1983... in my last video log, I just wanted to say...It would have been nice if you could have given that horrible shot after we got the gas. Umm, also I'm excited to see the world in 2083. I'm grateful for this opportunity even though I'm pretty sure I was about to pass out before the Nitrous Oxide, which is delightful by the way. Anyway, goodbye 1983. Oh! This is Dr. Nic Isbel... Nicole...Isbel, Anatomist. Pod twelve."

Even in the state of mellow detachment, it occurs to me that our final videos should have been recorded before the drugs were administered. I'm sure that whoever watches these, whenever they watch them, will cringe at my drugged-out rambling.

"Doctors," Mr. Fischer's voice sounds far away now, "please, put on your face shields."

Reaching up, I pull my helmet down snuggly over my head. A blue-tinted face shield comes down, which causes me to feel suddenly tired.

As the hissing sound of gas fills my pod again, I slide my parents' picture out of its hiding place. Tears blur my vision as Mr. Fischer speaks.

My eyelids flutter slowly closed as his voice fades, growing softer and more distant with each word. "Godspeed into the future. Good night and good luck."

CHAPTER 3

E verything is spinning. My eyelids are so heavy, that I can't open them, but that's probably a good thing. I feel like I've been violently pulled from a deep sleep, shaken, and spun around to the point of sickness.

Taking deep breaths, with tightly closed eyes, I try to talk myself out of nausea.

"You're not nauseous, it's all in your head. Mind over matter, mind over matter, mind over matter." I chant over and over again.

When the piercing, stabbing headache starts to fade to more of a dull, thumping pain, I peel my eyes open. The glass door to my pod is still sealed shut. I can't see out of it, though; it looks like there is some kind of gray cloth draped over my chamber.

"Hello?"

Reaching up, I pull my helmet and face shield off.

"Hello?"

The heat is sweltering. I can feel myself sweating in my suit. Droplets roll down my neck and collect uncomfortably under my body.

Pulling the emergency hatch inside of my pod, the door whooshes open.

"Hello? Is anyone here?"

Why isn't anyone answering me? As I sit up in the dark bunker, I can't wrap my head around what I'm seeing. Through the darkness, I can make out several pods but they look... broken. Is this a dream? Am I having some kind of cryo-sleep nightmare? They told us this wouldn't happen. They said it couldn't happen.

"Hello?" My voice is hoarse as I scream out into the eerily still silence.

My heart races as I sit, listening for anything. Why is it so dark? I can see the dim glow from the pods next to me, but beyond that, there's nothing. My chest heaves rapidly. I can't breathe.

Sweat drips down the back of my neck. It's so hot in here.

I'm not sure how long I sit here, listening, waiting, hoping that the lights flicker on and someone comes to check on us. If my pod malfunctioned and I was unfrozen somehow, there are supposed to be systems in place for our protection. LevenCorp told us that we would be closely monitored twenty-four hours a day.

Stumbling out of my pod, my feet hit the ground and my hands slide against the metal, slipping over a slick film coating the outside. It's not cloth outside of the chamber, it's...dust. Rubbing my fingers together, the thick grimy coating clumps together in my clammy hand. It looks like no one has been down here in years.

"Hello?" Each time I call out, I sound more frantic. My cracked, dry voice slips unheard into the dark.

My legs wobble as I stagger toward the next pod.

"Dr. Clarisse Schneider - Germany - Epidemiologist" I vaguely remember her from our training and briefings. She was funny and surprisingly carefree for someone who studies diseases for a living.

"Hello?" This time, I don't scream. I barely whisper. My eyes burn as the reality of this starts to become clear. Something is wrong. My brain is still in a fog, but I know this is not how the unfreezing process is supposed to happen.

Clearing the thick layer of dust from the glass on Dr. Schneider's pod, I look at her face. She's still frozen. The slightly blue tint her shield casts on her skin and the utter stillness makes her look like she's dead. It's unsettling.

Wracking my brain, I try to remember the very long and very technical explanation of this process. Letting my hand run over the pod, I let the dim glowing light strip guide me to the locked panel at the end.

"Fuck." How am I going to break into this?

Wobbling back to my pod, I search for something to crack the metal box open.

Feeling around, the only thing I have that would be strong enough to break the lock is my helmet and face shield. Not wanting to damage her pod and harm her in any way, I start hitting the lockbox on my pod.

With each swing, my body feels more and more exhausted. I need fluids and my stabilization medication. Those things should have been given intravenously while I was being brought out of sleep.

The loud clanking of metal echoes as my helmet grows heavier. The box finally dents enough that I can pull the door open. Each bag of solutions was created specifically for us. Taking the two bags of liquid from my broken locker, I hold them carefully. I don't want to lose even a drop.

Each pod is equipped with a medical supply kit if I can remember where it is. My memories are fuzzy. I remember the day of my mother's funeral like it was yesterday, but my father's funeral, which was only forty days later, is blurry.

Crawling on my hands and knees, I run one hand over the paneled sides of my pod, searching for the other doors that I know should be there somewhere. My fingers catch on a small metal latch. When I pull it open, the items inside bring a tear to my eyes. My backpack. The items inside make me laugh, even in this bleak moment. I definitely didn't pack for an emergency situation.

Pulling out my miniature blue shoe keychain, I press it to my lips. It's odd how something so completely useless can bring such a huge amount of comfort in this terrifying moment. It feels like my parents are here with me.

Tucking the keychain into my pocket, I continue to run my fingers over the metal until I come to another latch. The medical locker.

Pulling the small red bag into the dim light of my pod, I search for a kit to start my drip lines.

When I find a package labeled "PICC Line," I gather the bags of hydrating solution. My fingers tremble as I set everything up. I'm an anatomist. I spent eight years learning about the human body. I know every vein, every tiny bone, every system, and every function, but I have never placed an IV line.

Taking a deep breath, I insert the needle into the vein at the crease of my elbow and tape it down against my skin. Setting the bags of solution on top of my pod for elevation, I slump on the floor.

I don't understand what is happening here. Where is everyone? Why did I wake up?

Leaning my head back, I let my eyes flutter closed. For someone who has been asleep for so long, I'm so tired. My body rests, but my mind is in overdrive. Nothing makes any sense. I can't turn off my brain. I have to find answers to my questions. There must be some reasonable explanation for what I'm seeing around me. The fog of cryosleep is leaving me confused and unable to put all the pieces together.

Once I have regained some strength, I'll wake up Dr. Schneider.

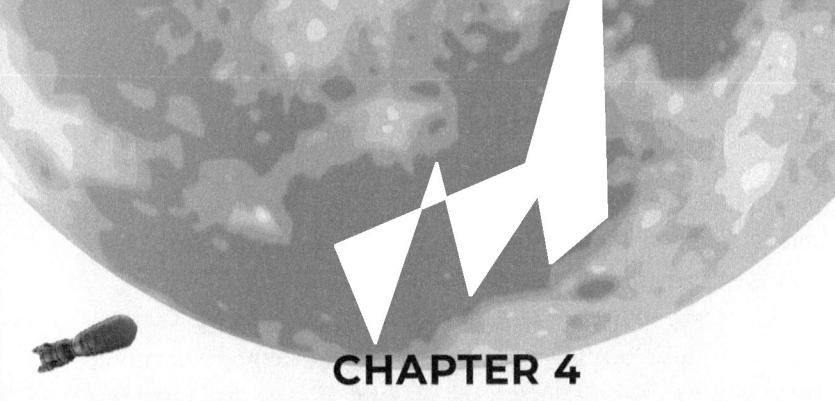

CHAPTER 4

Watching Dr. Schneider come out of cryosleep is like watching grass grow. I've been sitting beside her pod for what feels like hours. When her chamber finally opened after starting the unfreezing process, I started her solution bags. They've been empty for a while now and she still hasn't moved.

"Please, wake up," I whisper, leaning down to check her pulse again. I'm starting to feel desperate.

The quiet is so still and so intense that it's frightening.

Before I started her unfreezing process, I searched for a light switch or something to brighten the room. None that I found worked. In addition to mine, there are only three pods with lights on. Beyond those, the room is pitch black. I ran into several pods as I moved around the room, but I couldn't see inside of them.

"Look, Clarisse, it's time to get up! Get that blood pumping!" I try to cheer her on. Maybe she just needs a bit of encouragement.

Checking her pulse for the fiftieth time, I go back over the other illuminated pods. Dr. Arturo Santiago of Colombia and Dr.

Robert Newton of the United States... looking beyond their pods into the darkness, a shudder rolls down my spine.

There is a sinking feeling in the pit of my stomach, a rolling, gnawing anxiety that I'm trying to push to the back of my mind. Why aren't any of the other pods illuminated?

"How are things progressing over here?" I ask Clarisse enthusiastically, turning my attention away from the looming dread in my mind. If I don't think about it, it's not real. Reaching down to check her pulse, I am met with warmth. She still has no pulse, but her skin has lost the frigid stiffness that it held before.

"Holy shit, Clarisse! You're thawing!" I'm so excited that I momentarily forget the limitations of my body and try to jump up and down.

Pulling myself off the floor, my cheeks are burning—embarrassment over eating it in front of a bunch of frozen people.

"Are you ready Arturo? What about you, Rob? As soon as she's awake, you're next!" I ignore the silence and remove the IV from her arm. I find myself dusting the pods and straightening and re-straightening the medical equipment. The nervous energy I feel won't let me be still for even a second.

After several minutes of agonizing silence, I reach down again. I can't stop checking her pulse. It's probably a good thing she isn't conscious. I'm being incredibly annoying.

"Alright, Clarisse," I whisper as I press my fingers to her neck. The gasp that leaves my throat almost echoes in the bunker.

"Clarisse!" My voice is a shrill scream but I can't seem to control the volume. "You have a pulse!"

Turning to face the other pods, I shout excitedly, "She has a pulse!" No one joins in my commotion. It's so weak it's almost nonexistent, but it's there. A pulse, a heartbeat...signs of life.

As I pace beside her pod, I keep hallucinating movements. Was that a finger twitch? Did her eyelid just flutter? I need to stop staring at her. It's not waking her any faster.

Just to be sure, I recheck everything again. The medical supplies are still straight, and the men are still frozen. As I make my rounds, her pod starts to beep. It's a low, rhythmic tone, a heart rate monitor.

With each passing minute, the beeps become more steady, closer together. I count the beats thirty per minute, forty per minute, forty-five, then fifty-five. They even out at sixty-eight. I keep counting, over and over, checking that she's not slipping too low or climbing too high.

I must count the minutes at least thirty times. It's not an exact science as I don't have a stopwatch so it's left to my best guess to try to restart at the one-minute mark. I have no frame of reference for how long this is supposed to take. I think it's been several hours.

"Clarisse? Can you hear me?" I watch her closely, looking for any subtle signs.

A loud, hoarse, gurgling sound that seems like it might be an attempt at speaking startles me so that I scream. I was looking for a tiny clue, but this was more like a huge, flashing red light indicating progress.

"Dr. Schnieder? Everything is alright, try to stay calm." I completely lie through my teeth. Nothing is alright.

More gabbled, incoherent sounds follow until she finally peels her eyes open.

"Wo bin ich?" She groans and raises her trembling hand to her head.

"Dr. Schnieder, I'm Dr. Isbel, Nicole…I…"

"Where am I?" She pulls herself to sit. It looks like she feels much better than I did.

"We're in the bunker…"

"Where is everyone? Why is it so dark in here? Where is my nurse? Why are you waking me?" Her German accent is thicker than I remember it being.

As I shrug, I hear a strange squeaky sound comes from my

throat. I don't know what to say, sorry, it looks like they abandoned us, seems like the wrong thing.

"Who woke you?" She wobbles slightly as she gets out of her pod to stand beside me.

"I just woke up… I think my pod malfunctioned, but no one came. I've been awake for what I can only guess is a day. It's been dark and silent the whole time…"

For the next hour, she goes through the same panicked, frantic motions that I did. Screaming loudly into the abyss, checking all of the pods, pacing, pulling at her hair, mumbling under her breath in German… the stages of anguish.

She slumps to the floor in front of her pod and sobs. If her stages are anything like my stages, she should be almost ready to accept this.

"We should try to wake the others." She rolls her shoulders back after standing again.

"Should we do both of them at the same time?"

She shrugs, "I don't see why not…"

After we beat the lock boxes open and start the unfreezing process, we sit in our pods, facing each other.

"This is the most difficult part. It takes several hours and there really is no way to know if they're responding positively or if something is going wrong."

"That sounds nervenaufreibend…" she sighs.

"Um… yeah."

She chuckles, "nerve-racking."

"Oh," I laugh too, "it definitely is."

"Dr. Isbel?" She looks suddenly serious. "Thank you for waking me."

"Call me Nic, and, uh…" I suddenly become emotional, everything clumps together in my throat, making it difficult to speak. "Thank you for waking up…" my breath catches and try to smile despite the tears falling. The relief I feel at not being completely alone is indescribable. My whole body feels lighter.

There are so many unanswered questions, but at least I have someone to face this uncertainty with.

She nods understandingly and we sit in silence until she climbs out of her pod.

"I'm going to check the other pods…"

"Clarisse? Do you think it would be… awful if we look through the personal lockers… maybe someone has a flashlight or something we can use?"

"I was just thinking the same thing," she grimaces at the thought.

"I'll start here," I make my way into the darkness.

My skin crawls, it feels wrong digging through people's personal belongings— it's like I'm stealing. We need light to wake everyone else up. That is how I'm justifying this in my head.

"I found a flashlight!" She yells from somewhere beyond where I can see. "Well, fuck! It's not working… I think the batteries must be dead."

I drop my head down against the cool metal of the pod I'm searching through. I've been through six lockers and found nothing that's even remotely useful. On to number seven.

"I'm so hungry," I groan as I break into the next locker. "Why didn't anyone pack food?"

"I found a lighter!" She yells out again. At least her searches are more productive than mine. Jumping up, I make my way toward her as she clicks the lighter. It creates a large circle of light around her.

"Holy shit…"

The bunker is… covered in dust. The long metal staircase that leads to the door is broken and rusted. It looks like nothing has been touched in years.

We stand together in silence, taking in the bunker in disbelief. I feel her fingers against mine, our hands instinctively locking together as we step toward the closest pod.

"I'm afraid to look," her voice wavers.

"Me too, let's just do it, like ripping off a band-aid."

She holds her arm over the pod and we peer cautiously inside.

"Jesus Christ..." I step forward, looking more closely. I'm not sure what I expected, but it definitely wasn't this.

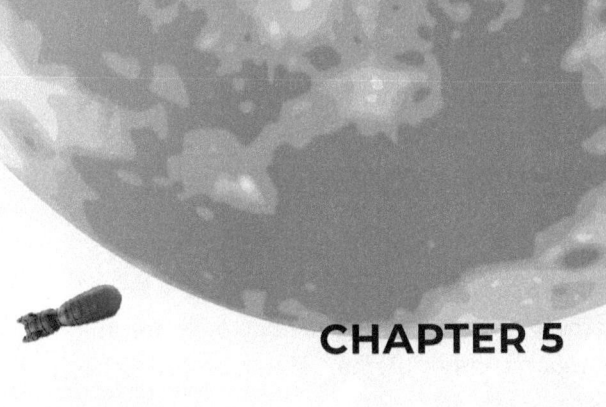

CHAPTER 5

We run frantically from pod to pod, holding the lighter over the glass. Each pod is the same.

"What the hell?" I think I might be sick.

"This doesn't make sense... for this to be real..." Clarisse starts counting in a frenzied panic.

"They've been dead for at least one hundred years." I don't recognize the croaky voice that comes from my own body. This doesn't feel real.

"How?" She sputters, shining the lighter over another pod.

Each pod is the same... dust and tattered pieces of cryo-suits. The aluminum helmets are the only things left intact.

"That amount of decomposition means... at least one hundred years. For the bones to be almost completely gone, it's been at least that, possibly more." I don't have the capacity to be gentle with this right now. "Everyone is dead. It's just the four of us left down here..."

Shouting in German, she starts to pace and pull at her hair.

I slide down to sit on the floor. A thousand scenarios run rampant in my mind. Did they just decide to forget about the project...abandon the whole thing and let us die? Was the government overthrown and there was no time to wake us? Was there a revolution? A war? A pandemic? A flood?

"Why did they all die, and we survived?" She eventually sits down in front of me.

"I don't know…"

"They said that we were each placed in blocks, remember?" She stands and starts to do math again. "If four pods are in a block, maybe ours was the only generator and solar panel that didn't stop working?"

"I thought it was five pods per block…"

She opens her mouth to speak, but the beeping starts from one of the men's pods. After a moment, the next pod beeps too.

I climb into my pod and she climbs in with me, both of us sitting cross-legged, waiting.

"I know we signed paperwork, but… I'm definitely suing." She purses her lips.

"You and me both! I think we've got a pretty solid case."

The wait feels shorter with her here. The desperation isn't as heavy. When their heart rates start to even out, a regular rhythm echoing through the bunker, I brace myself for the trauma we're about to inflict on them as they wake.

Dr. Santiago starts to move first, the deep, confused groan coming from his pod.

"Welcome back, Dr. Santiago."

Bewilderment, disorientation, anger, frustration, disbelief… he moves through the stages with quiet dignity. Only the furrow on his brow shows the different emotions he's working himself through.

He climbs out of his pod and follows Clarisse around the bunker, looking at the pods. He stops, paying particular attention to the rusted, broken staircase.

"We have to try to get out of here…" he starts pulling at some of the metal tables that line the walls of the room. "We're going to have to climb."

The sudden, loud beeping of Dr. Newton's pod catches all of

us by surprise. The rapidly growing rhythm reaches at least one hundred beats per minute in no time, then quickly surpasses that.

"His heart is beating way too fast," I search around helplessly for something that we use to aid him.

All of us work frantically, trying to wake him or move him into a position that might help. When the beeping stops suddenly, I start chest compressions while Clarisse tries mouth-to-mouth.

After several minutes, when all hope is lost, I stop. My arms can't keep up with the rigorous movements or strength needed to keep going. Clarisse stops and looks up with tears in her eyes.

"He's gone..." I sob and step away from his pod. Biting into the back of my hand, I try to stifle my cries. I can hear Clarisse and Arturo quietly sniffing and crying.

I didn't know Dr. Newton, but he survived all of this, whatever this is, only to die during reanimation. It doesn't seem fair. The circumstances that led to only four of us making it through this are still unknown but to have lost him, a complete stranger is breaking my heart in a way that I can't comprehend.

Slamming my hands down on the metal in front of me, I'm suddenly so angry that my body shakes.

"Why the fuck are we down here? Where is everyone... all the doctors and nurses that were supposed to be here, round the clock, watching over us? He shouldn't have died! There should have been people here to help him! None of them should have died!"

Clarisse comes to stand beside me. Her glossy eyes look toward the pods in the darkness.

A loud scraping sound startles us both. Arturo is dragging a table across the floor again.

"We can't wait around. We need food and water. No one is coming for us." He starts to put the tables together, creating a platform below the partial staircase.

"How can we help?"

"We're going to need to stack a table on top of these, that way we don't have to use so much arm strength pulling ourselves up." He shakes the tables, finding one that doesn't wobble.

The three of us lift and adjust the table so that it's sitting directly below the metal hanging onto the platform where the door is.

We each pack all the items that we can from tables and lockers, we don't know what we're walking into.

"Lightest should go first. The others will hold the table steady." He says as we both look at Clarisse.

She nods and climbs up onto the first table, then the second. The metal creaks as she reaches for it, pulling herself up onto the platform.

"Open the door and wait there. Be ready to grab her if the metal starts to separate!" He holds the table steady, gesturing for me to climb up. My palms sweat as I climb onto the second table.

"It looks abandoned…" she calls down after reappearing in the doorway.

Light is shining in through the open door, beaming down on us. Sunlight. We're almost there…if I make it.

The way the metal creaked when Clarisse grabbed it keeps playing over in my mind. I'm on the shorter side, so it might take some pulling to get myself up there. I'm definitely heavier than she is.

"Is this going to support my weight?"

"It will!" She sounds so sure as she kneels down in the doorway, holding her hand out to me.

Slowly standing up on the second table, I grab the handrail and swing my legs up onto the bottom step, crawling onto the platform and quickly out of the door.

"See! Easy!" She smiles, ignoring my winded panting.

"Alright, Dr. Santiago," I can't help the way my heart pounds.

"Please, call me Santi, my friends do," he smiles before climbing onto the second table. He looks nervous as he stands slowly, the table wobbling slightly below him. When he grabs ahold of the arm rail, I feel the ground shake beneath my feet. The metal screeches as he climbs onto the platform. On instinct, we both reach out and grab his arms, pulling as he jumps through the door.

"See," he puffs, "not so bad!"

As soon as the words leave his mouth, the loud clanging crash of the platform and remaining stairs hitting the ground echo through the bunker.

No one says anything, we just adjust ourselves and look around the room. This room is full of monitors, rows of desks with machines on each of them, covered in thick layers of dust. The large window on one side of the room is mostly broken.

"The door is locked." Clarisse shakes the handle, and it breaks in her hand.

"I guess we're going through the window." I use my backpack to knock the few remaining shards of glass onto the ground.

Stepping outside, we're directly behind a large, overgrown bush. Aside from the wind rustling through the leaves, it's eerily quiet out here, too.

"Sangre de Cristo!" Santi gasps.

When I turn to him, he's staring wide-eyed at the sky, using his hand to draw a cross over his body.

"What?" I turn to look in the direction of his gaze and I stumble back. "What is that?"

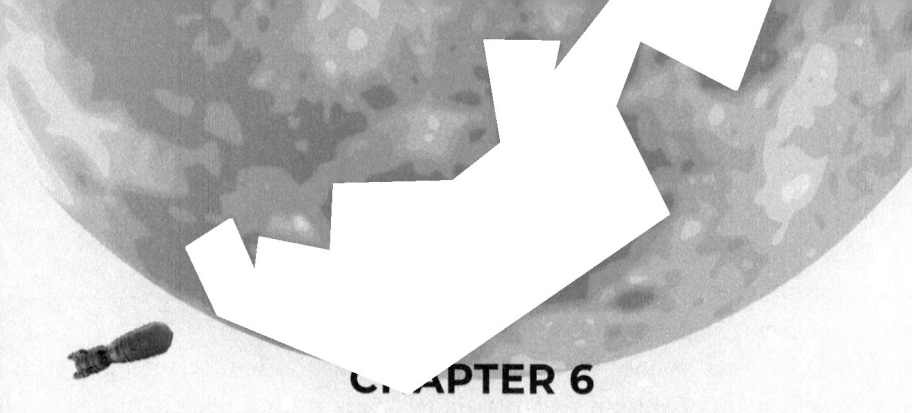

anging in the sky, directly above us, is a planet. It's so close that it looks like we could jump up and touch it. It has clusters of light spread across it, like looking at a city from far away.

It's beautiful and terrifying.

"Did either of you see Star Wars?" Clarisse is the first to speak.

"Did we get invaded by aliens? Intergalactic war... maybe that's the death planet..." Santi's voice is dazed and far away.

"The Death Star," I don't know why I correct him. Who cares?

Peeling my eyes away from the planet, I take in our surroundings here, on earth. It looks...new. Most of the LevenCorp building is demolished, with some heaps of rubble left. Beyond us, there is only grass and trees. Everything looks peaceful. Birds chirp in the trees. A gentle breeze blows through my hair.

"What do we do now?" I try to get their attention, but both of them are still staring up, mouths agape and eyes wide.

"I guess we should go look for help? Maybe...quietly, just in case?" Santi finally pulls his gaze from above.

"Come on, Clarisse," I take her hand and gently tug. I don't think she even realizes that we're walking.

After several minutes, my mind starts to wander. Where is everyone? Are we in danger here? A large planet is hanging over our heads that definitely wasn't there before but... what happened?

Santi stops, turning around to look between us and the ground. Isn't this where the road used to be? The entrance to the LevenCorp compound, the big gate... that should be right here, I think..."

He's right.

There is nothing here, no road, not even pieces of broken asphalt or part of the gate. It's like none of it ever existed.

"Apples!" Clarisse screams as she runs across the grass toward a cluster of trees. Santi and I quickly follow. I'm already salivating before I've even picked one.

"Maybe we should inspect them to make sure they're safe to eat?" He suggests as Clarisse takes a large bite.

"Tastes fine!"

I grab two apples and eat them so quickly I'm not sure I chewed once. For several minutes no one speaks, our ravenous eating is all we care about.

"Let's pack as many of them as we can carry," I open my backpack and start picking every fruit within reach.

"Should we just walk until we find someone?" Clarisse looks nervous like she's thinking the same thoughts that have been running through my head. What if we don't want to find someone...

"We could walk until we find a car or something..."

"What if..." I feel stupid for even suggesting this, but at this point, I don't have anything to lose. "We could walk toward my hometown. It's about a four-hour drive so it will take... a long time walking but..."

"Where is it?"

"Northwest of here, in Georgia. Spain, Georgia." I point to the left of where we're standing.

"Let's go!" Clarisse adjusts her small leather backpack that is more for fashion than actually carrying anything.

After at least a few hours of walking, I feel like I'm about to pass out from the heat. Cryo-suits are not ideal for hot Florida weather. I was born in the south and used to handle this heat and humidity. I guess I've become less tolerant in my old age. I can't help but chuckle at myself. Old age.

The grass starts to feel sponegy like it's full of water. Eventually, water pools around our feet with each step.

"Are we approaching a marsh?" Clarisse bounces on the squishy grass.

"We shouldn't be. There are a few wetland nature preserves in between LevenCorp headquarters and home but we shouldn't be inside of one. Unless I'm really lost..." I look up toward the sun. "This is the right way..."

With cautious steps, we continue on, walking through the increasingly wet grass. In the distance, the air above the ground looks distorted. It's either a mirage or there really is water ahead. It's not just the puddles we're walking through, there's a lot of water.

"Is that a lake?"

Movement out of the corner of my eye catches my attention.

"Look," I point to the right. Something is moving out there.

"What is that?" Clarisse takes a step forward. "It looks like..."

It hits me all at once. With a panicked yelp, I grab her arm and yank her back. "We need to get away from this water! Crocodiles, it's crocodiles!"

This makes no sense, there shouldn't be crocodiles this far north... in this area that didn't use to have water...

"We'll backtrack," Santi runs ahead, leading us further from the water. "It might take longer to figure out a way around, but we can't go through."

As the sun starts to drop in the sky, a purple hue streaks through the atmosphere. No one speaks, but I know they are watching it as closely as I am. The more the sun sinks, the brighter the purple begins to glow.

"Should we stop here for the night?" Clarisse looks exhausted, sweat dripping down her face.

"Maybe we should find a place with a bit more cover..." Santi suggests as we flop down onto the grass.

With a heavy sigh, he joins us in the grass. As we lie in silence, staring up at the sky, the distant memory of camping with my parents comes to mind. This sky would absolutely blow their minds.

"We haven't seen anyone all day," Clarisse whispers, and I'm not sure if she's talking to herself or us.

Both of us hum quietly in acknowledgment.

"We haven't seen anything, not a car, not a building... a few crumbled remains, but no intact structures..." I roll onto my stomach to see them. "Also, the water... there didn't use to be a lake in that location... or crocodiles this far north."

"So, maybe there was some kind of natural disaster." Santi points up toward the sky. "It still doesn't explain that."

The glowing blue and purple remind me of jellyfish. When I was a little girl, I went to the aquarium with my parents. The jellyfish exhibit was a dark room with recessed lighting inside the tanks. They were incandescent, glowing balls of blue, purple, and bright white. That's what the sky looks like, but it's coming from an unknown cosmic body.

"It's almost impossible to look away from it, isn't it?" Clarisse sighs, a dreaminess in her voice.

"It's like lying inside a lava lamp," Santi yawns.

When my eyes flutter open, it's daylight. The glowing purple sky has faded to blue and the sun is beating down on my already sweaty face. We've walked for two days and still not come across a single soul.

"Good morning," I sit up as Santi tosses me an apple. "We should make it to my hometown tonight."

He nods, biting into another apple.

I appreciate that neither of them has mentioned the very real probability that we will get to my hometown and it will be completely wiped away like everything else seems to be. Deep down, I know that's likely what we will find, but until I see it with my own eyes, it's nice to pretend.

Clarisse sits up and reaches for an apple. As she opens her mouth to speak a low, humming sound makes us all freeze. It sounds like the whirling vibration of a fan and it's getting closer.

Jumping up, we run, taking cover under nearby trees. After a moment, the sound disappears and I can't help but wonder if we are experiencing collective hallucinations.

"Let's go," Santi whispers, and ushers us back on course.

As the afternoon approaches, we're met with another strange sound.

"Is that…water?" Clarisse tilts her head, listening intently.

It sounds like rushing water. Each step we take brings us closer to the source of the sound. Between the trees, we can see it. A wide, rapidly moving river cuts directly through the forest. It looks like it popped up out of nowhere. There is no bank on either side, just trees, then an immediate drop down into the fast-moving current.

"What river is this? None of this makes any sense!" I grip a tree tightly to peer out over the edge.

"Look," Clarisse points to a huge hunk of cement sticking up out of the water.

"An overpass?"

This is the first manufactured structure we've seen since leaving the ruins of the LevenCorp bunker.

"Do you think we can use it as a bridge?"

We just stare at each other, nervously playing through every possible scenario.

"We could walk along the edge until we find a slower area,"

Santi suggests, but Clarisse is already charging ahead. He mumbles something under his breath, but I don't quite catch it.

When we reach the overpass, my nervousness grows. The cement looks corroded and I'm not sure it will hold our weight.

"We should go one at a time, just in case," I gesture to Clarisse. She is the lightest, after all.

"Go ahead," she takes a step back.

Taking a deep breath, I climb up onto the cement, using the exposed metal rods to get to the top.

The top is flat and smooth. Jogging, I quickly reach the other side and climb down, clinging to a tree to keep from falling.

Clarisse goes next. As soon as she reaches the top, her eyes widen. We all hear it, but it's too late. The cement crumbles at the base, falling into the water. Her scream pierces my heart as the overpass quickly sinks.

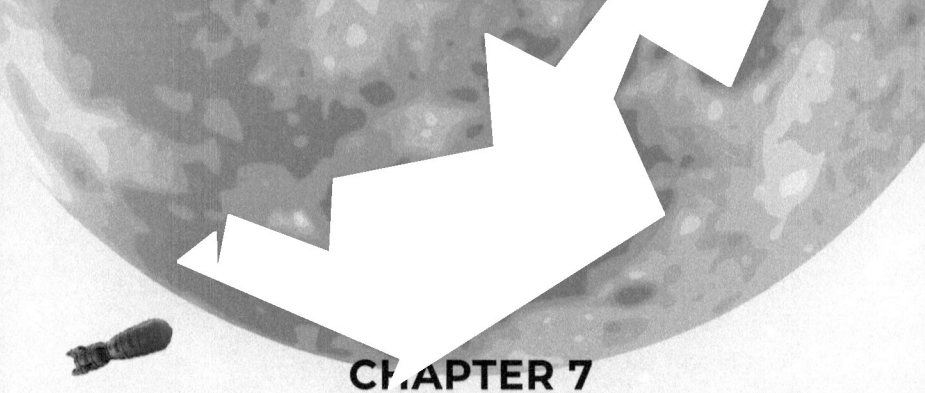

CHAPTER 7

"Clarisse!" I scream and reach out as if it would help somehow.

The cement rumbles and falls completely into the rushing river. My mind and body don't have time to process my next move before a flash of light momentarily blinds me. Squinting toward the sky, I'm met with… something floating above the water.

Is it a flying train car? A cryo-pod? It's difficult to tell.

Someone dives down into the water and reemerges only a few seconds later, with Clarisse in her arms. A metal ladder is lowered down and the person climbs up, one-handed, holding Clarisse.

A moment later, the same person is hanging on the ladder in front of me, gesturing for me to come. It's a woman…

My body is frozen.

I'm hallucinating. This isn't real.

When she grabs me and yanks me up into her arms, I'm so confused that I hardly realize that we're inside. She looks human but…not. She's too big, too strong… too silver.

She dumps me beside a trembling Clarisse and goes down the ladder again for Santi. With my arm around her shoulders, I hug her tightly while looking around the strange vehicle. It doesn't look like an airplane, but it's hovering in the air. There are three more... people in here with us.

One of them steps forward and speaks just as the woman climbs in with Santi in her arms.

He keeps speaking, but I don't recognize the language. Looking at the others, I can tell that they don't either.

When he steps closer, bending down, I can see his eyes and I gasp, stumbling back. The woman who saved us pulls a visor from her face and I can see her eyes, too. Blues, purples, and greens swirl together. It looks like the galaxy, speckled with stars. They all have long silver hair and silvery skin.

Well, for a moment they had silver skin. The woman's skin seems to be changing color. The silver is fading into a rich brown.

"Oh, my God," I gasp as the man's skin starts to change color, too. Santi frantically utters something in Spanish, and the man turns to him, replying in Spanish.

"You speak English?" The woman asks with a light, clear accent.

Clarisse and I stare with open mouths. I think I may have nodded my head.

"Are you of Earth?" Her head tilts to one side as she asks.

"Of Earth?"

"Yes." She offers no further explanation. Reaching forward, she takes some of my lifeless hair up between her fingers, studying it.

"Um... yes."

They turn to each other, speaking their language so rapidly that I can't even piece together enough to figure out where they are from. Are they speaking Russian? It doesn't sound like any language I've ever heard.

"He kept asking if we're from here..." Santi whispers. "They speak many 'earth' languages, he said."

"Do you have more companions?" The man turns to me, the same curiosity in his eyes as the woman had.

"No, we don't," Clarisse answers for me when I don't respond.

Of Earth.

Of Earth? Does this mean they aren't... of Earth? They definitely look...different. I want to scream, to run away, to escape them. Instead, I sit motionless, cold sweat rolling down my spine.

"We will take you to our leader." She nods her head and turns, walking away to speak to the others.

"Where are you taking us?" Santi asks the man as he turns to leave as well.

He replies with what I can only assume is the name of a place.

"I-Is that here? On Earth?" I'm frantic. They aren't taking us to space, are they?

"Yes."

The spaceship... thing, turns and starts to move, heading southwest.

"Where is everyone? What happened here?" I can't make my mouth stop talking. The need for answers is overriding my common sense right now. I don't know these people, I don't know what they want from us. I should be quiet, but I simply cannot.

"When we arrive, our commander will see you."

"Are you...aliens? Are you from that planet?" I point toward it.

If they hear me, they don't show it.

Giving up, I sit with the others, deciding its better not to annoy them. They might fling me out. Maybe that would be a good thing... After about fifteen minutes of quiet whispers and nervous glances, something catches my attention through the closed glass door.

"Holy shit! What is that?" I scream much louder than I meant to.

Outside, there is a vast open wasteland, a large crater-like desert that stretches out for miles. Crawling toward the door, I look down as we pass over the area. A tightness forms in my throat the longer I stare at it.

"Where are you taking us?" I turn back, looking at the woman.

"We told you," she repeats the name we don't understand.

"Yes but, where is that?" I try again.

She brings me a tiny, paper-thin television that fits in my hands. It looks like a clipboard, but it's electronic somehow. There is a map on it that is moving…

"Here," she points.

"Peru?" I study the map. "Is this red dot us?"

"Yes."

Turning in horror, I look at Santi and Clarisse. "We're over the Gulf of Mexico right now."

"Where is the water?" Santi is pressed against the door, looking down at the sand that has changed from barren emptiness to having speckled trees here and there.

"Soon," Is all she says before taking the small television from my hands.

Just as she said, we're soon sailing over the vast blue ocean.

"How are we moving so quickly? It doesn't feel like we're moving at all…" Santi looks around in amazement. "We will be there in no time at this rate."

"Do you think they're planning to kill us?" I whisper to Clarisse. The terror on her face tells me that she's wondering the same thing. It's a very real possibility that they are hostile. Did they wipe everyone out? Have they taken everyone hostage? Are humans slaves?

"Should we try to escape?"

I look around, searching for a way out when the woman comes back. We both freeze caught red-handed.

"Here," she points to the map again. We're flying over the Pacific Ocean, parallel to Colombia. We will be flying above Ecuador and into Peru in a matter of minutes.

Santi stands, a tear dripping from his eye before he can stop it. Looking out over the vast blue expanse, he hangs his head. "La Madre Patria."

Our... rescuers...captors...killers? I'm not sure what to call them yet. They watch him thoughtfully but with slight confusion on their faces.

I take this opportunity to really look at them. They have all removed their visors by now, revealing the same incredible eyes. Their skin tones are different, and the woman has softer, more delicate features, but they are otherwise the same. Their hair is long and silver, and they are all the same height with the same muscular build.

They are wearing tactical-looking uniforms... military, maybe? I remember how easily she carried each of us up the ladder, one-handed, never struggling. She didn't even appear winded after the third trip.

Their skin is so flawlessly smooth, not a single blemish or imperfection in sight, not a scar or mole... They are breathtaking in a chilling way.

"We have arrived," the man who hasn't spoken to us steps forward. "When we bring you inside, do not touch anything." He looks at us with thinly veiled disgust.

As he speaks, I tear my gaze from them to look out. We're approaching a city that only helps to confirm my suspicions. They are definitely alien. No human could build such structures. Everything gleams white against the lush green countryside. The soaring buildings look like castles or cathedrals built in lines that point straight up to the sky. The entire city is imposing and beautiful, inspiring awe and fear in the pit of my stomach.

We land in front of the largest, most stately building in sight. Three towers rise from the sides and center. Clarisse and Santi look equally amazed, their eyes flitting back and forth over everything in front of us.

"Remember, do not touch," he warns again before ushering us away from the crowd that is starting to gather.

As we are led inside we are surrounded by a sea of gigantic silver-haired people. They watch us with unsure curiosity. I feel like an animal caged in a zoo, a spectacle being observed for entertainment.

"This way to the holding cells," he says, and I trip over my own feet.

"Wait, holding cell?"

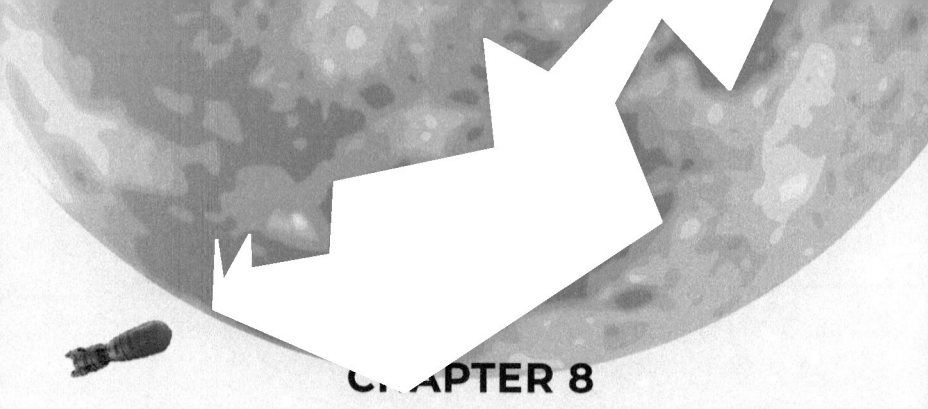

CHAPTER 8

Turns out that alien jail is a lot like a spa.

"Eyes closed," the woman who roughly scrubbed my body clean instructs before dumping water over my freshly washed hair. The large pool of bubbling water smells so delightful that I would never want to get out if I had a bit of privacy.

Looking down at my hands, I try to keep my eyes on my space at all times. I'm no stranger to the human body, but being stripped and scrubbed by a stranger in front of, essentially, more strangers is a bit much.

"Come," she pulls me out and begins pouring liquids from bottles onto her hands. When she starts to rub it in, I yelp. I can apply my own lotion, thank you.

Clarisse seems to have abandoned her feelings of fear and trepidation, relishing in the pampering that we're experiencing. Her contented sighs and relaxed groans fill the room every few seconds.

I am still tense. Being washed by someone else isn't something I've experienced since I was a little girl. I can't say that I'm enjoying it quite as much as she is.

I notice that the woman in charge of cleaning me appears to

be studying me. I can't see her body as clearly as she can see mine, but I'm using this moment to study her as well. As scared as I may be, I'm also fascinated. Their skin and build are so different from ours but somehow...not. As she scrubs me, I note how similar our skin color is, though she is free from the freckles that dot my face or any scars or visible pores. Fascinating.

I want to touch her hair. The silvery strands are perfect, lush, and pin-straight. There isn't a single broken piece. Her eyes are the same as the others, the Milky Way staring right at me.

The scientist in me wants to learn everything. Our sameness, our differences. I'm so curious that it's maddening. I have unending questions. I have to keep my jaw clenched tight otherwise, they might slip out. Why are they all the same height? Why do they have the same hair and eyes but different skin tones? How did they have silver skin before? What was that? Do men and women have anatomical differences? Their bodies are so similar...

"Your hair is... so odd," her face crinkles in confusion. "Why does it clump together?"

"I need a comb," I defensively run my fingers over the matted tangles.

"A comb?"

Using my fingers, I comb through my hair. "It's a plastic or metal item with prongs used to separate tangled hair."

"Tangled?" She says something in her own language as she inspects one of the knots.

The woman cleaning Clarisse comes over, picking through my hair. They mumble to each other and yank my head around while they study.

"Ouch," I pull back, angrily working a clump with my fingers.

"Do these hurt you?" One of them asks with wide eyes.

"Only when they're pulled..." I huff. This would be much easier with a comb. "Do you not brush your hair?"

"No, our hair doesn't clump."

Fascinating.

"Your strange body will not fit into our garments, but it is all we have." One of them hands me a neatly folded outfit.

My strange body...ouch. Rude but not inaccurate. Compared to them, I am short and stubby, with more curves than muscle. The material is so soft, and it stretches some. I struggle to get it over my hips, but eventually, it fits. The shirt is tighter over my chest than I'm used to, but not by much. The length is where I really run into trouble. I have to roll the bottoms up around my ankles and the sleeves over my wrists in order to use my hands and feet. Clarisse is taller than me but still has to roll her pants. I don't check on how Santi is faring.

When I'm dressed, I notice both of them staring at me.

"What?"

"Are you fully formed?" One of them finally asks.

"What? Of course, I am!"

They whisper back and forth in their language, watching me curiously the whole time.

"Are you fully matured?" The other one asks and I hear Clarisse failing to cover her laughter.

"Yes, I am."

This seems to confuse them even more.

"Is your male counterpart fully matured?" They turn to him.

"Yes, we're all fully matured adults..." He answers them, his voice clipped.

"How odd. You won't grow taller?" She looks back and forth between the three of us.

"No. I'm fully formed," my voice is a bit snappier than I meant for it to be.

"You are not the same height as your companions." This isn't a question, but she sounds confused.

"People can vary widely in height and weight. We don't have the same common traits: eye color, hair color, or body type as you seem to. Even people from the same family are varied. We are not related at all, so it stands to reason that we look different. We aren't even from the same country."

They start speaking quickly to one another again, walking out of the room, and leaving us standing alone.

"Can you imagine not having to brush your hair?" Clarisse is running her fingers through her thick blonde waves.

"No! I can't believe-"

"Come," one of them peeks her head back into the room.

"Oh, sorry," we quickly walk after them, barefooted.

"We do not have footwear for you. You will have to go without until appropriate sizes can be manufactured." She must have noticed that I'm staring at my feet.

"They think we're kids?" Santi whispers, leaning toward me.

"I guess we are much shorter than them…"

"They're acting like they've never seen a person before." his eyes are wide as he considers this. "How can-"

The women stop, bowing their heads slightly as the grumpy man comes out into the hallway, the one who told us not to touch anything. On instinct, I look down at my bare feet. Whatever he's saying to them, he doesn't sound happy.

The longer we stand here, the more nervous and uncomfortable I feel. I don't understand what they're saying but it's blatantly obvious that his irritation has something to do with us. After a moment he sighs and steps to the side, letting us pass.

Continuing down the hallway, I'm struck by the absolute enormity of this place. This corridor seems endless, turning and merging with others, door after door after door… The ceiling is so far up it's hardly visible. The vastness makes even them look small. I feel like a speck of dust, inconsequential. I rub my hand over the pocket on my shirt, feeling the picture of my parents, trying to draw whatever strength from it that I can.

When the hallway flows into an open lobby at the bottom of a long staircase, they stop again.

A woman appears at the top of the stairs. She motions with her hand, and we're moving again, walking up. People…

aliens… gather again. Groups of them stopped to watch us, the freak show on parade.

Santi's words play over in my mind. If they've never seen people before… does that mean that there was no one here when they arrived? How is that possible?

At the top of the stairs, we're met with a large room, a great hall, crowded with people. The towering mass of silver-haired aliens gathered to watch whatever is about to happen makes my stomach turn.

"Oh, god, they're about to kill us…" I choke. Human, alien, from the Colosseum to the witch trials… death as a mass spectacle must transcend species. They're about to kill us… or maybe force us to slaughter each other while they watch…for entertainment.

Flop sweat runs down the back of my neck. As we approach the end of the line, a single man is seated at the front of the room. We make eye contact and everything fades away.

My mouth hangs open, and I don't even care enough to close it. When he stands, the ground shakes beneath his feet, or maybe that was just my knees trembling.

I take a step forward on instinct.

Just like the others, he has silvery white hair, captivating galaxy eyes, and height, but there is something about him. He's entirely different. His power is tangible, hanging in the air. I feel myself shrinking, melting into the ground under the scrutiny of his gaze.

His face is emotionless. If he's angry, intrigued, or hostile, I can't tell.

He turns to the woman who rescued Clarisse. I hadn't noticed her standing off to the side. As they speak, she squares her shoulders. His voice is like thunder. It booms and shakes me to my core.

Another woman steps up from beside her. It almost looks like she's pleading our case. She physically puts herself between us, standing, her posture aggressive, with her back to me. Her voice grows louder and more agitated as they talk, but he never falters. His tone and volume never change, but they don't have to. He has the entire room hanging on his every word. I can't even understand him and I'm captivated.

After several minutes, he closes his mouth tightly, his jaw clenching. With narrowed eyes, he looks directly at me. My legs wobble and I choke on... nothing. He shakes his head, almost like he's disappointed, and turns, speaking to the woman again.

Without another glance, he marches away, disappearing.

The woman turns around, a wide smile on her face, "humans! Follow me!"

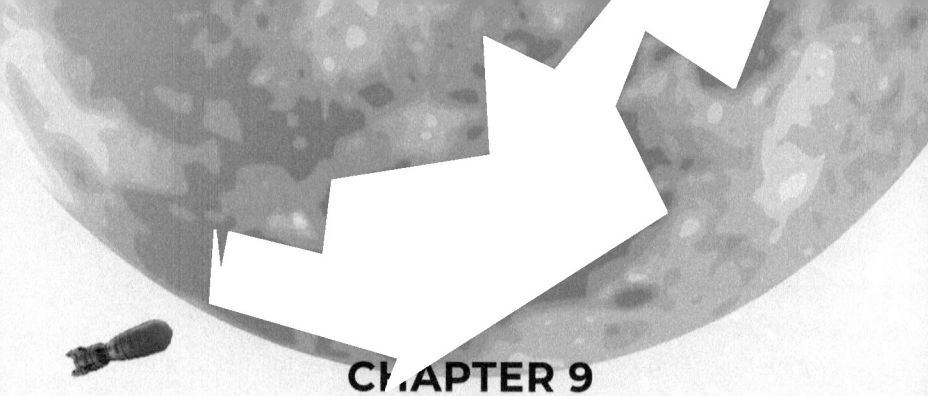

CHAPTER 9

The crowd disperses the spectacle clearly over for today.

"Would you like food before your interrogations?" The woman gestures for us to follow her.

"Interrogations?" Santi audibly gulps.

"Yes, do you need food first?" She smiles again.

Someone must have answered her because the next thing I know, we're following her through a side door. I can't think of anything beyond being interrogated. Are they planning to torture us? What do they want to know? I don't know anything... I'm the one with questions!

She leads us into a room that looks like a kitchen, maybe. One wall is lined with shelves with baskets full of colorful fruits. Some I recognize, others are definitely not from here.

We all stand uncomfortably in the middle of the room, no one daring to reach for anything.

"Eat..." She looks confused.

Stepping forward, Santi pulls an avocado from one of the baskets. Clarisse and I shrug. It's something familiar at least.

When he bites into it, pulling the rough skin from his mouth, she looks horrified. Quickly taking the fruit from his hand, she moves around the room, gathering items. When she pulls out a gleaming sword-like knife, we all take a self-preservational step back.

With effortless grace, she slices the avocado and lays the thin, perfectly symmetrical pieces onto a dish. After it's sliced, she selects several more odd-looking fruits from the baskets and slices them.

"Eat." She slides the dish toward us.

Avocado and banana, I know. The rest is unknown and slightly jarring. One of the fruits has dark blue skin and creamy almost custard-like flesh inside. Another is deep purple and shaped disturbingly like a hand. When she cut it, it oozed red liquid onto the plate. I'm not convinced that it isn't, in fact, a hand...

Clarisse reaches out and picks up a slice of something slimy. It looks like a green peach. When she eats it, her face changes from nervous to pleasantly surprised.

"It tastes like a mixture of orange and cherry," she shrugs and reaches for another.

Santi takes slices of the recognizable earth fruits. Not wanting to be rude or disrespectful, I reach for the dark blue...thing.

"This tastes like vanilla pudding," I take another bite. It's delicious.

The woman smiles and pulls several glasses down. "Water or A'shuur?"

"What is A'shuur?"

"It is a liquid made from the juice of the Shuur plant." She pulls out a clear bag full of iridescent pink liquid.

"We'll try that!" Clarisse smiles. I would kick her if I could.

"It's very refreshing." The woman smiles and pours a glass for all of us.

"Prost!"

"Salud!"

"Cheers!"

We clink our glasses together while she watches us with questioning confusion before taking a sip from her own glass.

As soon as it touches my tongue, the room spins.

I vaguely hear Clarisse and Santi choking and coughing beside me. One small sip of "A'shuur" and I feel drunker than I have ever been in my life. It was offered with water, and I wasn't expecting it to be alcoholic.

"You're so beautiful," Clarisse giggles as I trip over my own feet to see who she's talking about.

She grabs my face and smushes my cheeks between her hands. For some reason, this is hilarious to me and I laugh so hard that I snort. This makes these other's laugh so hard that Santi loses his balance.

The woman looks panicked, quickly running from the room.

"She poisoned us! We're dying!" Clarisse yells loudly right beside my ear. Then, to my horror, she gulps down the rest of the contents of her glass!

"Clarisse! What are you doing?"

"Can't let it go to waste!" She teeters on her feet toward the baskets, searching for more of the oozy blue vanilla pudding fruits.

The door opens and several women enter, shutting the door behind them. They are talking, the kind of rapid-fire babbling that happens when you're nervous. Why are they nervous?

"Are you sick?" One of them bends down to look at me at eye level.

"No, what's your name?" I can hear my voice slurring, but I can't stop it.

"Olexa," her lips pull into a frown. "Why are you unbalanced?"

"Maybe it was the cryo-sleep, but we clearly can't handle alcohol right now!" I giggle uncontrollably.

"Liquor?" She turns to the others, but they only nod in confusion.

"What's your name?" I ask the woman who pulled us up the ladder earlier.

"Gaia."

"Thanks for saving us, Gaia, but... are you going to kill us? Is the scary one going to kill us?" I do my best to sound serious, but Clarisse's babbling behind me is making it difficult.

"The scary one?" Her perfectly arched brow raises slightly.

"Yeah... the scary one..."

One of them says something in their language and all of them laugh.

"Do you mean my brother?" Olexa's huge smile assures me that I haven't offended her, at least.

Now that I'm looking at her, really looking, I can see the resemblance. While her power isn't as absolutely stifling, it's still there. She's regal... and stunning. Where he lacked emotion, hers poured from her eyes. She may be a gigantic alien with muscles to rip me to shreds, but I can see the kindness in her.

"He will not kill-" her words are cut off by the door. A man walks in and says something that wipes the smiles from all of their faces.

"We will see how scary he is. He is summoning you." She grimaces. Clarisse and Santi have taken to dancing in each other's arms.

I'm in enough control of my mind to know that this is not good, but not in so much control that I can really be afraid. My new friends Gaia and Olexa will protect me...probably.

As we walk out into the now-empty great hall, I can see that the sun has gone down outside. The glowing purple sky washes the room in a soft light that makes me feel tingly and warm.

"If he isn't going to kill us, why was he so upset?" I jog to match Olexa's strides.

"He intends to kick you out, to make you go survive on your own," she sighs.

"Are we prisoners here?"

"No... but you are not free to roam. He does not trust you."

I scoff, "Well, I don't trust him either!" I clap my hand over my mouth as soon as the words leave it. Even drunk, I know that was stupid. I can't get too comfortable, even if Olexa does have kind eyes.

I get a feeling from their curiosity and general accommodation toward us that they didn't have anything to do with why we haven't seen any people. Until I'm sure, though, I need to keep my guard up. They may just be softening us to make us more malleable before forcing us into servitude.

Her eyes are wide, and she looks nervous. "This will be interesting…"

CHAPTER 10

As we enter the room, Clarisse and Santi somehow trip over each other's feet and fall, dramatically onto the ground with a resounding bang that echoes off the walls.

The four men in the room jump up at the commotion. They look ready to attack until they realize it's just a couple of klutzy humans.

The mean one scowls angrily at Olexa and angrily gestures toward us while he's speaking. When our eyes meet, his jaw clenches and his shoulders tense. I can feel myself fading. The details of his face swirling around in my brain in a haze of silver and purple.

When my eyes flutter open, I'm engulfed in fabric. Where am I and how did I get here? Sitting up, I realize I'm in a bed. Crawling to the edge, I look nervously around the strange room. I'm alone. As I cautiously step down to the floor, I can't help my curiosity. There are only three walls, one side being completely open onto a large terrace.

I'm mesmerized as I walk forward, stepping out onto the balcony. As far as I can see, there is only the sky and the alien planet. I'm so far from the ground, I can hardly see it down below. It's breathtaking. If I fell, I imagine falling forever, never reaching the ground. With white knuckles, I grip the very thin rail that stands between me and the open air. This seems inadequate and dangerous, but I can't walk away.

I'm so absorbed in the view that I don't notice that I'm no longer alone.

"You survived through the night," a deep voice from behind me makes me scream.

On shaky legs, I turn to face him and my breath catches for a different reason. My already pounding heart beats even harder.

His hair is braided on the sides and pulled up. He isn't wearing a shirt and his skin has me transfixed. From his neck down, every inch of him is covered in tattoos, strange markings that look... well...alien.

"Have you recovered?" His voice radiates strength. He could crush me like a bug if he wanted to. I know it... he does too.

"Recovered?" I find my voice, but it sounds so small.

"From your sudden illness. Your companions have not yet awakened." His eyes sweep over my body slowly.

"Illness? I wasn't ill...just drunk." My cheeks burn as I remember last night. Olexa said he wanted to kick us out.

"What is drunk?"

"Umm... inebriated? You know..." Clearly he doesn't. "We drank that a'sjor...a'sh-"

"A'shuur did that to you?" He looks surprised.

I'm quickly coming to realize that our reaction isn't typical.

"Maybe we should stay away from that in the future..."

"You may partake if you wish. You fell unconscious rather quickly. Your companions, however, remained awake for hours." His annoyance is evident.

Clearing my throat uncomfortably, I shift on my feet.

"How did you get here?" The seriousness in his tone makes my spine stiffen.

"I don't... we're from here?" I don't understand the question.

"Yes, but we have lived on this planet for fifty-nine earth

years and have never encountered a single human. Where did you come from?"

I choke, coughing and sputtering I step back, hitting the railing behind me.

He steps forward, grabbing my arm and pulling me toward his hard chest.

"Be careful!" He snaps.

I'm too shocked by his words to care that his hand is still wrapped around my arm.

"Fifty-nine years? Where is everyone? What do you mean you've never seen a person? You didn't do anything to them? What happened?" I'm frantic, half-screaming. Before I have a chance to finish a thought, another rushes in on top of it.

"We assumed the explosion on Na'hara was responsible for the extermination of your people, but that was one hundred and fifty-nine earth years ago. Where have you been since then?"

"Wait.. what? What explosion? One hundred and fifty-nine years since what?"

He sighs and drags me inside. My feet hardly move as he leads me to the bed.

"Sit," he plops me down and then takes a step back. "There was an explosion on Na'hara, one hundred and fifty-nine earth years ago. It pulled our planet from its gravitational orbit. Debris impacted several surrounding planets, including Earth. One hundred years after the event, we came here to build. There have been no humans found, ever. Where have you been?" He sounds almost impatient, like he's explaining something that I should already know.

"There's no one left?" I jump up and brush past him, pacing circles. "Is that why the Gulf of Mexico-" I can't keep up with the flood in my brain. Gasping, I let my body sink to the ground as a sob rips through my chest. I feel like I'm being strangled, heaving and wheezing. I attempt to take a breath. Tears roll uncontrollably down my cheeks, dripping onto the floor as I openly weep.

For several minutes, I forget I'm not alone, wailing as I'm beaten down by so much pain I can't see straight.

I knew something happened. I knew it wasn't normal that in our days of travel, we never ran into a single person but... gone...all of them. Thinking something and being certain without a doubt are very different.

"How were you unaware of this?" His voice is softer, but it still surprises me.

"We... we were in cryo-sleep in an underground bunker. Since 1983 we've been asleep... it was only supposed to be for one hundred years... but everyone... everyone died..." my voice is croaky as it breaks and fresh tears fall.

I watch as he walks toward the door, a panel of lights glowing as he raises his hand to the wall. He speaks his language and someone, somewhere, responds. A moment later, a woman appears with a cart. She bows her head and leaves as quickly as she came.

"Water." he holds a glass out to me but I can't take it. My body feels heavy, weighed down, and broken. My lip trembles and I drop my head down staring at the floor.

He sits beside me on the ground, his hair brushing against my arm.

"Drink," he holds the glass to my lips.

When I look into his eyes, for some reason, everything becomes too much for me. Covering my face with my hands, I cry. Grieving the loss of everything. I had no family left, no ties to anyone, but I still mourn. We volunteered for the experiment in the hope that we would be able to cure diseases, to save people. Instead, everyone died, leaving us completely alone in the world.

I feel a large, heavy hand on my shoulder, gently patting me. I think he's attempting to comfort me.

When I've cried all the tears I can cry, I let my arms fall, dropping down at my side, dead weight. He's still watching me intently, confusion swirling in his eyes.

"Drink," his voice is very soft now. Taking the glass, I sip the water slowly. I can feel his eyes on me, but I won't look up to meet them. He's seen me, broken, literally on the floor, at my lowest point. In all of his power, the dignified strength that rolls off of him, I'm drowning under the pressure.

I wasn't even this broken when I lost my parents. This feels worse somehow. When they died, I felt alone in the world, like everything good had been sucked away. Having everything and everyone wiped away, no memory of their existence, it's like losing them all over again. They're gone. They didn't matter, no one did. Every person who ever lived, every contribution is lost, the world swallowing it whole and growing over it.

With a heavy sigh and a shuddering breath, I stand on my shaky feet.

"I was suspicious of you. It seemed impossible that you were, in fact, human. I believed you to be an enemy masquerading as human to trick us into a false sense of security. I see now that I was wrong. You may stay here, should you so choose." He stands, his shadow blocking out the sun.

"I... t-thank you..." I don't have the energy to think about that now. Do we even want to stay here? Where else would we go?

The silence between us is loud. I can feel it, like an itch under my skin. He wants to ask me questions... I want to ask him questions. Now is not the time.

"Will you take me to my friends? I...I need to tell them..." my voice cracks and I shudder. I don't want to be the one that tells them this, the one that breaks their hearts. It has to be me.

"Yes." His hand comes down on my shoulder again, softly, like he's holding its heaviness back on purpose.

As we walk down the hallway, I watch our shadows stretching across the gleaming white floor. I barely reach his chest. Small, insignificant...extinct.

When we reach the door, I can't bring myself to open it.

"What is your name?" He asks suddenly, distracting me from the turmoil that is consuming my mind.

"Nicole," I finally look at him.

He repeats my name softly with a gentle nod of understanding.

"Take a breath, Nicole," his voice is soothing, a hard, sturdy anchor to tie myself to as the current tries to wash me away.

When I turn to ask him his name, his long legs and brisk stride have already taken him down the corridor.

With a trembling hand, I slide the door open. I can't delay this any longer.

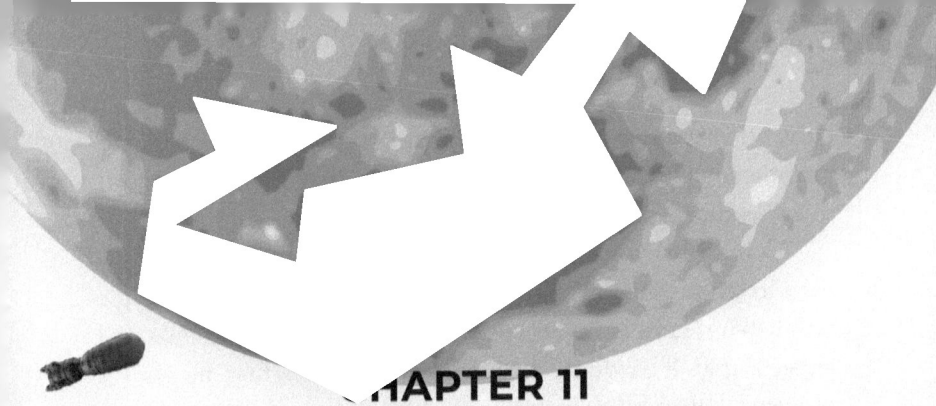

CHAPTER 11

T he three of us have been lying across the bed for untold hours. The sun rose high in the sky, then dipped below the horizon and no one has moved.

We cried, we cursed, we screamed, now we're perfectly still.

When the door slides open, I continue watching the purple glow from the night sky dance across the ceiling.

"My brother summons you," Olexa hesitates to speak.

Each of us makes a sound in protest, a hum, a grumble, a moan. I don't feel like being summoned right now. After several minutes of silence, the door slides closed again. Somehow, I doubt that will be the end of that. I don't know him; I don't even know his name, but I don't get the impression his calls often go unanswered.

The door slides open again, and I expect to be re-summoned. Instead, it's silent.

Lifting my head, I'm met with the commander himself, standing in the doorway, watching us.

"You need to eat." His eyes narrow, as if he already knows I'm not going to comply.

Santi sits up, his swollen, red eyes making my heart ache all over again. These two people, sprawled in bed beside me, are the only other people on earth. It's just us. For all intents and purposes, we're strangers, but right now, they give me comfort in a way that is only explicable by shared hurt.

"Come," his voice is heavy again. The authority he carries is hard to ignore. He says things like a man who knows that people will listen. There is no hesitation, no doubt. He commands and expects that it is done. I'm relieved to know that he isn't a monster that came down from the sky and murdered everyone on earth, but I'm not completely unafraid.

I peek up at him as I roll awkwardly out of bed. He is the definition of lethal. I haven't seen him do anything physically demanding, but he's dangerous and it shows. Every inch of him, of all of them, is solid sculpted muscle.

The longer I stare at him, the more my brain starts to buzz with questions. Are they like that naturally? It would seem so, since they all look the same. Is their hair made of protein like ours? It looks different, shinier, softer... I still want to run my fingers through it.

Following him down a long hallway, we're ushered into a room with a long table surrounded by chairs. Their architecture and designs are..... unusual, to say the least. Most things, like the table and our beds, just float inexplicably and impossibly above the ground with no legs or supports of any kind.

Enough food for at least twenty people is laid out in dishes.

He sits and then turns to us, waiting expectantly.

Santi steps up to a chair and pulls out the ones on either side of it. When Clarisse and I are seated, he pushes them in slightly and takes his seat.

"Are you incapable of sitting by yourself?" The commander looks utterly shocked.

"They are quite capable," a sad smile pulls at his lips. "Mi mama raised a gentleman."

"I do not understand." The confusion on his face is actually very cute.

"It's just the polite way for a man to treat a lady," he explains.

I hope that this is sufficient because now that I think of it... I don't know why we do this. Why do men pull chairs out for women? Or stand from their chairs when a woman stands?

"A lady?" He's still lost.

"A woman..." I clarify.

He nods, but I can see that he's still thinking about it.

Olexa and Gaia enter the room together. Gaia is stone-faced while Olexa has a large, happy smile on her face.

"I'm very excited to share your mourning meal," Olexa sits down enthusiastically.

"Our what?" All of us choke.

The commander says something in their language and her eyes go wide.

"We eat this meal to honor our dead. When the physical body perishes, we pay tribute by preparing a meal of difficult-to-harvest fruit." The commander gestures over the dishes on the table. Everything is... beautiful, glowing flowers, brightly colored fruits, strange and mesmerizing.

"T-Thank you," I sniffle as Santi grabs my hand under the table.

After saying something in their language, they abruptly stand. We awkwardly join them, waiting in the silence for whatever is supposed to happen next.

The commander turns to us, bowing his head slightly, "Begin to recite the names of your lost."

"Um, what?"

"Name the dead."

I didn't have any family left, so I started to name people that meant something to me.

"Mr. Ballard was my eighth-grade science teacher. He is the reason I'm an anatomist. Mrs. Hall, our elderly neighbor..." After naming different friends from elementary school and our old mailman, I turn to Santi.

With a tear in his eye, he begins to list his names, "Louis Fernando, Paola, Andrea, y Carlos Alberto Pena-Santiago."

When Clarisse starts, she lists nearly twenty names. "Dieter, Stefan und Elke..."

As we take our seats, I feel better—lighter. We're still the only three people left, but it doesn't feel as painful as before. The lives and contributions of others aren't lost because we remember them.

"Explain the mission directives," the commander demands in what seems to be his only way of asking a question.

Santi and Clarisse give him the details while I try to stare at him inconspicuously. He nods occasionally, listening intently while they speak. He eats with an atypical grace. I would be willing to bet that he never trips or spills things or kicks the frame of his bed when he's walking around his room. Not that they even have bed frames.

"And you?" He meets my gaze.

"And me what?"

"You are also a doctor, what kind?" His eyes narrow. I think he just realized that I wasn't paying attention.

"I'm an anatomist. I know everything there is to know about human anatomy."

"When we arrived here, we collected many items from your species. I have read your medical texts. We have many anatomical similarities."

There is nothing in his voice that gives the impression that he is joking in any way. He is simply relaying information, facts that he observed while trying to learn about humans. For reasons unknown, I snort hideously, laughing at his statement.

"This amuses you?"

"No," I clear my throat, but the laughter is there, itching, tickling, putting pressure on my neck. "It's just... I would be very interested to compare. For our similarities, there are striking differences."

"I see."

He turns back to Santi and Clarisse, asking them about their work. It makes my chest feel warm to see how passionate

Clarisse is when she talks about her field. He obliges and listens to her through the rest of the meal.

I eat in silence, listening, thinking...

After everyone has eaten their fill of the mourning meal, the sun has set. I can see the same exhaustion on the others' faces. The weight of the day has drained me.

"We will walk you to your rooms," Olexa offers the others. My room is on a different level and several hallways away. For a moment, I consider asking if I can stay with Clarisse or at least move to a room near theirs. I don't want to be rude or to put Clarisse on the spot. Maybe she doesn't want to share with me...

"Come," the commander gestures as we all stand.

Hugging them quickly, I follow him through the maze of hallways. I study his board back as he walks in front of me. You would never guess from here that he is so ornately decorated beneath his shirt.

"What planet are you from?" My nervous voice cuts through the silent hallway.

He pauses for a moment, answering without turning around. "An'eo."

When we reach the hallway that I'm almost sure is our destination, he opens a door that I'm sure isn't the room I was in before. When we step inside, I'm met with an office. The wall on the far side is made of glowing blue glass.

He leads me toward it, tapping his finger on it. The wall changes, several small pictures illuminating the wall. He searches them for a moment, then touches one of them. The screen changes again and he taps another picture, speaking words from his language out loud into the room.

He puts his pointer fingers to his thumbs and opens them in a square shape. A swirling solar system floats in the air around us. Putting up one of my hands, I pass my fingers through it... a hologram. We're standing in the center of the universe as the planets slowly orbit around us.

"Holy shit, this is like Star Wars," I mumble under my breath.

He speaks again, and the images move, Jupiter expanding and the different moons orbiting around it. He points to one of the moons.

"An'eo."

I recognize it as the planet that is now just outside my window. He says something to the... wall. I'm not sure how this technology works. The hologram moves again. Jupiter orbiting around us. A loud voice speaks, first in his language, then in mine. I assume it's saying the names of the planets in his language then in English. When it reaches his planet he nods as it speaks. "An'eo - Callisto."

"Callisto." I stare at the hologram of the planet I watch from my terrace.

"I can show you the event." The caution in his voice makes my heart pound.

If I try to speak, my voice would shake, so I nod instead. He walks through the cosmos, standing beside me as the solar system starts to spin. Mars explodes, sending debris and large pieces hurling violently through space. The shattered pieces impact several planets, but I can only watch Earth. At least five large chunks of Mars crash into Earth, hitting both the oceans and land. Nine moons of Jupiter are knocked out of orbit, each being ripped through the sky until they stop in different places in the universe.

When the simulation stops, I try to quickly wipe the tears from my cheeks but he notices before I can.

"Thank you for showing me this," I attempt to smile.

"You are welcome." He nods. The gentleness in his voice surprises me. It's not the first time I've heard it, but it still catches me off guard. It's as if he has a switch for his power, like he can turn it off when he wants to.

We walk silently down the hallway. The spectrum of emotions that a person can feel in a given moment is extraordinary. I feel everything. I'm broken and grieving, but there is still hope in my chest. We lived, this is not the end for us. I'm filled with curiosity. I want to learn and understand everything I can about these beings.

When we reach the door, I want to say something, to thank him for…everything. I'm struggling to find the words to adequately express my gratitude for tonight's dinner. It was what we needed to have a moment of recognition for everything we lost.

Feeling brave, I look up, only to find his gaze already fixed on me. Whatever I wanted to say is completely forgotten. His face is kind of perfect—flawless— in a way that makes him simultaneously beautiful and frightening. I need to go inside and try to sleep; I'll end up standing here all night.

"Goodnight, Commander," I feel my cheeks heat. Why does he make me feel so…fluttery?

The corner of his mouth ticks and, for the briefest moment, I think he might smile.

"Goodnight, Nicole."

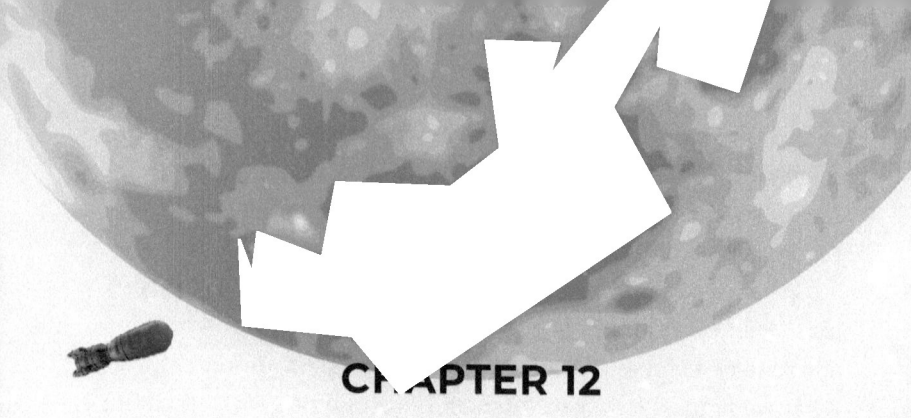

CHAPTER 12

'm not sure what time it is when I'm awakened by the door sliding open. I lay perfectly still in the bed, my eyes straining in the dark for a moment. I hope that it's Clarisse or maybe even Santi.

That hope is quickly dashed when a tall, muscular silhouette comes into focus against the purple glowing light.

"Who's there?" My voice shakes.

All at once the figure stops moving, and I hear a gasp. A woman's voice speaks rapidly into the darkness and a dim light turns on growing slowly brighter. I don't recognize the woman standing at the foot of the bed. She turns, looking out over the balcony and then back at me.

"Why are you here?" Her voice is angry and aggressive.

"I…" I don't know what to say. The hazy confusion of being ripped from sleep mixed with my nervousness has me sputtering instead of speaking.

In an angry mixture of their language and English, she starts shouting at me. I can't read between the lines enough to understand what she's trying to say. The bits of broken English aren't giving me enough context. It's apparent that she is getting more upset and more agitated with each passing minute.

"Where is-" she keeps repeating that over and over, the rest of the sentence, the most important part, I can't understand.

"I'm sorry!" I jump out of the bed and rush toward the door. All I can think is that there's been some mistake and I am sleeping in her room.

I run down the long hallway, trying to remember the way to Clarisse's room. After several minutes, I come to a staircase that I don't recognize. I must have made a wrong turn somewhere. Turning back, I try to retrace my steps to the room so that I can start again, but after I come to a dead-end hallway, I realize I'm lost.

Wandering around in the dark, I try to be as quiet as possible. I don't want to disturb anyone in the middle of the night. I find myself at the top of another staircase. This place is a gigantic labyrinth of white, the floor, the walls, and the ceiling. There are no distinguishing features, art, decor…nothing.

While I contemplate whether or not I want to go down to the next level, I hear something in the distance. Footsteps in the dark.

"Nicole?" It's Olexa.

My tense shoulders slump. A friendly face.

"Are you hurt? Or ill?" She sounds concerned.

"No, I'm just looking for my friends… I think there was a mistake with my room."

"A mistake?" Her hand comes down on my shoulder, gently pulling me away from the stairs.

"She was so upset. I think I must have ended up in her room by accident…" I explain everything. At some point, she stopped walking, standing tensely while I tell her what happened. She looks angry, her shoulders hunched aggressively.

"No." With no further explanation, she turns around and pulls me after her toward the direction we just left. When we reach the staircase again, she practically runs down. At the bottom of the stairs, there is a small hallway with two doors. She opens one of them quickly and shouts something in her language.

I'm taken aback by her anger.

The dim lights grow brighter until the whole room is illuminated. The commander is sitting up in bed, his bare chest catching my attention first. He looks shocked as the two of them speak angrily at one another.

"He will fix it," Olexa finally releases her grip on me. With an indignant smirk, she leaves without looking back.

I shuffle on my feet, staring down at the ground.

"Explain the incident." His voice sends a shiver down my spine. His usually rich, clear timbre is rough. He's tired.

"Oh, I… a woman came to the room and was very upset. I couldn't understand her, but I thought maybe I was in her room or something." I feel ridiculous. Was this really such a big deal that the commander had to be disturbed in the middle of the night? Surely, this could have waited until morning.

"I'm really sorry she woke you up. I'm fine. I don't need you to do anything. I'll just wait until morning. It's no big deal." I ramble as he pulls himself warily from his bed.

The gasp that leaves my throat was probably heard by everyone within two miles. My cheeks burn as I stare at my tangled fingers.

He's naked.

I am a doctor of human anatomy. I've seen naked bodies, tons of them. I've studied cadavers. I've looked at the naked forms of both men and women countless times. I've been in relationships. Nudity is not something that makes me uncomfortable.

Seeing him so unexpectedly makes me feel like a thirteen-year-old watching a dirty movie for the first time, not a professional who doesn't bat an eye at nakedness.

One thing is undeniably true, I have found a very large difference between their males and human males… No similarities there…nope, in shape, sure, but in size…definitely not.

"There was no mistake," he's angry, I can hear it. I'm so busy staring at my hands that I don't notice him approaching. His hand rests on my shoulder, gently guiding me toward the door. He has pants on. I breathe a sigh of relief.

"Oh, she just seemed so upset to find me there…I can understand if I came home in the middle of the night and someone was sleeping in my bed-"

"Those are my quarters." He cuts me off.

"What!" I don't mean to shout, but it flies out of my mouth before I can stop it. "Why am I sleeping in your room?"

"You were ill."

"No, I was drunk! I'm fine. Oh, my god! Please, don't let me keep you from your room! Put me anywhere, a broom closet! I'll take a couch… please…"

"You will not sleep in a closet." He sounds shocked by the suggestion.

As I open my mouth to speak realization hits me like a slap to the face.

"Oh, my god!" I mumble to myself. The woman was a…visitor. "I'm so sorry," I groan, "Please, take your room back."

"You enjoy the view. I saw you."

"So what? That doesn't mean I should get to steal your room! Please, Commander, take your room back. It was very…sweet of you, but I can't take it now that I know it's yours. I don't want to inconvenience you."

He opens a door to another outdoor terrace with steps that lead down to a grassy lawn.

"Why do you call me commander?" He ignores everything else I said.

"I don't know your name…"

"You have not asked my name." I can actually hear the amusement in his voice.

Stopping mid-step, I turn to him. It's true, I haven't asked. "What's your name?"

"Ronäìn Te Kxìr'r Käuze'eyä."

"I'm sorry, can you repeat that?" I hope my face doesn't look as bewildered as I feel. I don't want to disrespect his name or his language.

"Ronan."

"Ronan," I repeat quietly. I don't know why, but my stomach flutters. Knowing his name feels like sacred information somehow.

"May I call you that? Or is there something more formal or appropriate that I should call you?"

"You may call me Ronan."

My heart pounds against my ribs. The purple glow of the sky makes his eyes look even more brilliant. Shifting on my feet, I let my gaze drop from his eyes to his bare chest. His tattoos almost glow in the dark. I'm at eye level with the base of his sternum, a circular swirling pattern etched into his skin there is so striking I can't look away.

Without realizing it, I take a step toward him, hypnotized. I don't understand the meaning of his tattoos, but I can feel that it's there. Something powerful has been printed on his skin, but it's beyond the scope of my understanding.

When he whispers something in his language, I look up at him; the trance breaking.

"Come."

In the same way that he always does, his hand rests on my shoulder, leading me toward a building across the lawn.

"What is this?" I gasp as he slides the door open.

I'm suddenly violently doused in heavy emotion. A sob and a laugh battle in my throat.

"Ronan," my voice cracks, but a smile so wide it makes my cheeks ache spreads over my face. "What is this?"

I stand frozen, unsure of what to look at first. Shelves filled with books, a store mannequin, a dining table with dishes, a bicycle, a lamp… The whole of human history, our inventions, the leftovers from lives lived and lost.

Taking a shaky step forward, I take my time looking at every item. There are several things that I don't recognize. Electronic-looking items that I've never seen before.

"What is this?" I point to something that looks like a thin television on a stand. The glass is cracked, but it seems otherwise intact.

"A computer." he stays back a few steps, giving me space to explore.

"This is a computer? From earth?" I can't believe it. This looks nothing like our computers when we were put to sleep. This is so sleek and small compared to the large boxes that we had.

"We have been able to identify almost everything here but…" he stops and walks behind a shelf. "What is this?" He steps out and laughter bubbles up in my throat.

"That's an iron." I giggle as he holds it in his hands.

"An iron? What is its purpose?"

"When you plug it in, it gets hot, then you rub it over your clothes to remove wrinkles."

He spins it in his hands, studying it. "interesting."

I pull a book from the shelf. It's in Spanish. It looks like a fictional story, but I can't be sure. Opening the cover, I look over the publishing information and my eyes widen.

"This story was published in 2049!" Doing the math in my head, I look at him in shock. "That's sixty-six years after we were put to sleep… how long were we frozen before the 'event?'"

"I never calculated the timeline in earth years. It was 4280 on An'eo." He looks up thoughtfully like he's trying to do the calculations now. I watch his fingers move while he runs the numbers in his head.

"What earth year did you freeze?"

"1983."

He hums and continues counting. "It was 2061 on Earth at the time of the event."

"So, that's…" I count on trembling fingers. "Seventy-eight

years... we were frozen for seventy-eight years... then another one hundred fifty-nine."

"Two hundred and thirty-seven earth years." He nods.

Black starts to creep in, starting from the edge of my vision, growing quickly until I can't see anything.

CHAPTER 13

My eyes flutter and I hear frantic talking all around me.

"What do you mean she just fell? People don't just fall!" It's Clarisse, and she's panicking.

"Did she hit her head?" Santi is here too.

"I caught her. We were speaking, then she fell…" When Ronan speaks, I feel it vibrating in my skull. "You are both human doctors. Help her."

"I'm fine," I groan and blink my eyes open. It's only now that I realize why his voice sounded so close, why I could feel it rattling under my skin. He's holding me, pressed against his bare chest.

"Nic, what happened?" Clarisse sounds so upset. I think we're all a bit fearful of something happening to one of the others.

"I think I fainted. I'm so sorry for scaring you. I'm fine. I just…we figured something out, and it upset me. That's all."

"What did you figure out?" Santi looks afraid to ask.

"We were asleep for two hundred and thirty-seven years… Ronan showed me a simulation of the event. It was… awful."

They look shocked as they try to process everything.

"I would like to see the simulation if that's possible," Santi asks cautiously.

"Of course," Ronan's chest rumbles, and I realize, much to my horror, that I'm still in his arms!

"Oh, Ronan! I'm so sorry!" I wiggle, dropping my legs down to the ground. "I'm fine! You don't have to carry me."

"Ronan?" Olexa raises her brows at him, then says something we can't understand.

His jaw ticks, and he takes a step back.

"If all is well, I will be returning to bed," Olexa smiles.

Jerking my head toward the window, I see the purple and blue sky still very clearly indicating night.

"Please, go back to sleep! I'm sorry you were woken up." When I walk toward the door, Santi follows, entering the room across the hall.

"Come," Ronan sets his hand on my shoulder.

"Ronan, I can't take your room. Please, stick me somewhere else."

"I will not 'stick you' somewhere. You like the room, you will have it."

We walk down the hallway in silence until he stops me at the stairs.

"Are you certain that you are well?" His eyes search my face. His expression is stern, but his eyes aren't.

"I am."

Following him through the dark, my mind wanders back to how all of this started.

"Was that woman your girlfriend?"

I want to fling myself from the nearest staircase as soon as the words leave my mouth.

"Girlfriend?"

"Um," I feel stupid. Why did I ask him this? "A romantic companion? Someone you love or commit to. It's like a friendship, but more intimate." I'm rambling.

"No, she is not my girlfriend."

He offers no further explanation. If he thinks it's odd that I asked, he doesn't show it. After walking up the stairs, he stops me again.

After walking up the stairs, he stops me again.

"Why do you have different accents? Each of you is different."

"Well, we're not from the same place. Santi is from Colombia and Spanish was his first language. Clarisse is from Germany and I'm American."

This answer doesn't seem to explain anything.

"You are all of earth…"

"Yes, but we're from different countries."

"Do you not speak their languages?" He still does not understand.

"I speak some Spanish."

"You do not speak all human languages?"

My mouth falls open, "of course not! Do you speak all the languages on your planet?"

"We only have one language. Everyone of An'eo speaks An'eoc."

"Everyone on the planet? Is your whole planet one country?" I'm fascinated.

"We have several regions, but we are one planet, one people."

"We had a lot of division here," I start to explain how we separate ourselves by ethnicity, race, and nationality.

"That sounds foolish. If your planet was attacked, you would be uncoordinated and easily invaded…." The way he's looking at me makes me feel small and stupid. That's how he sees me. "I read your texts. This caused many wars, did it not?"

"Yes, it did." I hang my head. I don't know how to stand in defense of my people. When we went to sleep we were in the middle of the cold war. Clarisse's own country was torn in two…

"See? Foolish. On An'eo we don't fight our brothers."

"We were far from perfect but a lot of people… most people, tried to be good, to be kind… We didn't set up our world that way. We were born in whatever county we were born in…" I'm sputtering, grasping at straws.

"That sounds like an excuse. If you admit it was flawed, why did you not change it?"

"I'm only one person! What could I have done? How dare you place the shortfalls of humanity at my feet!" I feel both boiling rage and shame. "I was just an ordinary person, I wasn't born into power… What could I have done to force world leaders to hold hands and sing kumbaya?"

His expression changes. "you are very small and weak. I suspect you are correct…"

My mouth drops open. "What the fuck?"

"I said 'you are very small and weak, so I believe you are correct.' You would be incapable of forcing anyone to do anything." His voice is completely calm, and matter-of-fact.

"Good night, Commander." I step into the room and slide the door closed. I grumble under my breath as I make my way to the shower. A sliding door is decidedly less apt at conveying anger than a slamming one.

He blamed me for the division of people, then he called me weak and useless.

Scrubbing my skin in the shower, I force all thoughts of him down. Or at least I try to. His stupid, flawless face keeps popping into my head. I'm not an idiot. I would never assume that I am anywhere, even close to his abilities or strength. To hear him say it out loud, so pragmatically… We clearly have differences in etiquette. Insulting people with low opinions of their capabilities and intelligence is generally frowned upon here.

I don't know why my feelings are so hurt. He insulted me, yes, but it's more than that. He's hard to read, but I thought we were forming a friendship… of sorts. He sat beside me on the floor while I cried, and showed me the simulation and the museum…

I'm acting like a teenager with a crush because he let me call him by his name.

I need to get my shit together. He's the commander of an alien race, a perfectly formed extraterrestrial specimen. We are not friends.

Climbing into bed, I open my backpack and dig through the items until I find my notebook. I need to change my expectations. He asks me questions to learn about the human race. I will do the same. Scribbling down an anatomical survey, I write everything I can think of that I can ask to learn more about them.

Maybe Olexa will let me do a macroscopic anatomical study?

I wonder if they have microscopes to do a microscopic study.

I feel better after spending an hour considering educational topics. I might not be strong like he is, but I'm not stupid. I don't need him to be my friend. I will learn from him and let him learn from me. Santi and Clarisse are my friends. That's all I need.

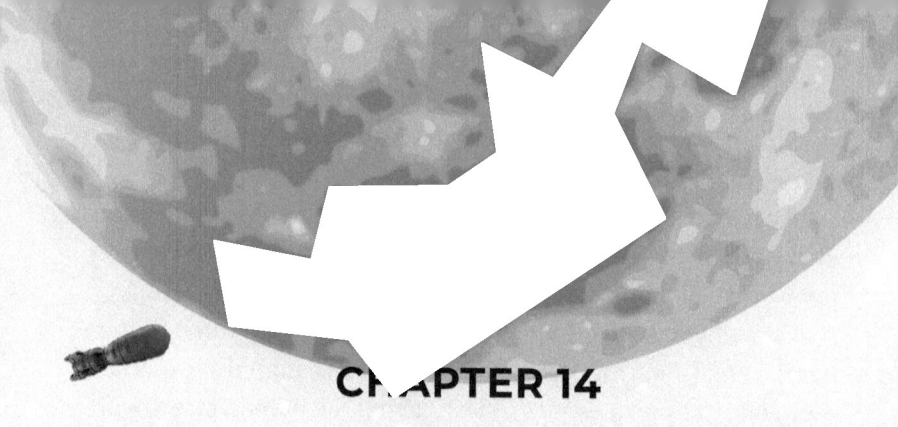

CHAPTER 14

With my notebook in hand, I wonder about the halls, lost again. I thought I could find my way to the dining room, but even in the light of day, I can't.

Rounding the corner, I collide with someone hard. My body tumbles back but before I can fall, I'm grabbed and effortlessly lifted from the ground.

"Your body is very small." I look up to find the grumpy one that brought us here, holding me tightly with one arm wrapped around my chest. His signature scowl etched into his face, of course.

"I'm sorry, I didn't hear you coming." I steady myself and let go of his arms.

Scooping up my notebook and pen, I almost hope that he will continue on his way. When I've gathered my belongings, I give him a tight smile. Shit. Now I'm going to have to tell him I'm lost.

"The Commander attempted to gather you from your quarters this morning. He is searching for you now." His grouchy face has a confused furrow between his brows.

"Oh, wonderful." I sigh.

"Come," he turns on his heels and begins walking down the hallway. I jog beside him to keep up with his long strides.

"What is your name?" I question breathlessly. No one has asked our names. We have to ask them first. If we don't ask, they don't offer the information freely. I figure I might as well meet him officially.

He stops and I run into his back. He doesn't even flinch like an ant bumping an elephant.

"I'm Nicole." I hold my hand out to him when he turns.

He frowns and grabs my hand between his thumb and pointer finger like one would hold something gross that they don't really want to touch.

"Um, no. Sorry. I—like this," I pull my hand out of his grasp and put them together. "This is called a handshake. It's how you introduce yourself on earth. Do you have an introductory custom?"

He pulls his hand away from mine. "We only share our given name with familiar relations. My title is Elite Navigator. You may call me that."

"Oh," my cheeks heat. I wonder if they think I'm rude. I've been so hyper-focused on his bad manners, that I've not considered my own.

He told me I could call him Ronan…

My shoulders slump as we continue walking. I know everyone is busy, but maybe Olexa or Gaia can spare a moment to discuss social etiquette. They never offered their titles.

He stops again, turning to me. "You are unhappy." He's not asking.

"N-No, I just… I didn't know. I hope I didn't offend you before…"

"My name is Macsen."

"Thank you. It's nice to meet you formally. I will continue to call you Elite Navigator, if that is what makes you the most comfortable."

He nods and begins to walk again. "What is your title?"

I'm surprised he asked…

"Doctor."

"You are a medic?" For the first time, the irritation on his face slips away, replaced with shock.

"I wasn't a practicing physician. I worked as a medical scientist."

When we turn the corner, I recognize this hallway. We're next to the dining room. I should draw a map in my notebook.

He slides the door open and I follow him in. Clarisse, Santi, and Olexa are already sitting at the table. Ronan and Gaia enter the room just behind us.

"Thank you, Elite Navigator. I appreciate your help."

"Doctor," he tips his chin down and leaves the room.

As I sit down, I force my eyes down. Don't look at him. Instead, I wish everyone a good morning and begin to put fruit on my plate.

"I'll take some of that, please." Santi holds his plate up and I serve him several fruits, then put several on Clarisse's plate too. While I place the dish down, he fills my glass with water. Clarisse takes a different dish and adds things to all our plates.

As I bring fruit to my mouth, I catch Olexa and Gaia sitting across the table, staring at us in confusion. My eyes automatically peek toward Roman. He has the same expression as he stares at us.

"Is this customary human behavior?" Olexa is the first to speak.

"What?" The three of us look at one another, trying to figure out what we did wrong.

"Filling the plates and glasses of your companions." Ronan actually sounds slightly angry.

"Oh, in family-style dining, like this, it is not uncommon to serve others, no." I don't know why the look on his face is bothering me so much. He looks upset.

"On An'eo, this is a highly respected way to express intimate love. In a male and female union, the male serves his female only." He looks between us, his agitation growing.

"On earth, it is not practiced only between intimate partners." Santi tries to ease this awkward tension. It seems to work with the women, but Ronan still seems angry as we move on to other topics of discussion.

"Is your diet exclusively vegetarian?" Clarisse asks, as, once again, there is no meat on the table.

"What is vegetarian?"

"Plant-based. No meat." As the words leave her mouth, their faces wrinkle in disgust.

"Meat? From what?"

"You know... animals or fish..."

I want to melt into the ground. They look absolutely horrified.

"Meat and eggs are an excellent source of protein." She doesn't look even a bit concerned by their grimacing faces.

"If you seek more protein, we have this." Gaia picks up a dish and passes it over the table. The brown, jiggly slices of... whatever that is looks as appetizing as the dish it's sitting on, but we each take a slice, anyway.

I continue to eat around it, hoping to avoid it as long as I can.

"You have not tasted it." Ronan tilts his chin toward my plate.

Plastering on a fake smile, I take a bite and swallow it down without chewing. I feel it sliding down my throat, coating my mouth in the unexpectedly garlicky flavor.

"Wow," I continue smiling, "I wasn't expecting it to be so viscous." With my jaw clenched, I slice another piece, eating it under his watchful gaze.

"Or to taste so strongly of garlic," Clarisse croaks.

"What are your titles?" I decide to change the subject. I don't want to force down any more of this slimy brown jello.

"I am Chief Engineer." Gaia sits a bit prouder.

"I am Elite Combatant," Olexa usually softer features look more serious.

"Is that how you would prefer to be addressed?"

"No, you may address me by my given name," Olexa smiles and Gaia nods in agreement.

I can feel Ronan's eyes on me. As we finish breakfast, I mentally map out the route back to my room. Down the hall, take the first right, then left at the dead end, then up... then at the top of the stairs... I'm almost sure it's another right.

"Now that our meal is finished, I would like to show you the grounds," Olexa offers with a smile and I'm quietly filled with relief. Ronan says something in their language and Olexa tips her chin.

"You will join me, Nicole. I will reunite you with the others momentarily." He turns to me and despite my best efforts, my face falls. I don't want to act like a petulant child, but I am hurt. I thought we were becoming friends, and he thinks I'm a spineless weakling who does nothing to stop the injustices of the world.

"You are angry at me," he looks surprised.

"N-No, not angry." I'm not angry, upset maybe, but not angry.

"Why?" Olexa looks back and forth between us.

"I'm not angry," it feels warm suddenly.

"You have avoided my direction today."

"I have also noticed," Gaia adds and I grit my teeth. Cool, everyone has apparently noticed that I stare at him.

"Did he do something?" Santi sits forward, looking furiously between the two of us.

"What? No!" I can't say that I don't appreciate his immediate anger over Ronan possibly stepping out of line but, nothing could be done if he had. Ronan would squash Santi like a bug with very little effort.

"You seem unhappy about my suggestion that we speak before you join the others, why?" He is going to keep pushing this in front of everyone.

"How would you feel if I blamed you for everything wrong with your society, then decided that no, it couldn't be your fault because you are too weak to be blamed? It's not my fault that humans have wars and I don't want to be blamed, but I also don't appreciate being called effectively useless."

"It would be preposterous for you to call me weak, as I am not. You are. It is factual..."

Wow, so he's doubling down on this then.

"What the fuck?" Clarisse mumbles.

"That is what she said last night, what does that mean?" He looks at Clarisse.

"It means... it's an expression of surprise," Santi steps in when we don't answer.

"You are surprised? Do you not know your physical limitations and fragility? I doubt you could even hold one of our weapons, let alone use it against an enemy." His brow furrows further.

"It's just not a very nice thing to say to someone, like commenting on their weight or appearance... calling someone weak is... rude." The realization of how ridiculous this conversation is hits me.

"I did not realize it was ill-mannered to mention your lack of strength and power." He nods.

Clarisse huffs and shakes her head in disbelief. "He really keeps digging deeper, doesn't he?"

I chuckle, waving my hand. "It's fine. Let's forget it. I'm not mad." This past hour has felt very long and we're only just starting the day. Etiquette lessons all around. I'm exhausted.

Elite Navigator enters the room and speaks quickly in their language. Ronan and Gaia stand and quickly excuse themselves without much word. Everyone looks worried.

"We will begin our tour," Olexa smiles, but I can see that she's distracted.

We walk for miles and we never leave the building. I can't imagine venturing out into the city. She explains how only the sovereign family and the warriors live and work in this building. We are shown libraries, offices, meeting halls, and ceremonial rooms. It's a lot to take in.

"Is everything alright?" I walk beside Olex as the others look over the vast collection in the library.

"We are constructing another city to the north. We received word that there was an accident where three An'eo were injured."

"Oh no, are they alright?"

"I do not know." She suddenly looks very upset.

"Do you know them?"

"One of them. She was Gaia's... she and Gaia were once together." She looks riddled with guilt.

"Do your people play instruments or listen to music? Are there singers?" Clarisse and Santi come back, completely unaware of the conversation we just had.

"We have instruments."

"Do you put on music and dance?" Santi starts to hum and move his feet.

"No, we do not do that." A smile tugs at her lips.

He lunges forward and grabs me, humming a rhythm, while he spins me around. Now that they bring it up, I realize how much I miss music. There is nothing like turning on the radio and singing at the top of your lungs in the car.

When he spins me again, my dizzy vision catches someone in the doorway. Ronan and Elite Navigator are watching us.

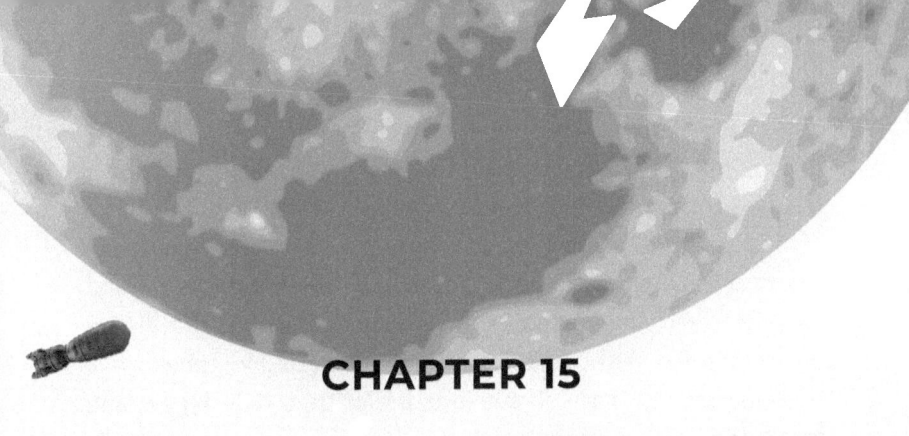

CHAPTER 15

C learing my throat, I quickly step out of Santi's grasp and straighten my clothes.

"What is that?" The confusion on their faces makes me smile. I guess watching people dance would look strange if you've never seen it before.

"Salsa!" Santi starts to move again, this time grabbing Clarisse.

"They are dancing," Olexa's voice is full of amusement.

"I do not understand the appeal." Ronan watches Santi as he moves his hips from side to side while swaying his arms in front of his body.

"It's fun," I try to explain even though the look on his face tells me it's a wasted effort.

Elite Navigator watches us thoughtfully before turning to talk to Ronan quietly. They watch us, then whisper, then watch some more. When he leaves the room, Olexa looks at us eagerly, like whatever she knows, is something we want to know, too.

"We have converted some audio files from discs. Would you like to hear them?"

"Audio files?" I can tell that the others don't know what that means either.

"I believe it is music."

The buzzing excitement is immediate. We follow him down the hall to a room that Olexa didn't show us. It looks like a control center of some kind. It's circular with a large, glass tube in the center that looks like it's somehow filled with liquid and lightning. Elite Navigator is already here, tapping the illuminated pictures on the wall. I used a computer a few times while working on my thesis. It reminds me of that, only bigger and better and beyond what I'm capable of using.

A cheerful beat starts to play behind the voice of a woman singing in Spanish. Santi doesn't waste a second grabbing our hands in his and leading us to the center of the room.

"Do you know this song?"

"I've never heard it before," he laughs as he starts to dance, situating himself in between us to show us what to do.

"Right, left, right, left," he instructs us on which foot to step back on. "More hips and add your arms." He exaggerated the movements until we start to catch on. "Now, step back and turn, right, now back and turn left."

By the time the first song ends, I've forgotten that we have an alien audience to our dance lesson. Clarisse and I are howling with laughter over our uncoordinated spins as we try to remember the steps.

As the second song starts, Santi gives up on us and grabs Olexa by the hand. She happily dances with him. It would appear that she was watching his instruction closely while he taught us because she does each step perfectly.

"See!" Santi spins her around, "this is how you cumbia!"

I attempt to spin Clarisse the same way but she steps on my feet instead.

The next song starts with an upbeat rhythm that sounds different from the last few, this sounds like pop music. When the singer starts in, we dance around the room with no choreography or steps, just moving.

As the songs transition in and out, from the third to the

fourth to the fifth, we dance, like we're the last people on earth. I don't care about Ronan watching me. I don't care that I'm a terrible dancer. I don't even care that I've never heard any of these songs. For the first time since waking up, I feel normal. If I close my eyes, I can pretend that I'm at a party with college friends, laughing and dancing.

My chest feels like it's full of champagne bubbles, tiny tingly bursts of joy. I don't know the artists or what year the songs came out, but here we are, dancing to them. Everything isn't lost. Even now, years later, we're listening to this small piece of our history.

I'm suddenly so grateful to Ronan for showing us these songs. Without thinking I grab his hand and pull him into the center of the room. He lets me pull him forward but he doesn't move, he just stands there while I spin and jump around him.

The scream that comes from both Clarisse and me when 'You're The One That I Want' starts seems to startle everyone.

"I know this song!" I grab both of his hands and start to loudly sing the lyrics while I spin around the room with him. Never in my life did I think a song from the Grease soundtrack would make me this excited.

Ronan moves around the room with me. I try to show him the dance from the movie, using Clarisse to teach him his part. He looks amused as he watches us fumble with the choreography. He never actually smiles, but he almost does.

My mind wanders back to my high school prom. I was a shy, nervous wallflower who didn't dance to a single song the entire night. If I could tell that girl that she would be twirling in the arms of a physically perfect alien almost three hundred years later, I doubt I would have believed it. I can hardly believe it's happening even now.

At the end of the song, I bow gracefully and thank him for the dance.

"I think I understand the appeal of dancing now," he says quietly, only to me. My cheeks burn and my heart flutters.

Damn it.

Olexa picks up my discarded and nearly forgotten notebook from the floor. Any tingly feelings Ronan was making me feel are pushed to the side.

"This belongs to you," she hands it to me, but I can see the curiosity. She's been looking at it all day.

"I actually wanted to talk to you about this." I hope this isn't going to end up being an unacceptable request. "As you know, I am a doctor of human anatomy. I would love the chance to do an anatomical study where I could gather some information about your body. Just for educational purposes."

"Would you like to study me?" She offers immediately.

"I really would," I sigh, relieved. "We have so many similarities, but I want to learn about the differences too."

I was hoping she would be willing to do this, but I wasn't expecting her to volunteer so quickly. The more time I spend with Olexa, the more I like her.

"I will come to your quarters tomorrow."

was awake before the sun this morning, getting everything ready for the anatomy study.

I'm not sure if she will want to lie down or stand, but I make sure that my bed is perfectly made in case she chooses that. I read and reread my question again and again.

I'm so nervous.

I've done these studies before. In college, I had to do one at the coroner's office while he performed an autopsy. This feels scarier than that.

I am about to study the body and functions of an extraterrestrial being. Any scientist would be giddy. This is a nerds wet dream! The stuff of science fiction novels. I am about to be the first human, ever, to study alien anatomy.

A sound from the hallway outside makes my heart pound. She's here.

When the door slides open, my heart drops from my throat, down to my stomach.

"Where is Olexa?"

"She was called away in the night. Gaia requested her presence in the north. She informed me of your desire to study our anatomy. She sends her apologies." Ronan tips his chin, emphasizing the apology.

"Oh, no worries." I try not to let my relief show. I thought he was coming here for the study. That would have been-

"You may study my anatomy instead."

Fuck.

"That's very-"

"It is necessary to have a male and a female, correct?"

My palms sweat as I search his face. There is no humor or smugness in his voice. He isn't offering to make me uncomfortable. He's trying to be helpful. Everything about him is logical and practical. I just need to act like an adult and this will be fine, probably.

Be a professional, Nicole.

"Thank you, commander."

He slides the door closed and turns, waiting for instructions.

"I want you to be comfortable. If you want to stand, that's fine, or you can lie on the bed. I don't know if you wear underwear or...if you're uncomfortable with nudity..." My palms sweat. "I also have a series of questions, a survey, to gather information about certain functions that I can't see with my eyes alone. Which would you rather tackle first?"

"I will stand. I would prefer to complete the visual study first." He pulls his shirt over his head and I audibly gulp. My mouth drops open as he pulls his hair up, tying it on top of his head, out of the way. Why is that so attractive...

You are a doctor; I remind myself; this is about science!

As his pants fall to the floor, I take a deep, cleansing breath. Clearly, he's not uncomfortable with nudity. Peering up over the top of my notebook, my stomach clenches. Roughly sketching his form on the page, I focus all of my energy into making sure everything is correct and proportional.

With nervous anticipation, I inch forward as I carefully examine every small detail. His feet are large and wide, but otherwise human in appearance. Stepping behind him, I start from the ground up. I'm drawn to his calves. Where the muscles in a human calf are straight up and down, his appear to slope downward at an angle. Fascinating.

Moving up his back, I stop for a moment, appreciating his ass, not scientifically, but as a hot-blooded woman standing before a perfectly shaped backside.

The small of his back is narrow and grows wider as it moves into his upper back and shoulders. Lost in the structure of his muscles, I step forward, my fingers running over his spine at the center of his back. I can't tell without an x-ray, but his spine feels different. I try to count his vertebrae, but they aren't palpable. There seems to be a smooth, flexible bone covering the spinal cord from top to bottom.

His broad shoulders are as sturdy as stone, deep ridges of muscle rippling under his skin. He is so lean that the muscle fibers are visible through his skin, even with the tattoos.

"When we were rescued, Gaia's skin was silver. What is that?"

"It is body armor that protects our skin from the elements, as well as weaponry."

"And it just... appears when you need it? It looked like it was melting away..."

"We control it." He starts to turn silver before my eyes, like a blot of ink on a page, the smooth silver spreads over his skin in a matter of seconds.

"C-Can I touch it?" It's beautiful.

"You may."

It's cool to the touch, like metal almost but still soft like a shirt. I can't believe this is real... His tattoos are covered, it's not just their skin changing color, it's an actual covering. Just as quickly as it appeared, it fades away.

It's hard to wrap my mind around. He's real; standing before me. Natural body armor, eyes like the stars... it feels a bit like believing in Santa Claus. I can reach out and touch him but it's almost beyond comprehension that he exists. For my life, my parents, and everyone that came before us, there was life out there...

Before I move to the front, I stall and use the joint of my finger to measure an inch. Starting at his feet, I move up. Approximately six feet six inches.

"198.12 cm," I mumble as I write the measurements down. For the sake of thoroughness and definitely not to avoid standing in front of him, I measure his back and waist.

I want to ask about his tattoos, but I'm afraid that my voice will shake if I speak. They cover him like a long-sleeved shirt, reaching low on his hips, up to the base of his neck. I can't make sense of them; they could be words or symbols.

My knees feel weak as I walk around to face him. Starting at his feet again is probably the safest choice.

The further up his legs I go, the tighter my throat feels.

Keep your face neutral. I plead with myself as I move up to the one place that I desperately want to study. The place I've been most avoiding.

My eyes glaze over as I reach the mid-thigh. There it is. The longer I stare at it, the bigger it seems. For my own sanity, I don't measure it...

Science and professionalism are starting to slip as I feel desire pooling between my legs. Jesus Christ, Nicole... he's an alien. Are these feelings even ethical? Sex between different species is wrong, right?

I've studied attractive men before, I've seen plenty of muscle and handsome faces, plenty of penises too... He is something else entirely. He is raw power. As I stand here before him, I can imagine his skin against mine, the heavy weight of his body as it presses against me; as he holds me down. Shit.

Peeking up from my notebook, I gasp and my eyes shoot up to meet his. He's rock-hard.

When did that happen?

His thick, heavy inches stand straight up. Ethics be damned.

That won't even work if I wanted it to. He is not made for a human woman.

"This is surprising." He looks down thoughtfully. "I had not expected mutual attraction."

Mutual what?

"It's a biological reaction…" he doesn't seem embarrassed but I try to comfort him anyway, mostly as a distraction for myself.

"No, it is mutual desire," his voice is a bit raspy than it normally is.

"What?"

"We cannot become erect without a partner's reciprocated desire." when he steps forward, I step back.

"Reciprocated desire?"

"Yes."

"Wait, so no one can have sex unless both parties want to? How can you possibly know if I want to?" I raise my hand to my burning cheek. He can probably tell by the way that I'm panting and drooling…

"I can smell you." he takes a long, slow breath, his eyes laser-focused between my legs.

"Oh, my god," I turn on my heels and run. My mind is in overdrive as I run as fast as I can toward what I hope is Clarisse's room.

CHAPTER 17

C larisse is still asleep when I burst into her room. I'm so wound up that I don't even celebrate the fact that I actually found her room on my own.

She sits up, groggy and startled as the lights grow brighter.

"What's wrong? What happened?" She pulls herself out of bed frantically.

"Oh, God, Clarisse... I'm..."

She grabs my shoulders, studying my face. "Are you hurt... sick? Is Santi alright?"

"No, nothing like that. Physically, I'm fine... Santi too..." I realize suddenly that coming here was a bad idea. What am I going to tell her? I want to fuck the commander and hey surprise, he wants to fuck me too!

My cheeks burn as I replay the way he inhaled. He could smell me? That's humiliating.

Relief washes over her face as she plops down on her bed. An awkward silence hangs in the air. I don't know what to say. I burst in here, waking her, and now I'm not sure how to explain what happened.

I'm afraid she'll judge me if I tell her the truth.

"Does this have anything to do with a ridiculously tall, silver-haired alien commander who stares at you with sex eyes every chance he gets?" She smirks as my mouth falls open.

"Sex eyes?" Of course, that's the only thing I truly heard.

"Yes, he gives you major fuck-me-eyes." She wiggles her eyebrows suggestively.

"I don't think that's true." I don't want to give too much away. I came here in an emotional frenzy, but I don't want to spread this around. He might not want everyone to know that he desires a 'small and weak' human.

"Listen," she pats the bed. "I'm not going to tell you what to do, but if, hypothetically, a muscular alien with the face of an angel wanted to fuck me...there would be no holding me back."

"Really?" I crawl into bed beside her. "You don't think it's—I don't know, wrong?"

"What's wrong with it? If, again, this is hypothetical, a fully grown, consenting alien wanted to rock my world, what would be the problem? This is all assuming that we're compatible with them...physically." She looks at me expectantly, waiting for me to give away what I know.

I just shrug. If I tell her that I've seen his penis, she won't let it go without hearing all the details. At least I know she won't judge me...

Rolling over and wiggling underneath her blanket, I close my eyes. No matter how hard I try, I can't stop thinking. Next time I see him, I'm going to have to force my mind to control my body. I can't let him know or smell that I want him.

I haven't had sex in hundreds of years. He's liable to kill me! I need to remember that it should help keep any wanton thoughts at bay.

"So, you're really not going to tell me?" She huffs after a few minutes of silence.

"There's nothing to tell." I lie through my teeth.

"Sure, that's why you burst in here with terror in your eyes," she chuckles.

Groaning, I roll over to hide my face. What she thought was terror was actually salacious lust.

I spend the rest of the day keeping myself busy. It might look like I'm avoiding him, but that is not the case. I just have so much to do. Currently, I'm flipping through the pages of a Korean language children's textbook from I don't know when.

I could be an adult and go talk to him. As always, I have so many questions, but I'm afraid of the answers. Things were simpler when he didn't know about my attraction to him. He has the upper hand here.

A sudden thought occurs to me, and it's like a zap of electricity to my spine. Slamming the book closed, I jump up and leave the small library.

He doesn't have the upper hand. I've seen his cards, and he's seen mine. If anything, it's an even playing field. For whatever reason, he wants me too, enough to have a steel-plated hard-on.

As I march down the hallway with newfound purpose, I round the corner, stopping just short of colliding with Elite Navigator, again.

"I have been sent to retrieve you." He looks slightly less grumpy than usual. The scowl is there, but it's softer.

"You know, a map of this place would be helpful. As Elite Navigator, are you the guy to see about that?"

"I navigate the terrain. I have Earth's coordinates and conditions memorized. I am qualified to lead a squadron through any mission. I do not draw maps of our metropolitan buildings." He looks mystified that I would even suggest such a thing.

"Geez, relax, I was kidding."

"Oh, that was jest?" He looks relieved that I'm not as much of an idiot as he thought I was.

"Yes," I chuckle as we turn the last corner. Just as we reach the door, he stops me, looking down at me seriously.

"Doctor, against my own understanding, I feel the urge to warn you. The Commander is in a foul mood today. I find that it is generally fitting to not further vex him."

"O-Oh, alright. Thank you…" Do I generally vex him?

Speak of the devil and he shall appear. At that moment, he stomps angrily down the hallway. When he sees us his brows furrow.

Elite Navigator takes a giant step away from me, "Commander," he nods before turning to quickly exit this uncomfortable situation.

After a second of staring at one another, he steps forward, grabbing my shoulder, and ushering me into a room across the hall from the dining room.

"R-Ronan," I sputter as he drags me.

"Did I insult you? Did my hardness insult you?" He bends slightly, bringing his eyes closer to mine.

"What? No."

"Then why did you run?

"I…" I stutter, searching for the right words. "Can we wait until after dinner? I'm sure the others are waiting. We can talk after."

He looks upset, but he nods.

When we enter the dining room, Clarisse and Santi are already there. Olexa and Gaia are still away, which unfortunately makes our entrance all the more awkward.

Dinner is unusually quiet. I don't look up at him once, but I can feel him watching my every move. Now that I know about their…sexual tendencies, I keep feeling self-conscious. Can he smell me? Am I aroused? Can he sense it before I can?

While I never look at Ronan, Clarisse can't stop staring at him. She keeps looking between us, then smirking.

Way to be inconspicuous.

Several centuries pass while everyone finishes eating. The gnawing suspense in my stomach leaves very little room for food. I've been pushing things around on my plate for about thirty minutes.

When everyone else's plates are clear, I release a breath that I started holding when we sat down.

"Want to hang out? We can go on a walk or something?" Santi suggests as we finally stand up from the table.

"You slept poorly, didn't you, Nic?" Clarisse smiles sweetly. "I'll walk with you, Santi."

"I... yeah," I lie, "I'll join you next time."

The thought of being alone in a room with him again makes my heart pound so loudly, that I can hear it. I'm so anxious that I feel nauseous.

What if he tries to kiss me? Will he? Will he scoop me up in his large arms and hold me against his chest?

God, I hope so.

A deep, low rumbling groan comes from his throat and I let my eyes slide over the ground to look at him.

If a look could melt the skin from my bones, this would do it. There is fire in his eyes that scorches my skin.

"Nicole," there is a wobble in his deep voice, a break that lets his desperation show for a brief moment before he shuts it down.

His hand on my shoulder, he leads me down the hallway and up the stairs. Fuck! We're going to my room... well, his room, but mine.

When he opens the door, I walk out onto the terrace. I need space. Maybe if we're outside in the fresh air, the breeze will carry away the scent of the sticky area between my legs before he smells it... oh god... this is humiliating.

"Why did you run? I do not understand. Do human pheromones smell differently? Am I mistaken, and you do not desire me?"

Pheromones? That's what he's smelling... not my actual... closing my eyes, I take a deep breath.

"Ronan, will you explain to me how sex works on An'eo?"

can see the thick outline of his massive cock pressing against his pants but I force my eyes up.

"When we feel the desire to have intercourse, if both parties release the pheromone for lust, our brains release the block that holds back our physical body."

What?

"Wait, so what if the parties are both females?"

"It is the same. Our sexual components are controlled by the pheromone. We cannot engage without it."

"So..." I'm intrigued and confused. "What happens when one person wants to have sex with someone who isn't interested?"

"Nothing happens, if only one is interested, they are not released." He looks like he doesn't understand why I'm having a hard time grasping this.

"But it does happen? You can want sex and the other person doesn't want you back?"

"Is that what you call intercourse? Sex?"

"Intercourse isn't wrong, it's just...very formal." I squirm. This conversation isn't exactly sexy, but he is still extremely hard.

"To answer your previous question, naturally, it happens. Do humans desire everyone they meet?" His brows raise slightly.

"No, of course not! I guess I'm just—" I sigh not sure how to ask what I really want to know. "Ronan, did you want me before the pheromone or did you only want me once I released it first?"

God, I sound ridiculous. Insecure and pathetic...

The corner of his lip twitches, and his eyes look lighter. "I wanted you. Your body is unusual. I am curious about it."

That is definitely not sexy.

"Unusual. Well, thank you." My voice is completely flat.

"My body is very hard, and yours is very soft," he takes a step forward. "I imagine every part of you is very soft. I want to feel it against me." The growl in his voice makes me clutch my notebook.

Alright, it is sexy.

Clearing my throat, I quickly flip through the pages to my questions. The piece of me that is clinging to the idea that sex between us is wrong is getting smaller by the second.

"How do you reproduce?"

He groans and rolls his neck stiffly. "Do humans often leave their desires unfulfilled? I have never been so erect and left wanting."

"Uh, well, on earth, just because you're attracted to someone, it doesn't mean you have sex with them. We barely know each other." I gulp.

"You wish to continue with your questions, then?"

"Y-Yes." I'm lying. My pants are about to burst into flames—metaphorically and physically. I feel so hot everywhere I'm going to combust.

He nods. If he's disappointed, he doesn't show it.

"Unlike human reproduction, we do not need a male. A woman is always necessary, but not a male. Two females can produce offspring together." He says casually as my jaw hits the floor.

"Do your females... Do they have penises?" I'm scribbling furiously in my notebook.

"No," he looks confused. "When experiencing orgasm, do your females not secrete fluids?"

"We do, but it doesn't contain sperm. Do you have sex for pleasure and reproduction, or only for reproductive purposes?" My voice wobbles at the end.

"We have sex for pleasure." he takes another step forward. "We have methods to block conception so that we can engage in sex solely for pleasure."

"W-We do too, birth control." My throat is so dry.

"I have taken a blocker," he nods and I almost faint.

"Wait, men can take birth control too?"

"Yes."

I know I shouldn't ask this, but I can't stop myself. It's for science... I need to know.

"Sexually...are we compatible? Do you have sex the same way we do?"

He takes a slow breath through his nose and his eyes flutter closed. If he's trying to smell the pheromones, he's about to get smacked in the face with them. I'm a mess.

"I believe so," his voice is low and raspy. "We may need to perform another anatomical survey to know with certainty."

My knees wobble and I look up at the purple sky.

"If you remove your clothing," he steps forward, "I could look between your legs."

"For science," I barely whisper.

He nods and takes another step toward me. At this point, we're only an arm's length from one another.

"I have ached for hours, your scent is imprinted on my brain." His hand flexes like he wants to touch himself, but he doesn't. "I have thought of nothing but spreading your legs."

"Ronan."

"I want to unite my body with yours, to feel the suction of

your sex stretching to accommodate me. I yearn to drink from the pool between your legs."

I feel lightheaded as he speaks. The pulsating thump is too much to bear. Squeezing my thighs together, I try to make it stop but that only intensifies it. I'm so wet between my legs that my pants are soaked.

My eyes flutter closed and I feel like I'm floating. It's as if the breeze is pushing me toward him. Mother Nature herself is sending me into his arms.

In a moment of clarity, I realize how badly I really want him, how my body craves his. Call it lust or something more, it doesn't change how this feels. There is no fighting this. If I stop it now, I'll only be prolonging this torture. We're inevitable.

I surrender.

Suddenly, I'm weightless, swaying. Everything tingles as gentle pressure urges me forward. I can feel his breath on my skin, the tips of his fingers grazing gently over my forearms.

I let my head fall back. It's hopeless to fight this. He's not touching me, but I can feel him like the ghost of his skin across my skin. The heat that flows from him is like the sun against my face. When I open my eyes, a breathless gasp burns in my throat.

We're eye to eye, my body levitating, hovering above the ground. I feel like I'm floating because I am.

My stomach churns, boiling and throbbing with such fiery intensity that I'm not even concerned with his magic tricks. I'm wound to the point of hysterical lust. I care more about his cock than the fact that I'm actually floating in the air…

His hands slip behind me, grabbing tight-gripped handfuls of my ass as he plucks me from the sky. His face falls into the crook of my neck and he groans, kneading me almost painfully. Parting my legs, I bring them up, hooking them around his waist.

"Oh, God," I can feel him, pressed against my soaking wet, acutely empty pussy.

My fingers thread through his hair. It feels like strands of silk, soft and smooth.

His eyes are wide with shock when he moves his face out of my neck. Our mouths are so close that it would take only the smallest movement to bring our lips together. I want to taste his skin, to explore it with my tongue.

With one hand holding me up, he uses the other to tug the hem of my shirt up. To help him, I grab the hem and pull it over my head.

A strained groan, then softly spoken words in his language tumble from his mouth as he stares at my chest.

"You can touch them," I almost beg. The look on his face makes me feel more powerful, more beautiful than I've ever felt before. Goddess, woman, Mother Nature, some divine entity in the flesh.

With a surprisingly gentle touch, he cups me in his hand, his thumb running over my nipple. This nearly nonexistent action feels like ecstasy.

As his touch becomes more aggressive, my body starts to search for the friction that I desperately need.

I want him to kiss me, suck my skin, and run his soft tongue over me. His eyes come up to meet mine and I can't help but to wet my lower lip.

In an instant, he's on me, his tongue swiping over my lip, mimicking my previous action.

"You taste sweet," he whispers as he kisses me in a way that is so overwhelming that I forget to breathe.

With his free hand, he starts to pull at my pants. Dropping my legs down, I help kick and tug until I'm naked. I've been naked before men in the past, but this feels distinctly different. He is not a man. I can feel his desire... the overwhelming, all-consuming need like a hand on my throat. His eyes touch me physically.

As he sinks to his knees before me, he pulls his own shirt over his head.

This colossus mass of muscle looks between my legs as if he is standing at the gates of heaven, all he has to do is enter.

Reaching forward, he pulls me into his arms again, wrapping my legs around his waist as he lowers my back to the ground. The glowing lavender sky that surrounds us is warm and sticky against my skin.

When his mouth meets mine again, I let my fingers explore him, grazing over his broad shoulders and back. I'm vaguely aware of his pants coming down. It's only when the blunt end of his massive tip brushes between my legs that I realize how close he really is to being buried inside of me.

I close my eyes, bracing myself for the inevitable pain of what is about to happen.

When nothing happens, I peek one eye open. He's sitting back, staring down at me with one hand outstretched as if he wants to touch me but can't.

"You are very small," he marvels, like he's discovering the wonders of the world.

"And you are not," my lips twitch.

I'm about to beg him to just do it, to wreak whatever havoc he wants on my body. I don't mind, in fact, I'm desperate for it. Before I can say anything, his mouth is pressed to mine. One hand bites into my waist while the other slowly sweeps down my stomach, stopping right before the place I want him to touch me most.

His mouth moves down, nipping at my throat.

His fingers gently explore me, softly opening me up. The sound of his fingers and my wet skin squish in the quiet. I don't think I've ever been this wet or desperate. I've never been kissed this thoroughly before. It's as if he's claiming me with his mouth. The wildness of his mouth doesn't match the tenderness of his hands.

Just when I'm sure I can't take any more of this soft teasing exploration, he stops. Lifting his head, he speaks in his language and the walls respond.

"What just happened?"

"I have ordered breakfast to come here in the morning. We will be too exhausted to leave your quarters."

Holy hell.

Reaching out, I run my hand through his hair, stopping at the base of his skull to grip it tightly. I need something to hold onto.

He holds himself against me with his hand. We both take a deep breath at the same time, probably for different reasons. I'm preparing myself to be torn apart.

My eyes pinch shut, and I instinctively open my hips wider as he presses forward. He moves slowly, each inch sinking into me.

He rumbles something low that I don't understand, and I open my eyes to meet his.

I know that there is no way to physically enter my uterus but it feels like he has. When I look down between us, I'm shocked to see at least two inches remaining.

"What the fuck..." I start, but then he drags himself back and the words turn into a moan in my throat.

When he slides forward again, I can feel him pulsating.

"Ronan."

He growls and slides out again. With each thrust, he moves in a bit further.

Relax, relax, relax. I repeat over and over in my head, taking deep breaths. If I tense for even a second, he's liable to rip me apart like an axe cutting through a log. My body wants to clench, to protect itself, to push him out.

"O-Oh my god-" I whimper as he makes a low growling sound that reminds me as if I could forget that he is not a human man. It's rough and deep, an animalistic howl, primal, like an instinct.

I can't tell if this is pain or pleasure. My back arches up from the ground and he slips his arm underneath, holding me. Our bodies fit together like puzzle pieces. His face in my neck, his hips between my legs... our skin melts together.

When I close my eyes, I can see him... I can see me... layers of pictures, colors, and sounds. When I touch his chest, I feel the pressure on my own skin. It's like I'm in his mind... his body is a part of my own. It's terrifying and incredible.

Tears prick my eyes, burning there as I drown in unknown waters.

This is beyond sex. This is a union of our metaphysical selves. Soul, essence, consciousness, being, whatever it is, mine is fused to his. A deep, strained sound tugs in his chest as he chokes out a string of words in his language. While I don't understand the words, I understand exactly what he's saying. It's too much, all of it...

"Look," he pants, and I follow his gaze down. He's watching himself disappear inside of me. Slowly, he slides in and out, my slickness coating him. "Watch your body, see how it opens up for mine." You are so small, but look at how you stretch around me." He's mesmerized. "So soft and warm..."

"Ronan..." I grip the base of his neck and a shudder rolls down his spine and I feel it against my skin, goosebumps forming everywhere.

He releases me from his arms and leans back. His thrusts grow faster, but he's holding back, only allowing half of himself in. His tip rolls through me like a deep massage. I feel my body starting to spasm. My body is so tightly wrapped around him that not even the tiniest space can exist. The heat and friction are overwhelming.

Digging my heels into the ground, my chest rises off the ground, my back arching almost painfully.

I'm suspended on the edge, the tight, suffocating, mind-melting moment before orgasm, but instead of building, cresting, then easing up, I'm stuck. The tension is building, rising higher and higher until my body is so rigid I can't even draw in a breath. My mind goes completely blank, bright white and void, an empty abyss.

My eyes flutter and roll back. He whispers against my ear

and rocks forward, pushing himself into me until our hips slam together.

"Ronan... fuck," I think I'm screaming, but I can barely hear beyond the blood rushing through my body. I have no control over my body. This feels violent, more like an exorcism than sex. "Please-" If I don't come right now, my poor heart will most certainly stop beating from the strain.

A loud, grunting moan from deep in his chest vibrates through me. A zap of pulsating pleasure hits my desperate clit and my body snaps, like a rubber band that's been stretched too far.

Finally. Finally, everything shatters. I'm not sure if I'm conscious or even touching the ground. My body shakes and he pulses inside of me. He roars into the purple sky; the sound echoing around us. I can feel the warm, wet spurts of his release pumping into me and overflowing.

His large hand comes up to my face, holding my cheek while his thumb grazes my lips. Soft whispers, words that mean nothing, but somehow everything floats around me.

My eyes burn with exhaustion as he pulls me up from the floor, carrying my limp body to the bed. Physically, I feel almost brutalized. My body is battered and beaten, but my heart... my soul is full to the top with a kind of deep contentment that I've never known before.

The silky, cool blankets engulf me only a moment before he does, his rigid body pulling me to him as I lose the will to fight against sleep. The slow thumping of his heart by my ear is like a tranquilizer that plays in my dreams like a song.

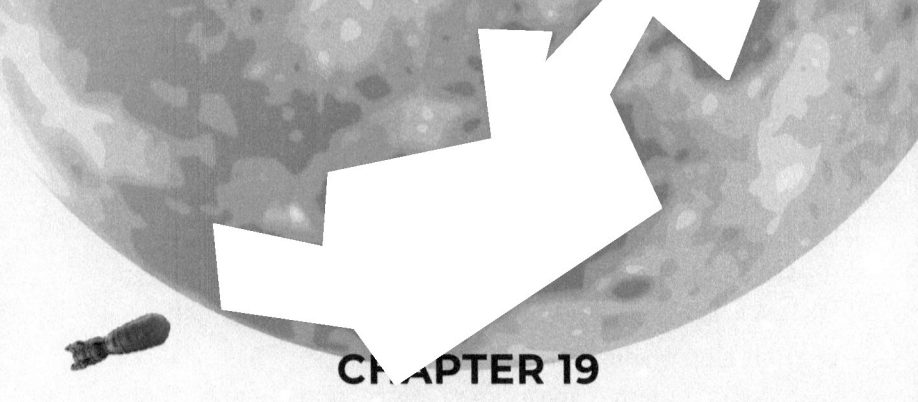

CHAPTER 19

Quite whispering wakes me from a death-like sleep. Blinking my eyes open, I see a woman pushing a cart into the room and quickly backing out. Ronan is inspecting the contents of the cart, a pair of pants hanging low on his hips.

When I move to sit up, a shockwave of pain radiates from my aching, swollen sex.

"Nicole?" His voice is soft and full of concern.

I groan and roll over, covering my face in the blanket. "It's fine, I'm fine."

The bed dips and his body slides under the blanket next to mine.

"You are hurt," his hands gently scoop me up, pulling me so that I'm curled into him.

"Just sore… I'm fine…" My nose nuzzles into his neck.

His fingers slide down my waist to my hip, squeezing the skin there. My body hurts, my mind is racing, and my skin tingles under his touch.

"Let me see," he suddenly says, and I nearly choke.

"See what?"

He's already sitting up, pulling the blankets down.

"Oh, my god! Ronan!" I shriek, trying to grab the fabric that has slipped past my stomach.

His eyes move down my body and I feel flushed. I have a million questions about last night and my body feels like it's been ripped to shreds and then put back together with tape. Everything hurts, my arms and legs feel wobbly and the muscles I haven't used in almost three hundred years are aching.

"Ronan, I can't-" I start to protest. The memory of his body on mine, the sounds he makes, the look on his face, my body's biological reaction is going to get me killed.

"I will not enter you," his voice is tight as he studies me with intensely furrowed brows and a deep frown.

"O-Oh ok," I don't know why I sound disappointed.

"Are you hurt?" His voice carries an irritation that catches me off guard. Is he mad at me?

"Um, it's sore."

"I hurt you." His voice is still clipped, but the anger isn't directed at me.

"Not hurt. I just—I'm sore. It aches, like an overworked muscle. You didn't do anything that I didn't want." I force myself not to wince as I sit up beside him. My fingers slip into his hair, and his chest rumbles. He's like a cat purring.

"I dreamt of your body last night," he groans before pressing his face into my neck. "I have never known such pleasure as what you gave me."

Probably because my body wasn't designed to handle the battering ram hanging between his legs.

"Let me fix the pain I've caused," his lips kiss down my throat as I release a whimpering sigh.

"Fix it how?"

"Open your legs," the authority in his voice makes my stomach clench. A fluttery tremble shakes beneath my skin, anxiousness, and excitement making me dizzy. He slides off the bed and I nearly choke. He's on his knees as he takes my legs carefully, pulling me toward the edge. Slowly, methodically, he places my thighs on his broad shoulders so that I'm completely surrounding him.

I can feel his breath against my swollen, ravaged skin. Oh, god, my poor vagina.

A soft, sweeping motion against the sore opening makes me gasp. His warm tongue spreads me open with such tender care that my eyes flutter involuntarily.

"Wait!" I gasp and lift my head. "I should shower!"

"Unnecessary, you taste of our joined bodies."

I shudder, "exactly."

"It is delicious to me." He dives back in with gusto, licking and sucking me with his full face yet somehow, still gently.

It's as if he's inside my mind. Anticipating my every need before I can even think it. Slurping, squelching, kissing. He's lapping away the pain with every swipe of his tongue. My sore muscles tense and shake as he pushes my body up, up, up to the place where only pleasure exists. Gripping his hair, I clamp my legs around his head. A sweet, salty, earthy taste coats my tongue, flooding my mouth as I come.

The muscles in my belly and thighs scream in protest as they clench and flex. His whirlwind tongue draws every drop forward, like last night, it feels like he's trying to suck my soul from my body.

"Ronan," I wheeze as the numbness starts to leave my limbs. "What the fuck is going on? Why does it feel like… I… we're…"

Leaning back against the headboard, he gestures for the cart with his hand and it rolls across the floor toward us.

"Ok, see! That's what I'm talking about… how? Are you telepathic or something? You lifted me up last night…is it magic or…or mind powers?"

"It is not magic."

"How then? You just rolled a cart with your mind!"

"Our power source is everywhere. It is in the air, in the water, in the very structure we live in. Our brains are connected to it. You've seen it. It's contained in the control room."

"Your power source?"

"Yes, our lights, heat, and cooling sources, the intelligent interfaces we use for communication and travel."

"Like... electricity?" My human brain can't understand.

"The closest example would be nuclear energy here on earth. Unlaar is mined on An'eo and used to power everything. It is connected to our consciousness like a continuation of our being."

"Unlaar," I repeat slowly. "Is that how you speak and the lights turn on?"

"Yes."

"So, you can just...lift things..."

"Yes."

"How do you connect to it?" I'm still not completely sure I understand it. Is it... a living thing?

"We just are. It would be the same to ask how your consciousness is connected to your physical body. It just is."

I can accept that.

That doesn't mean I don't have at least fifty questions to ask about all of the other absolutely illogical occurrences.

"Why did it feel like we were connected? Some moments felt like... I don't know, it was as if I could see myself through your eyes. When I touched your chest, I felt it against my own skin. How?"

"My body was inside of yours. Two could not be joined more closely. Of course, our consciousness connected. It was a strong connection, more so than I have ever felt with another."

"So, that is normal for you?" I can't imagine being able to connect like that to anyone I slept with.

"No," he scoops fruit from the trays and places them onto two plates. "Our bond was deeper and more profound than anything I've ever experienced. My heart now beats in time with yours. I did not expect to feel bound to you in this way." He stops and looks at me, saying something in his language that makes tears prick in my eyes. I don't know why. It's as if my body knows, even though my mind doesn't.

"Eat." He hands me the plate as I blink the tears away quickly.

"Thank you," I'm starving. As I clumsily shovel a bite of food into my mouth I happen to look up to catch him watching me. He's smiling at me thoughtfully, in the way that someone looks at a puppy or a baby...

"What?" My cheeks tingle with embarrassment. I'm sure there is fruit juice dripping down my chin.

"You are uncoordinated." He still has that endeared look on his face.

"I think we need to work on compliments, Ronan. My body is unusual and now I'm uncoordinated..."

"What do you mean?" He is completely lost.

"It's impolite to point out people's physical deficiencies, like... that they are weak..." I bite into my lip to keep from laughing.

"I insulted you?"

"For a minute, you're just very... blunt." I let my fingers trace over the tattoos on his arm.

"Insulting you was never my intention." He looks upset.

"Ronan, it's fine."

This is a lot to think about. Did he just tell me that he loves me? His heart beats in time with mine? I want to ask questions, but I'm afraid. In order to preserve my poor heart, I push it aside to deal with it later. Taking the conversation high and to the right, I change the subject completely.

"Do your people..." I hesitate to bring it up. "Are there no assaults on An'eo?"

"Assaults?" He's confused.

"Of a sexual nature. If your partner has to share the feelings for it to be even physically possible, is rape even a thing on your planet?"

Somehow, it feels even worse to talk about such things after what we shared last night. What we did was so... so.

It was the antithesis of assault. It was so connected and reciprocated and warm. It was everything that a sexual experience should be. My curiosity won't let go of this no matter how I try to push it down.

"What is rape?"

"Forcible sexual assault. It doesn't happen exclusively to women by any means but statistically…" I rub my palms against the soft sheets. "It's when an unwilling person is forced, physically to participate in sexual… experiences that they don't consent to."

Anger takes over his face, "people force themselves on unwilling partners?"

"Yes, unfortunately, they did."

"That is abominable!" He actually growls. "What would you do when this happened to you?"

"Oh, God, no! It never happened to me! It was a common problem, but it wasn't something that happened to every single person. The majority of society wanted sexual experiences with people that wanted those experiences with them."

His face softens, "I see. So what punishment was given to those who committed such atrocities against another? Surely, death is the only acceptable option."

"Well, there were factors taken into account. It's more nuanced than that…"

"How could it be?"

Wow, this is a difficult thing to explain.

"I have never heard of this before. It is distressing." He looks lost.

"It is."

I don't know what he's thinking, but I have effectively killed the mood. His large hands grip my waist, pulling me like a child onto his lap.

"Touch my hair," the request is soft, but I can feel the urgency behind it.

"I really like your hair," I whisper as I scratch gently at his scalp.

He groans and leans down to press his nose and lips against my cheek. I don't know what is happening, but it feels like it's moving at the speed of light. It's like jumping into a lake. You're submerged all at once. I don't know which way is up. He's a rip current, sucking me under the surface and carrying me away.

CHAPTER 20

'm not sure how much time passes while we hold each other but eventually, the walls talk. It's difficult to put into words how startling that is when you're not used to it.

Ronan sits up and grumbles under his breath.

"I am being called to the northern city." He holds his hand out to me, pulling my aching body from the bed.

"Was there another accident?"

"No. Emotional turmoil is causing a spectacle." He sighs, clearly annoyed. "Olexa will return within the hour. I will sort the issue and return as quickly as possible."

"O-Ok," I don't know why I feel nervous and fluttery. Clingy is not a word I would have ever used to describe myself, but I'm feeling very needy. I don't want him to leave for an undetermined amount of time so quickly after last night. I still have so many questions.

Swallowing down my emotions, I plaster on a fake smile. "Have a safe journey."

"When I return, I will come directly to you, day or night. Is that acceptable?" His heavy hand rests on my shoulder.

"Yes."

"This pleases me," he nods before walking away.

As soon as the door is closed, I slide slowly down to the floor. I want to find Clarisse and Santi, but I'm going to need to do some serious stretches if I'm going to be able to walk more than a few steps. My muscles ache as I spread them over the floor and reach for my toes. Each second that passes, holding my body in a deep stretch, I feel myself loosening up.

In the silence of the room, I lose myself in thoughts.

I had sex with an alien last night.

His words come flooding back to me. My heart beats in time with yours. What does that even mean? And more importantly, does he say that to everyone he sleeps with?

Tucking my feet into a butterfly stretch, I'm suddenly struck with a realization that almost knocks me over.

"Oh, my god!" My hand claps over my mouth.

He served me food this morning. He put fruit on a plate and brought it to me in bed.

"Ok, ok, ok calm down," I hold my hands up, talking to myself. "Don't read too much into that. We told him that it was normal and not romantic. He was just being polite."

Wow. One night together and I'm an absolute mess! All I need is a notebook to write Mrs. Ronan Commander all over and I'm right back to junior high.

Scraping myself off the floor, I take a shower to further relax my body. When I step out, Clarisse is sprawled across the bed. I cringe at the thought of what she might be lying in…

"You missed breakfast this morning," she tilts her head. That's it… no question. Just the statement left hanging in the air.

"I did."

"Is it because you spent the morning vögeln?"

"I don't know what that means, but no, I didn't spend the morning doing that." My face is on fire. I know I'm as red as a tomato.

"I can't believe you're not going to share the details with me…" she pouts.

"It was wonderful and I'm sore and confused." I cover my face with my pillow.

She perks up. "I knew it would be… there's just no way they walk around all perfect like that and don't know what they're doing in bed! Why are you confused?" The smile drops from her face and she gets serious.

"I don't know. It was so…" I feel like I'm about to start crying. "It was so intense, Clarisse. It wasn't just physical, it was mental and emotional, too. I don't even have anything to compare it to. It was so…"

"Alien?"

"So alien! And this morning he was so sweet, and I ruined it by talking about sexual assault and now he was called away so I'm just left here to try to piece everything together…"

"Scheiße, you talked about sexual assault? Why?" She looks horrified.

"Well, they don't have that. It's not a thing, physically, it can't happen." After I give her the vague details of their sexual process, she falls back on the bed.

"That's amazing…"

Without giving her any specifics or details about Ronan, I share my anatomical study findings. She is particularly intrigued by the silver skin armor.

"I need to do a study. I wonder if Olexa would speak with me? Do they have diseases? What about reproduction?" The scientific parts of our brains take over and we get lost in deep conversation about bodily functions, muscles, and skeletal structures. I still have so many questions to ask about them…

"Nicole?" Olexa's voice from outside my door stops us from speculating about different theories.

Realizing that I'm still only wearing a towel, I quickly jump up to get dressed while Clarisse opens the door.

As soon as I come out, I know something is wrong. She looks awful. Her breathtakingly beautiful face is marred by a heavy sadness.

"What's wrong?" I'm instantly afraid for Ronan.

She sighs and her shoulders slump forward. "Do you recall the accident I mentioned?"

"Of course."

She closes the door and speaks into the room. One of the side walls opens and a seating area with plush chairs slides out onto the floor.

How long has that been there?

She sits down like her bones are made of lead. Her usual pin-straight posture is slumped back against the back of the seat. She looks like she needs a shoulder, someone to listen while she vents.

"One of the injured, Secondary Engineer, was an intimate partner to Gaia. Their relationship ended without my interference, but I was blamed for the division. She succumb to her injuries and her family wants retribution. They claim it is my connection with Gaia that distracted Secondary Engineer and caused the accident."

Forcing my open mouth to close, I try to understand what she's saying.

"Wait," Clarisse speaks first. "So, Gaia's ex-girlfriend had an accident and died and her family is blaming you?"

"Precisely."

"That's awful! It wasn't your fault, you weren't even there!" I need to focus on the relevant facts, not the fact that I had no idea that Olexa and Gaia are in a relationship… I feel like a fool for missing the signs. Now that she mentions it… they're always together, they sit together, they share loving glances…wow. I've really been wrapped up in myself.

"Secondary Engineer and her family believed that Gaia chose to end their union because of me. This is not the case, but in their grief, they cannot see reason."

"I'm sorry this is happening to you." I reach forward and take her hand in mine.

She stares at our hands with an odd look on her face. Feeling uncomfortable, I withdraw, pulling away until she grabs me again.

"This is nice. You have the hands of a small child."

"I… ok…" I pat her hand, unsure of what else to say.

"How was the anatomical survey? Were you able to complete it before Ronan was called away?"

"Mostly, I still have questions. They can wait though, they're not that important…"

"Please," she perks up, "ask me. It will distract my mind from the strife in the north."

"Do you reproduce the same way we do? Are you born the same way we are? Do you menstruate? What are your lifespans like? Ronan mentioned that you don't need men to reproduce. How does all female reproduction occur? I've never seen a child here… do you… are you born as babies and grow or…"

"Do you have illnesses and diseases?" Clarisse adds.

She looks surprised by our rapid-fire questions but smiles, relaxing slightly.

"Your medical texts gave only brief descriptions of your reproductive functions. We share similarities but also many differences. Over time, we have evolved to eliminate the suffering that earth women feel."

"The suffering?"

"Yes, during reproduction we do not feel pain."

"Wait," Clarisse interrupts her and jumps up from her seat. "Wait…" she starts to pace. "Are you trying to say that you don't feel pain during childbirth?"

"Yes, we have eliminated that."

"What the fuck?" We both shout.

"What do you mean you 'evolved to eliminate' that? How?" I'm practically down on my knees. They have clearly found the secrets of the universe. "Share the wealth!"

"Share the wealth?" She's completely lost. "I do not understand."

"Holy shit…" I can't wrap my head around this. They won the anatomic lottery, and they don't even realize it.

"We are born immature, as you are."

"Where are the babies and kids? What do they look like? Are they… buff, like you?" My mind is spinning a hundred miles an hour.

"Buff? What is this?"

"Muscular." I'm awkwardly half sitting and half standing, suspended in the air while I wait for her answers.

"No, our young are small, like you. They reach maturation after fifteen earth years."

"Where are they? Why haven't we seen any children?" Clarisse is just as wound up as I am.

"This is the Capitol Hall. It is a place of training and legislation, not for children."

Oh. Well, that makes sense.

"But you live here? Does no one here have children?" Clarisse is able to articulate her questions better than I am.

"Those without dependents live here."

Sitting down, I lean back in the chair. Forcing my eyes closed, I try to quiet my mind. This is too much information to take in at once. Olexa and Clarisse talk about diseases. I vaguely hear them discussing their ability to heal. I can't stop thinking about my new obsession. I have to see an alien baby.

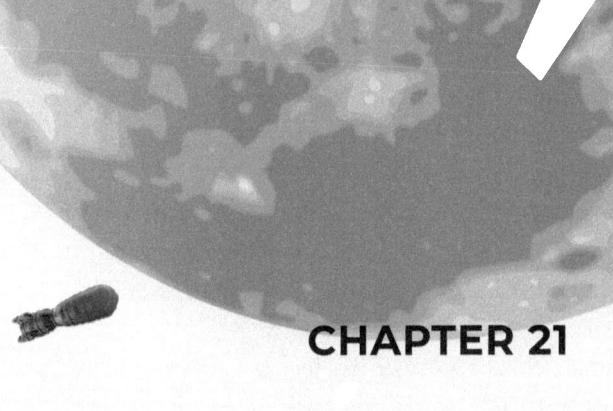

CHAPTER 21

One day was fine. I was busy with my soreness and writing everything I learned about their anatomy. Two days was mostly alright, I kept busy. When two became three, which bled into four, five, and six. I'm starting to think Ronan is staying away forever.

Maybe this is the way of the intergalactic one-night stand? Is he a cosmic playboy, ravishing the women from planet after planet, collecting his menagerie of extraterrestrial notches in his bedpost?

I knew men on earth who were smooth with the lines. Maybe all of his heartbeat talk was just talk.

Tying my hair into a frizzy ball on top of my head, I climb into my bed—which is really his bed.

With a sigh, I cover my face with the pillow. Maybe it will smother me in my sleep and put me out of my misery.

I feel my body drifting, consciousness becoming hazy as I fall into dream-addled sleep. He haunts my thoughts, both waking and sleeping. I can't escape him.

I dream of his hands, his skin, and his silky hair. I'm engulfed in him, surrounded and filled. He's everywhere.

Shooting straight up in bed, there is nothing but deep purple silence. Outside, rain falls from the sky, glowing drops like tiny, flickering flames. As I stand from the bed, I can't tell if I'm floating or walking.

Standing just inside, under the cover of the ceiling, I stare out at the endless sky.

"Nicole," his voice behind me doesn't startle me for once. I knew he was here. I could feel it.

His body tucks in close to mine, his feet on either side of mine, his bare chest pressed against my back, his arms circling my shoulders. My skin tingles under his touch.

"I thought of you constantly," he reaches one hand out, catching a drop of water in his palm and bringing it in for me to see.

"I missed you, too."

All the nervousness and doubts, the insecurities, are washed away by the gentle touch of his hands.

Leaning my head against his bicep, I run one of my fingers through the tiny droplet. I can't tell if the water is purple or if it's just reflecting the sky.

"Is everything alright?"

He sighs and squeezes me tighter against him. "For now. I tried to return each day, but it was not possible. Everyone presented me with obstacles that forced me to stay."

Spinning to face him, I press a kiss to the spiraling mark in the center of his chest. Quickly lifting me, he brings his mouth to mine. His grip on my thighs is soft, but his mouth is not. His lips are aggressive, nipping and sucking on mine. He steps out from under the protection of the room and onto the balcony. The warm drops of rain cool my burning skin.

From the pit of my stomach, a gnawing ache grows, spreading, corrosive, and devastating through my veins. Surely, he can reach it, he can massage it away.

With nimble fingers, he pulls the tie from my hair, letting my wet strands fall around us, sticking to my face and his, as the rain soaks it completely.

"You are wearing my clothing," he growls as his hand runs up my back, over the fabric of his shirt.

"I missed you," I moan as he tugs it up, rendering me naked in his arms.

The rain runs down his skin, dripping from his chin. He's beautiful. Towering and strong yet still soft. The universe swirls in his eyes as he reaches down with one hand to yank his pants down. With a groan, he's free, pressed between my body and his.

"Ronan, please," I start to beg, but he's lifting me before I can finish.

Holding my thighs, he lowers my body down, impaling me tortuously slow.

With a tight grip, he lifts and lowers me, using only the strength in his arms to create the friction we both need. With white knuckles, I hold his shoulders. He doesn't need help to support my weight, but if I don't hold on to something, I'm afraid I'll float away.

"Your vagina has bewitched me," he groans. My eyes jerk open, meeting his.

"My what?" I choke out the words in a laugh.

"I read your medical text. Is this incorrect?" He slows his arms.

"Not incorrect, just not sexy."

He stops moving completely, waiting for me to explain.

"The medical terms are correct, they should be used in professional or scientific settings, but right now, there are different words that we can use." I'm panting under his intense gaze.

"What words?" The growl in his voice makes me tremble. "What should I say in reference to you?"

"Pussy."

My cheeks flush, but the look on his face makes it easy to ignore.

"Pussy," the strain in his voice vibrates all the way down to my toes. Is it possible to orgasm like this? "And for me?"

"Cock or dick," as the words leave my mouth he twitches, tugging inside of me, making the excruciating pounding pulse between my legs almost unbearable.

He hums, a resonant sound that draws me closer to my breaking point.

Resuming his movements, he lifts me up and drops me down. My body swallows him whole each time. It burns and stretches and aches, but inexplicably it has me begging for more.

"Harder, deeper, faster," I moan and call into the sky.

Thunder booms and a bright flash of light cracks across the sky as the rain beats down harder. Pelting drops hit our skin as he meets the movement of his arms with thrusts from his hips. My head falls back, the rain drowning out the scream that claws its way from the back of my throat. I shake like a leaf in his hands.

He continues his movements, forcing aftershocks like earthquakes to hit me, one after another until he stills. He pulses inside of me, releasing everything he has with a long, low growl.

Stumbling inside, he drops us down into the bed, narrowly avoiding crushing my body below his.

"Fuck," I whimper and pull myself to sit up beside him.

"Is this word multifunctional?"

"Yes," I chuckle and lean into his chest. My fingers trace the lines of his tattoos, moving over his heart toward the spiral.

"Are tattoos normal on An'eo?" I haven't noticed them on anyone else. Then again, I haven't seen anyone else shirtless…

"No," he leans against the headboard, letting me see him better. "These markings are for the aristocracy, but they are not uncommon."

"So, only the upper class have them?" I'm surprised.

"Yes, is earth different?"

"Yes, tattoos are taboo."

"What is taboo?"

"Kind of forbidden. Tattoos are a rebellious thing. Criminals and rock stars… " I shrug. I don't want to offend him. I never cared about tattoos, it didn't make a difference to me.

"Rock stars?"

"Entertainers, musicians, especially rock and punk. There is a stigma, but yours are…"

Fascinating? Beautiful? Panty-soaking?

"My mother came from a nation of warriors. My marks tell of my lineage, they tell the history of my blood. My father's lineage is sovereign." He points to his right arm. "My father is here." He holds out his left arm. "My mother is here. They meet in the middle, my beginning."

The longer I stare at the symbol on the center of his chest, the more it starts to make sense. The right and left sides of his body flow from that symbol in the middle. His history, his family…

Depending on how you look at it, it seems to flow both ways. He expands from his family, or his family expands from him.

"It's incredible." I continue tracing over his heart.

"Tomorrow, there will be a meeting of the council. I would like you to attend." He pulls me closer, lifting my legs over his.

"A-Alright," a feeling of unease presses on my chest.

"I will be beside you." He rolls over, facing me. His eyes flutter closed, and I can see how tired he is. Whatever is happening tomorrow, I have a sinking feeling that it's not good.

CHAPTER 22

should have said no. Absolutely, without a doubt, I shouldn't be here.

Sitting in a large conference-like room, I am on one side of a gigantic table. Wedged between Ronan and Olexa. On the other side, eleven very angry-looking An'eo look like they would enjoy ripping my limbs off.

I haven't understood a single word since we sat down, but each sentence is spoken louder and with more rage. I've picked two of my cuticles into painful open sores and I'm working on a third.

I don't want to offend anyone, so I just stare at the table, trying to figure out what it's made of. It's not wood, metal, or plastic… I wonder if it can float on command or do anything other than be a table.

A particularly loud shout catches my attention, and I make the mistake of looking up. The man is gesturing to me while he yells.

Ronan stands from his chair slowly. The room grows very quiet suddenly and I'm sure everyone can hear my heart thumping in my chest. When he speaks a shiver runs down my spine. He's so calm. The kind of calm that's frightening. The kind of calm that makes a cold sweat drip down your neck. His voice is as smooth as silk, not loud or shaking, completely even.

Everyone looks afraid now. I don't have to understand the language to know that whatever he's saying is striking fear into the hearts of the very large, muscular alien gladiators sitting across from me.

"Nicole," he turns to me and holds his hand out.

With my eyes trained on the floor, I take his hand and walk between him and Olexa out of the room.

"I will find you soon," he nods to me before turning and walking briskly down the hallway.

"Come," Olexa's hand comes down onto my shoulder and she leads me in the opposite direction. "The others are outside. Santi has discovered a plant that seems to excite him greatly."

I want to ask her what the hell just happened, but I ignore it. If she could tell me, I'm sure she would. Ronan will tell me later…probably.

As we walk, I notice her pace slowing significantly. I'm barely moving. Typically I have to jog to keep up with their long strides. When I look up at her, she's already looking at me like she has something to say.

"Is everything alright?"

"Has my bother…" she stops, turning to face me. "Sa'nu."

"What?"

"Do you know Sa'nu?"

"Is that a person?"

"No, it is a connection. My brother has never said it?" She bends down, making herself eye-to-eye with me.

"I don't think so…" She's freaking me out.

She hums and stands again, walking at her usual brisk pace. She leads me out, onto a terrace much like the one off of my room. A garden surrounds it. Santi and Clarisse are sitting in the grass with large canvas bags beside them. They are sorting through whatever is inside.

"Nic!" Clarisse jumps up and points to the bags.

"Coffee!" Santi is practically screaming. "We found coffee cherries! Elite Navigator is setting up an area where we can dry them in the sun!"

"Oh, my god!" I bounce on my toes.

"You are excited about this plant as well?" Olexa looks mystified as I nod.

"How long will it take until we actually have coffee to drink?"

"Well," Santi's excitement level drops. "It will take about twenty days to dry the beans, then we have to hull them, then roast them. I'm told they have a power source that will get hot enough to do it. All told, probably twenty-five days."

"Wow, that's a lot of work for a cup of coffee."

"It will be worth it. These are naturally grown Peruvian beans!" He runs his hand through the bag of red balls.

"Where did you find it?" I need to get out and explore more. I've been too busy having my insides rearranged to get a lay of the land.

"There is an area just beyond those trees," he points out. "There are coffee plants everywhere!"

"I'll have to come pick some of the cherries so I can pull my own weight! I can't drink the coffee without putting in some of the work."

"Let's dump these bags, and we'll go pick more." Clarisse leads me toward an area where the sun will directly hit the beans. We spread the cherries out on the warm ground and try to explain coffee to Olexa.

Suddenly, the sun is gone. I'm cast in a dark shadow. Ronan.

"What are you doing?" His voice from behind me doesn't startle me the way it used to. He makes me feel safe now.

Turning, I look up to see him staring down at me thoughtfully.

"We're drying coffee cherries, to hull, then roast, then drink!" I explain the process smiling at Olexa.

"Bean water that makes you buzz..." She shrugs toward her brother, who looks confused.

"It's..." my words catch and my spine stiffens when I notice four of the angry men from the meeting standing in the distance.

"They wish to observe humans." His explanation doesn't make me feel any better.

"Where are the rest of them?"

"They are not invited," the unmistakable irritation in his voice tells me that these are the four who never spoke during the meeting. "Come, eat."

While we were picking beans, a whole buffet was set up on the terrace. We are introduced to Elite Inspector, Secondary Navigator, Chief Originator, and Secondary Commander.

The more I stare, the more I'm sure Secondary Commander is Ronan and Olexa's brother. I'm also sure that he hates me. He has spoken Spanish with Santi and German with Clarisse but not a single word to me. He hasn't looked at me once.

My palms sweat.

As we eat, Elite Inspector peppers me with questions. Some are fine but some are... inappropriate, to say the least.

No matter how I phrase the answer, he still doesn't believe that I am a fully grown adult woman. I'm trying not to roll my eyes.

A gentle breeze blows across the table, and I watch as several wispy white seeds float in the air. Everything around me fades away. I'm a little girl again, blowing dandelion wishes in the garden with my mom. I follow the white tufts as they blow by. One of them lands in Ronan's hair.

Reaching up, I pull the soft fuzz that almost blends in with his silvery strands.

The shocked gasps that come from around the table have me freezing, my hand suspended in midair. I expect to turn around to see some kind of snarling alien monster waiting to attack us. When I look, there is nothing. Well, not nothing. Several horrified faces are looking at me.

Santi and Clarisse are looking back and forth between everyone, trying to understand what just happened. I can't figure it out...

Everyone is staring at me, so it must have been something I did but I can't think of what it could be. Looking at the little seed still in my hand, I quickly toss it. Are dandelions bad or something?

"Nicole," Olexa rises to her feet, "Santi, Clarisse, I will bring you to your quarters."

"O-OK." I meet Ronan's eyes, hoping for something, anything, to tell me that everything is fine.

"I will come to you," the small tug at the corners of his mouth tells me all I need to know. He's not mad. Whatever I did or didn't do, he and I are fine.

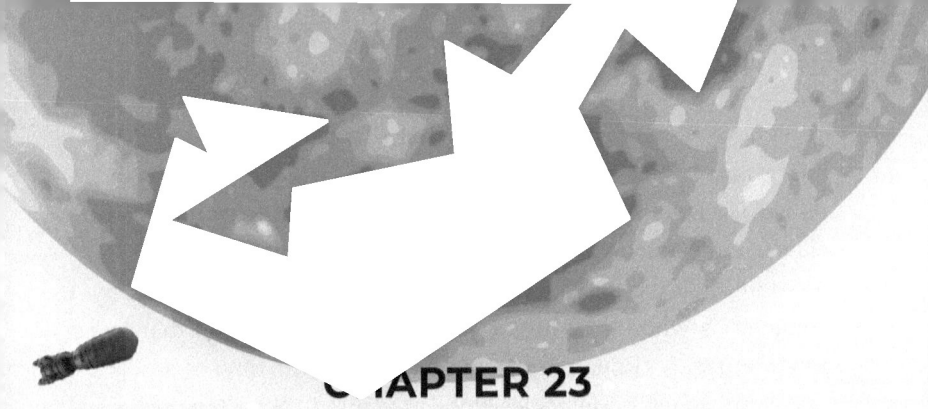

CHAPTER 23

"O lexa, please." I'm practically begging as soon as we drop Santi and Clarisse in their rooms. She won't tell me what happened, but I can see that she wants to. She's holding it back. I'm hoping that if I pester her enough, she will break.

Down two hallways and up one flight of stairs, I keep at it. Asking, begging, annoying.

"Did I do something wrong?"

With a heavy sigh, she places her hand on my shoulder and almost pulls me toward my room. I'm winded and in a full run by the time we get to the hallway. She slides the door closed and puts her hands down on both of my shoulders.

"You touched his hair." Her eyes look like they're about to fall out of her head.

"What?" I wasn't expecting that to be the grave offense.

"Ronan. The Royal Commander of Earth Fleet. You touched his hair..." She emphasizes each word like that is supposed to somehow illuminate the horrible atrocity that I've committed.

"And that is...bad?"

"Nicole, it is unthinkable what you did," she sinks down onto the end of my bed.

"Olexa, you're scaring me. What did I do? Is touching his hair illegal or something?" I'm panicking. That twisting, nauseous feeling of uncertainty and impending punishment claws at my stomach.

"On An'eo, hair is sacred. The only time it is touched by someone is when they honor you by washing it. Even that is a rare occurrence. Ronan never allows anyone who offers."

"Wait, what?" Memories flood my mind. "I've touched his hair lots of times... when we got here... those women that washed us..."

"They asked for the task. They wished to honor you, people of earth."

I can't dwell on how sweet that is. There is too much panic now.

"What does this mean? What happens if you touch someone's hair?"

"In my life, I have never seen it done the way you did it. Once during a combative struggle, one An'eo cut the hair of his opponent. He was immediately killed."

Killed? I sit down on the bed beside her and my chest tightens. He asked me to touch his hair... I can almost feel it, phantom silk in my hands. The memory of his body pressed against mine, warm and strong, while I gently scratch at his scalp tugs at my heart.

A gentle breeze blows against my skin and the warmth of the sun sweeps me up. He likes it when I touch his hair. A sacred, precious thing... he lets me, of all people, touch it.

"Nicole?" She drags me away from the gooey, warm feeling in my heart and back to reality.

Humming, I'm not sure I trust my voice. I feel a bit like crying, or laughing, or singing maybe.

"I fear for him," she sounds close to tears, too, but I doubt it's for the same reason.

"Why?"

"He has been challenged. The angriest voice at the meeting of regional heads was the brother of the deceased woman. He believes Ronan is unfit to command due to his leniency on me... and Gaia. Her family is out for blood. He will not punish us because we have done no wrong but they will not let it go." Her eyes well up with tears. "I was not concerned until now..."

"Hold on," I jump up, "Her brother challenged him? What does that mean?"

"They will battle."

"Battle? What does that mean, Olexa? I need specifics!" Now is not the time for their irritatingly vague answers. Give me details!

"They will fight before the regional heads. The winner will command the Earth Fleet."

"Ronan will win, right? Why are you concerned now? Because I touched his hair? What does that have to do with anything?" I can hear my voice growing louder but I can't stop it.

"You will distract him. A Sa'nu is sacred, but the bond makes you weak initially. It distracts... it consumes all thoughts." She looks absolutely distraught. "This is my fault. Her family is trying to punish me by harming him."

"What is Sa'nu? I'm not going to do anything to distract him! I'll go to sleep in Clarisse's room. Is the challenge dangerous? It sounds dangerous. What happens to Ronan if he doesn't win?" Tears drip down my face as I heave in a breath.

"The fate of the defeated lies in the hands of the victor. He will surely choose death. He will see it as a recompense for the loss of his sister."

"What about your brother? Secondary Commander? Can he do anything to help?"

"Ronan has told you about Caelum?" She looks completely shocked. Her shoulders perk up. For whatever reason, she sees this as a good thing and I'm going to have to disappoint her.

"Um, no. He looks just like you, I assumed."

She sighs and slumps down again.

When the door slides open behind us, we both jump up. Olexa doesn't even wait for him to close the door before she's practically screaming.

I may not speak the language, but I get the gist. She's very upset.

"Why are you crying?" He steps past her.

"Ronan, you're being challenged! Is that guy going to kill you?" I'm yelling, just like Olexa.

He stops walking toward me, a strange look on his face. When his head falls back and he lets out the most beautiful laugh, I've ever heard, I'm somehow enraged and...incredibly turned on.

"Tiny earth woman, you do not need to worry about me. Elite Technician is no match for my strength in any challenge."

I've never seen him smile like this before. Is my worry really so hilarious?

"But what about the Sa'nu? And I touched your hair in front of everyone! I—" My frantic rambling dies in my throat. The look on his face is like a hand squeezing my neck. I can't speak... I can hardly breathe. His laughter stopped as soon as the word, Sa'nu, left my mouth. I wish I could unsay it, or melt into a puddle on the ground.

Without taking his eyes off of me, he says something hoarsely to Olexa, who quickly turns on her heels and leaves the room. When we're alone, his long strides bring him toe to toe with me in a split second.

"Did Olexa explain the meaning of that word? Sa'nu?"

When the word leaves his lips my knees wobble. Not figuratively. They actually wobble and I have to grab his arm to keep myself upright.

"Whoa..." I try to shake to dizziness from my head. "Um, no, she didn't."

"Sa'nu is a rare connection. An'eo are given the ability to bind to their partner. It is an elevated level of attachment. Sa'nu is higher, more. It is precious and uncommon. When that level is achieved, that pair is intertwined forevermore. Through life, after death, and into the beyond. They share the same heartbeat, the same vision. Their blood mixes from two, joining to create one."

My toes barely touch the ground as he holds me by my upper arms. If someone walked in right now, they would think he was about to shake me. Maybe he is.

It might have been minutes or a few days, I couldn't say. We just stare at each other, his large hands holding me tightly.

I'm not going to speak first. I will bite a hole through my tongue before I open my mouth. Does he think that we are Sa'nu? I'm not about to ask! If he was just explaining the meaning of the word and my brain somehow twisted it around that he was calling me his, I would die of embarrassment. He has to say it, loud and clear.

"Nicole?" He moves his arms, lifting me slightly closer, our chests touching with each breath.

"Ronan."

He's staring at me, waiting for a response.

"H-How do you know if you've found... that?" I don't dare say the word out loud again.

"I assumed I would know in an instant if I was gifted a Sa'nu but... I have done research. I met with a history keeper. No An'eo has ever has a Sa'nu that was not also An'eo."

My chest deflates. Do I even want to be his Sa'nu? What is wrong with me? I've known him for a month! He gave me his room and made us a mourning meal. He let me touch his hair and served me food. Is that really enough to be intertwined with someone forevermore?

"I have traveled the universe and seen the sunrise from planets at the end of this solar system. I have met Kings and commanded a fleet. I am the son of a warrior and a king. I never expected to find you here. A small, soft woman from Earth. I never knew I was searching the cosmos for you."

A hiccupped sob escapes my lips, and I lean forward,

pressing my face against his chest. I need a minute, a second, where his swirling eyes aren't watching me.

With his arms around me and his heart beating beneath my head, I close my eyes and listen. Not just to his heart or the steady inhales and exhales of his breath. I listen to my heart, to my body.

My parents were soulmates. They were each other's second chances. My mom believed in fate and divine intervention.

I was born hundreds of years ago and survived a catastrophic event to be right here, right now. With him.

"What does this mean?" I glance at him.

"It means I will please you every night. It means that the universe has given us a gift. A connection so deep it cannot be severed."

"Ronan, I have so many questions," I whine into his shirt.

"Ask."

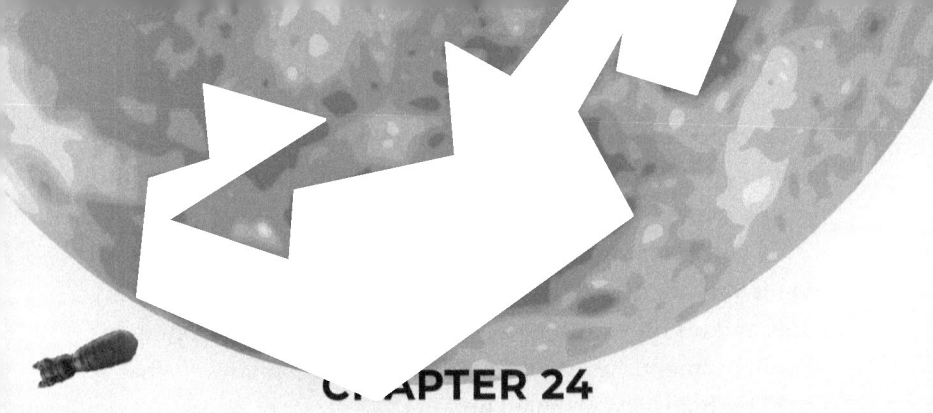

CHAPTER 24

"Did you know before we had sex or after?"

"After." Blunt as always.

"Is that how it works? Does everyone find out only after they have sex?"

"Yes. I believe humans and An'eo are different in their attractions. We do not feel the desire to sleep with almost anyone. It is not uncommon for years to pass between compatible sexual attraction." His hands weave through my hair, rubbing the ends between his fingers.

"Interesting. I think you've got us wrong, though. We don't want to sleep with everyone we meet, either." I chuckle into his chest. "Why didn't you tell me about hair being sacred?"

"Our first night together, you ran your fingers through it. It was passion and lust, but also innocence. You did not know of our customs. Your desire was uninhibited. When you ran your fingers through my hair, it was as if I had never seen the sun, and your fingers gave me sight. I want you to touch me whenever you want to without hesitation." His hands move down to my hip, trailing slowly over the fabric of my pants.

"Am I going to be a distraction to you with this challenge?"

"Yes. But I will still win." He sounds completely sure.

"Ronan. I'm serious." I sit up so that I can see his face. "If I need to go hide out in Clarisse's room, I will. You can't get hurt because of me."

"If you keep yourself from me, I will be distracted more so than if you are near." His fingers slip down past the hem of my pants and his other arm moves up, under his head. Stopping his slow movement, he sits up and picks up the pillow. "What is this?" He holds my keychain up.

"Oh," I smile, the way I always do when I see it. "That's just a keychain."

"What does it do?"

"It's just a little… personal flare, like a decoration, for your keys." Why are some things so difficult to explain?

"What is its purpose?" He still doesn't get it. I've noticed they don't really 'do' decor. Nonessential items like decorations or trinkets don't have a place here.

"It doesn't really serve a purpose. Some people collect them, some were functional, like a bottle opener or a tiny flashlight, or a Swiss army knife. They are just cute or silly."

"Why was it in the bed?"

"When you were gone, I felt lonely at night. That keychain is comforting to me, which is ridiculous, I know." I take it from his open hand. "My dad bought it on our last vacation before my parents died. We went to Myrtle Beach. Beach towns or touristy places always have little souvenir shops that have the same junk in each store, but my mom liked to look, anyway. In one of them, we found this keychain. I was wearing shoes that looked just like these. Blue Chuck Taylors with little flowers embroidered on them. We all thought it was funny…" I trace my fingers over the little shoe.

"You had no siblings?"

"Nope." I pull him back down into the pillows. "It was just me. My parents were older. They had both been married before and had no children. They divorced later in life and met each other. They always said that they were each other's 'second chance.' I was a miracle baby." I cringe, thinking of myself as that.

"Divorce?"

"Uh, to end a marriage? Do An'eo get married?"

"An'eo have unions—partnerships, but believe it is not the same."

"Well, my parents were both married to other people. My mom always said that it was fate that they even met. Her ex-husband had been very controlling, and he didn't allow her to drink."

"How did she survive?" He looks shocked.

"Oh, no, um, alcohol. She still drank water." My lips roll into my mouth to keep from laughing. The word 'cute,' does not come to mind often when I think of Ronan, but sometimes he really is. "That's just a sort of universally understood way to say you abstain from alcohol. Saying ' I don't drink' is understood to mean someone is sober."

"For what reason was she forced to abstain?"

"Control, I guess. He wasn't a nice man. But that's how she met my dad. On the day the divorce was finalized, she stopped at a bar for a drink. My dad was there with his brother. It was the first anniversary of his divorce and he hadn't been on any dates so my uncle forced him to come out. He always said that he thought an angel walked through the door when Mom walked in." My chest tingles, the way it always does when I think about my parents.

Reaching for my backpack on the floor, I pull my most prized possession from the front pocket.

His nose scrunches slightly as he stares down at it.

"How did you make this?"

"It's a picture, a photograph. You take it with a camera. I don't actually know how a camera works if I'm being completely honest." I can only shrug. "Do you not take pictures?"

"Not of people. We capture scans of the terrain to create electronic files for mapping, routing, or planning. What is this used for?"

"It's just to remember. I haven't seen my parents in a long time, but I can look at this picture, and I'm right back there. I can hear my dad's loud, infectious laugh. I can smell the cinnamon in the air. This was Christmas Day 1976. I had just turned twenty. I didn't know it at the time, but we only had one Christmas left together."

"They seem very happy."

"They were."

He pulls me toward him, placing his chin down on the top of my head.

"My mom started noticeably forgetting things in the weeks after that picture was taken. At first, we thought it was just forgetfulness, but one day she called my dad by her ex-husband's name. The doctors said it was a rapidly progressive dementia. She died less than two years later at sixty-eight. Thirty-six days later, Dad was gone too. They said it was heart failure but I think it was a broken heart that took him. He couldn't survive without her."

I'm not sure why I'm telling him all of this, but it feels good to talk about them. After they died, I threw myself into school. I never talked about them to anyone.

"I cannot comprehend the sadness you must have felt," his arms engulf me, holding me against the warmth of his chest.

"It was very hard, but in an inexplicable way, I was relieved. Dad didn't have to be without her."

"But then you were alone."

"I was but you have to sacrifice sometimes for your loved ones. They needed each other."

"What did you do?" His fingers rub against my skin.

"I continued going to school, finishing my Ph.D. program, and ultimately volunteering for the research project that led me here. I really hoped that we could figure out a way to stop and reverse dementia."

After a moment of silence, he sighs, "Secondary Commander is my brother."

"Ronan," I crane my neck to look at him. "I would love to hear about your family but please don't feel like you have to share with me because I told you about mine."

With his fingers gripping my chin, he tilts my head back further to kiss me. He takes the breath right out of my lungs. A soft, warm feeling spreads through me, starting in my chest and flowing outward to my limbs.

Unlike our previous kisses, this is romantic, sweet, and caring. All of my senses are dull, completely overpowered by the building urgency in my blood.

Just as suddenly as he began the kiss, he ends it, pulling back, and swiping his tongue over his bottom lip.

"Your lips distract me." The subtle scratch in his voice is aiding in the release of my pheromones.

Dropping his head back into the pillow, he takes a deep breath. "My brother challenged me when I became commander of the Earth fleet. After winning, I sent him on a scouting mission to set the location for our next metropolis. He has remained there for two Earth years. I believe he is instigating the Elite Technicians challenge."

"Olexa thinks that he will demand your death if he wins." The thought makes my insides flip-flop.

"I do not doubt he will."

"Your brother would instigate a challenge that would see you killed if you don't win? Why?"

"I will win." His large hand comes up to hold my face, running his thumb over my lips. "I out-trained him. He believes our father gave me an advantage by training with me, but I woke early every day to meet him at the training grounds. Caelum was welcome to join. It was his choice. When I was named commander, he felt he was robbed of the opportunity."

"What an asshole!"

The thunderous laughter that fills the air around us makes my insides flip flop again, but this time for a different reason.

Lunging forward, I grab his face and pull him forward. On instinct, my body draws closer to his, wrapping around him, melting into him, pressing together everywhere. Breaking the kiss only to pull my shirt over my head, I control the tempo, the depth, and the length of each sweeping pass of our lips.

Spreading my fingers through his hair, rubbing against his scalp, his composure starts to crack.

"Nicole," he warns as I press down, letting my need rub against his.

"Ronan, I need you now." I bite his earlobe gently and he flips us over on the bed, trapping me below his body.

"I am supposed to train with Macsen tonight," he growls, thrusting his hips forward and rubbing himself against me. "He can wait until tomorrow."

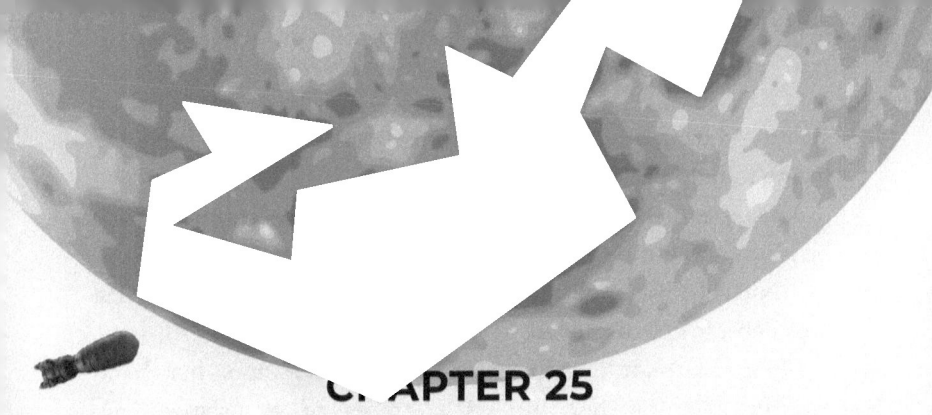

CHAPTER 25

Tapping my pen anxiously against my notebook, I stare at the door, hoping that he will come in and inform me that the challenge has been canceled altogether.

"Nic," Santi reaches over and flattens his hand over mine, stopping my nervous fidgeting.

"Sorry."

"What's going on with you today?"

Groaning, I drop my face down against the table. "Well, Ronan is training today with Elite Navigator for the challenge that might kill him. So, you know, nothing much going on with me. Everything is fine."

"I've been meaning to talk to you about him," he says in a hushed tone.

When I sit up, I'm met with concern on his face. Unsure of where this is headed, I start to feel nervous. The look on his face is telling, whatever he's about to say, it's not good.

"I think you should be careful, Nicole. I've seen the way he looks at you. I'm not sure if you've noticed it but he seems, I hope this doesn't upset you, but he seems like he's-"

I'm not sure if it's the look on my face or the grunt sound that comes from Clarisse that makes him stop speaking, but we all sit silently, staring at each other. I'm in shock. Clarisse desperately trying to hold back laughter.

His eyes flick back and forth between us several times before he gasps and jumps up.

"Nicole! Please tell me you are not involved with him!" He looks absolutely disgusted.

"She's an adult, Arturo," Clarisse stands too, her hand angrily gripping her hip. Any traces of amusement are completely gone from her face, anger replacing them.

"Who cares? Are you kidding me? She is an adult *human*. He's an alien! You can't possibly condone that!" He snaps at her. The way he emphasizes human makes my stomach turn.

"Oh, please. You can't be serious," she scoffs.

"I'm completely serious! Are you sleeping with him? Nicole, that is so unethical. It's like a cat and a worm trying to mate! We're doctors!" He throws his hands into the air.

"Hey, whoa!" I'm yelling more loudly than I should. "Who is the worm in this scenario, buddy? I am an adult, he is an adult, this is not like a worm and a cat, you jerk! I am of able mind and body and I can do as I please!"

"I'm shocked at both of you. It's disgusting! Is he forcing you? They are bigger and more powerful. Do you feel like you can't say no? Did he threaten to kick us out if you didn't?"

"What? No! Did you hear me? I am not being forced. How dare you-"

"How dare I?" His sharp yell startling me. "We're the last people on earth and you're screwing an alien?"

"Are you jealous or something?" Clarisse is yelling now, too. "Did you think that the three of us were going to repopulate Earth together? Hurensohn! You don't get to dictate our bodies under some kind of a twisted notion that as the only man left, they somehow belong to you!"

"I know you don't belong to me! It's just disgusting to think that you would have sex with something that's not even your species! You know it is wrong, that's why you've been hiding it from me!"

"Not 'something,' someone." My voice is shakier than I would like it to be. "I wasn't hiding it from you. I just don't make a habit of talking openly about my sex life. Clarisse and I don't sit around discussing it. She just knows."

Tears prick in my eyes, welling up before spilling down my cheeks. What I feel about Ronan, it's not disgusting or unnatural. Maybe this hurts so much because somewhere, deep down, I'm afraid that he's right. I had reservations at the start.

"Are you sure it's even safe? You said Olexa told you they have babies, but are you sure? What if he's using you as some kind of breeder or something?"

"Jesus Christ!" Clarisse is furious. "I saw a baby yesterday. Mac- Elite Navigator took me to meet his sister and her son, you idiot."

Our eyes go wide. If we weren't in the middle of an argument, I would have questions. Santi shakes his head, repulsed.

"It's like wanting to have sex with an animal or something. It's wrong!" He takes a step toward me. He's not much taller than me, but he looks bigger, stronger in his anger.

"Stop it!" Clarisse begs him, "You're upsetting her!"

As soon as the words come out of her mouth Santi is no longer standing in front of me but pinned to the wall beside me. Ronan has him by the throat, and his legs kick, searching for solid ground.

For a moment, the room is silent. Ronan's shirtless back moves as he inhales. Otherwise, everything is still. Fear and horror shine in Santi's wide eyes.

"You will not raise your voice to her," Ronan finally speaks.

Clarisse slips her hand into mine, her body shivering at the tone of his voice.

"Ronan," my voice shakes, "we're just having a disagreement. I'm fine."

"He was approaching you aggressively." He growls, never breaking his gaze.

"He wasn't going to hurt me," I'm only half sure that's true.

Santi's feet touch the ground and the tension in my shoulders releases. The relief I feel is short-lived, the anxiousness building again as Ronan speaks, low and ice-cold.

"Our private relationship is none of your concern."

Clearly, he heard more of our argument than I thought.

"Today and only today, I will allow you to walk away from this because I can see that your misguided concern is genuine worry for your friend. She is safe with me. I will not allow anything to harm her."

Anger radiates from both of them as Santi jerks himself away.

"It's obvious that you're much bigger and stronger than we are. You hold all of the cards here. The power is completely unbalanced, one-sided," he glares at Ronan. "Are you sure that your relationship with her is fair?"

"Our union and the nature of it is none of your concern," he repeats.

"Ridículo," He throws his hands in the air and stomps away.

"Don't worry about that jealous asshole," Clarisse wraps her arm around my shoulder.

Ronan is making me nervous. He hasn't blinked since Santi walked away. The deepset scowl on his face and the slight hunch in his shoulders would give away his anger to anyone, but I can feel it. Like heat in my veins.

"Come," his voice is stern but much softer as he places his hand on my shoulder.

I jog beside him for a moment before he stops in the middle of the hallway, lifting me up like a child and crushing me into his chest.

"If he would have struck you, I would have removed his head from his body." There is a desperation in his voice, in the way that he's holding me. Gripping into my skin like he's afraid I'll fade away.

I press a kiss to his temple, then his forehead. He groans and takes a slow, deep breath against my neck. Every time he does that it sparks something in me. No matter how I was feeling just a moment before, I'm feeling drippy and hot.

"I need to train. I have rage in my veins. If I fuck you right now, I will hurt you." His chest shakes as he speaks.

His riled-up state, heaving chest and spot-on use of the vocabulary I've been teaching him has me practically drooling.

When he reaches the training area, he yells angrily into the quiet room, his voice echoing off the walls. The ceiling splits in half, retracting to reveal the slightly purple sky.

He speaks again and a long silver bar flies from somewhere directly into his open hand with such speed I'm sure it would have ripped my arm off.

Elite Navigator runs toward us out of nowhere. A silver bar gripped tightly in his fist.

Ronan smiles before turning on his heels and sprinting. Both men are running so fast that I'm sure they will sustain life-threatening injuries if they collide. As the space between them shrinks, I start to panic. My hands come up to cover my mouth, forcing the frightened sounds back down my throat.

When they leap into the air, reaching a vertical height that is at least as tall as they are, I watch, open-mouthed - stunned.

They crash into each other with a bone-crunching thud.

Did they forget about the armor they have built into their skin? Why aren't they using that?

After several heart-stopping moments, I realize that while they are absolutely trying to beat each other up, Elite Navigator isn't going to injure him, at least not too badly.

Sitting against the wall with my knees up to my chest, my thoughts drift back to Santi.

I can understand his concern but some of the things he said were downright cruel. Everyone here has been nothing but welcoming and helpful to us. He spoke about them as if they were vermin.

After running and chasing and hitting, they stand calmly beside one another. Ronan holds his silver spear out and Elite Navigator taps it with his as they bow their heads. As he walks toward me, I pull myself up.

I'm not sure why, but seeing him makes me supremely annoyed. He's not even sweaty or winded. If I ran to the other side of the room, I would be out of breath and as red as a tomato.

"I should have ensured your well-being before training. What can I do to make you feel better?"

The irritation I felt is gone in an instant.

"I want to shower."

He nods, "come," he starts to lead me away.

"Together."

He stops and turns to look at me with wide eyes. "Would you like to bathe with me?" He looks confused.

Biting into my lip to keep myself from laughing, I take his hand, pulling him out of the room behind me.

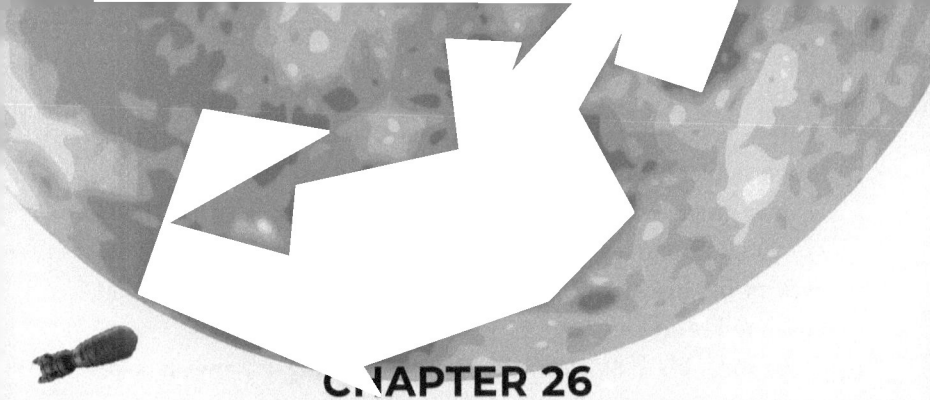

CHAPTER 26

Adjusting the dial for the water takes me a while. I'm still not used to their strangely high-tech showers, and the water is never the right temperature.

I finally turned around to see him naked, standing in the doorway, watching me. The smile on his face makes my knees weak. I'm sure my frustrated grunts and huffs have something to do with it.

"Come here." I drop my pants and kick them off, stepping into the warm, lightly perfumed water as steam billows around me.

He still looks unsure. I've gathered that showering together is not something that they do on An'eo. I'm about to teach him a thing or two.

"Can I wash your hair?"

"I would be honored." He drops to his knees in front of me, giving me access to the top of his head. His eyes never leave me as I pour some of his strange shampoo into my hands. It's almost as if he's holding his breath, waiting.

Reaching out, I run my fingers through the thick, wet strands. His eyes flutter closed, and he tips his head back slightly. I'm acutely aware of how quickly he's getting hard. Stepping forward, I let his tip graze my legs as I massage his scalp.

His groans and sighs cause physical reactions in my body. I'm longing and desperate. Each low, sensual sound from the back of his throat triggers a memory, a flash in my brain, skin, lips, hands and tongues.

Rinsing his hair clean, he stands, reaching for me. It takes everything in me to stop him. I have plans.

"Wait." One finger stops him in his tracks as he watches me pump soap into my hands. Working the soap into a thick lather, I step forward, starting at his neck and working my way down. I wash him.

With slightly parted lips and panting breaths, he watches my every movement. I can feel his eyes on me as I run my greedy fingers over the dips and ridges of his muscles. Everything about him is hard but soft. Steel wrapped in smooth skin.

Looking up to meet his gaze, I wrap my hand tightly around his cock, right at the base. A relieved guttural growl and a heaving exhale work like vibrations against my already throbbing sex.

Sliding down to his tip, I replace my first hand with my second, over and over again.

His head falls back as he runs his hands over my waist, cupping my breasts.

Waves of energy wash over me. I feel taller, stronger, bolder. My muscles twitch as my eyes flutter closed. Raw power radiates from my fingertips. I could run a marathon or scale a mountain. The blood in my veins buzzes, electric and alive. My eyes fly open to meet his. I have never felt like this before. I don't understand it but the grin on his face shows that he does.

"What is this?" My voice doesn't even sound like my own. It's thick, weighty authority in each word.

"It is my strength, take it," he leans forward to press warm, soft kisses to my chest.

Holding my hands out in front of me, they tremble. The

strength coursing through them is too much for my body to handle.

"Get up," I sound demanding, in control, like him.

Without drying off, I pull him by the hand, leading him to the bed. I can't tell if he's just letting me pull his body or if I really am stronger, but there is no resistance. Turning so his back is to the bed, I push against his chest with both hands. He falls back with more force than I intended.

"Sorry, I'm not used to this," I stare down at my hands.

Droplets of water roll over my skin, puddling on the floor as I stand and watch him. I know what I want to do, but I'm nervous. I'm hardly a first-timer, but he isn't human. His length and thickness are concerning.

The thumping between my legs spurs me on. Crawling across the bed, I stop between his legs.

His breath catches as I lean down. With my eyes on his, I lick the tip, his body immediately tensing and squirming. Gently kissing, sucking, and licking, I tease him, enjoying the way he begs. The slightly sweet, sticky fluid leaking from him rolls down over the sides of his shaft, coating my fingers.

I love to watch his desperation, to hold him on the edge but not go further. I know what he wants, what he really needs, but I won't do it, not yet. Giving me his strength might have been a bad idea. I'm clearly easily corrupted by power.

Stroking him with one hand while I lean down to lick his balls, he starts to fall apart. The sheets are clenched so tightly in his fists that they rip, tears running through the fabric. His heels dig into the bed as he pushes himself up, thrusting forward, truly begging me.

Between my legs, the dripping wet mess grows with each passing second. Deciding that it's finally time to continue on the mission I've set for myself, I leave a quick, sloppy kiss to his tip before crawling further up the bed.

"Nicole," he grips my hips with bruising force. He's not going to let me continue teasing him.

Taking a deep breath, I adjust my hips, hovering over him.

The muscles in his stomach tremble as I sink down, letting him split me open.

With my hands planted firmly on his chest, I rise up slowly. Loud, uninhibited moans echo off the walls, our panting breaths and sighs float on the wind. I'm consumed by fire, burning from the inside out. Every roll of my hips brings me up higher. I'm delirious, drunk on the smell of his skin, the taste of his lips, the feeling of him deeply embedded inside of me.

If anyone was listening, they would think he was hurt, the tortured sounds that claw their way from his chest, scratching all the way up through his throat. He sounds miserable, aching and pulsating inside of me but holding himself back.

I don't know how he's keeping himself from orgasm, but I'm determined to shatter that control.

Bouncing faster, I ride him with no concern for how sore I will be later. My thighs burn, but that only makes me want to speed up. My newfound strength gives me the boost I need to really handle him.

"Ronan, come, please," I sob, my toes curling as he slams upward growling out the sexiest-sounding phrases I wish I could understand.

With his head pressing into the mattress, his back arches, his whole body contorting painfully. He feels bigger, harder like he's about to explode, but he forces it back, still. He's waiting for me.

"Fuck! I'm coming." My head tips back and I claw into his chest. Overwhelmed by the unexpected flood of pleasure that shakes me to my core when he presses his hips up to meet mine.

He chokes on my name, crying out as he pulsates in the depths of my stomach.

"Ronan- Oh my god," each deep jerk is like a vibration that zaps my oversensitive clit, rippling up my spine.

He fought with Elite Navigator for almost an hour earlier and he was barely affected. Right now, he's panting and breathless as he pulls me forward, kissing me so hard it bruises my lips.

Lifting up, he slides out of me and a gush of fluid follows after. My thighs and his stomach are wet and sticky as we grope and lick each other.

"I like your body very much, the softness, the way it bends and arches." His hands glide down over my ass, squeezing the thick, soft skin.

"So, you're an ass man?" I giggle against his chest.

"A what?"

"Nothing," I curl into him. "I wish we could go for a drive." Admittedly, I feel much better about the argument with Santi lying here in post-sex bliss, but a drive would be the cherry on top.

"I can take you in the airbridge. We will need someone else to accompany us, as it is not a single flyer."

"Thank you, it's sweet of you to offer." I pull the sheet up over us. "It's just not the same. Putting the top down, turning the radio up, and cruising, it can't be beaten. I used to just jump in my car with no destination in mind, just following the road. I love driving."

"Is there anything I can do?"

Sitting up, it hits me. "Actually, yes."

"Name it. I will see it done."

"Can you take me to see a baby?"

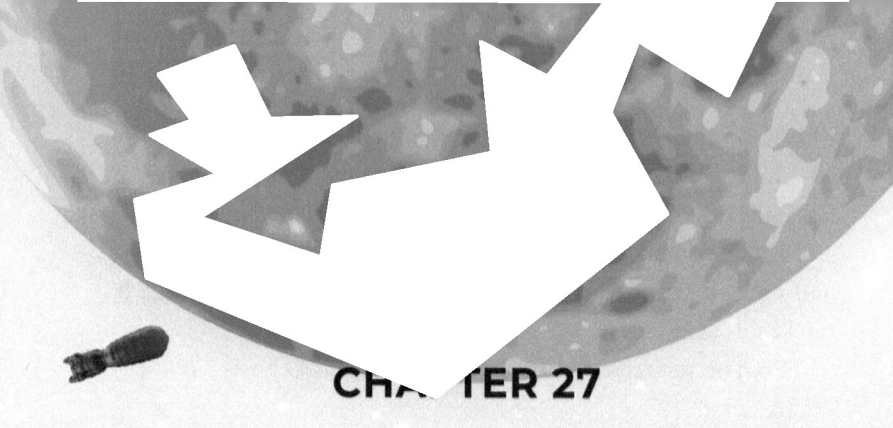

CHAPTER 27

E very day this week follows a predictable routine. We wake up and spend an hour wrapped around each other before Ronan has to train.

While he is busy beating different trainers to a pulp, I study, walk with Clarisse or Olexa, or accompany Elite Navigator on quick surveys around the capitol and surrounding areas. No one mentions Santi, and I'm grateful for it.

Eventually, I will have to talk to him but not yet.

While I love exploring with Olexa or gossiping with Clarisse, my outings with Elite Navigator are my favorite. His grasp of sarcasm and humor is improving, probably by the aid of a certain foul-mouthed German, but he still has a long way to go.

A few days ago he told me that we would soon be passing over a cluster of volcanoes and the air would smell strongly of sulfur. I responded, sarcastically, that I couldn't wait. He did not understand the joke and spent the rest of the ride questioning human olfactory senses.

"Doctor," he comes to sit beside me while the airbridge zooms through the sky. "Would it be inappropriate for me to ask for advice?"

"Not at all, please, ask." I dig my nails into my fist to keep my face neutral. I've bothered Clarisse for days but she won't budge. She gets a big, goofy smile that she can't get rid of whenever he is mentioned but she's been shockingly quiet. Considering how nosy she was for details about my situation, I didn't expect her to be so private about her own.

"I am told that human women have not evolved to allow for painless delivery of a child. Is this true?"

I choke on… spit or air or possibly nothing. This was not the direction I was expecting him to go.

"Why? Is Clarisse-"

"No!" He looks horrified.

"Oh, ok." I place my hand over my chest, hoping to slow my rapid heartbeat.

"I would very much like to engage in a copulatory relationship with her, but I fear for her safety."

Rolling my lips into my mouth, I stare at him. He's obviously large, but he's different from the others. He's quiet, serious, and extremely logical. The fact that he's so concerned for her is completely unexpected and very sweet.

"Can you take birth control?"

"A blocker?"

"Yes. You could take those, couldn't you?"

He nods, but his face is still etched with worry. "What if the blocker fails? You are the only other human woman here. We cannot be sure."

"Do your blockers fail frequently?" I'm feeling very warm.

"No, never. Yet, I cannot ease the distress in my mind."

"Have you tried to talk about this with her? Maybe you just need to sit down with her and talk through your concerns."

He sighs and rubs his large hand over his face. "I have tried. Whenever we approach the subject." He takes a shuddering breath.

The pheromone.

"I see."

"I can think of nothing else."

"Well, I'm not sure it's my place to talk to her for you so, maybe, you can write it out? Give her a letter?" I pull my notebook out of my bag, handing him my last remaining pencil.

He holds it between his fingers, moving his hand to study it.

"I have never written anything. We do not write."

"O-Oh- how do you communicate with people who are not nearby?"

He picks up the tiny screen from the seat beside him and presses buttons. A moment later, Ronan's face appears.

"How?" My eyes bulge.

"Nicole?" Ronan's voice is as clear as if he was standing right in front of me. He shouts something in An'eoc and Elite Navigator takes the screen. They speak rapidly for a moment before he hands it back to me.

Ronan sighs, "I feared for your well-being."

"Oh, sorry," I cringe, "I'm fine. I just wanted to know how you communicate from a distance. I'm sorry."

"Do not apologize. I have asked that you return. Is this satisfactory?"

"Yeah, we can come back."

The airbridge is always fast, but it feels like we've sped up, zipping over the tops of the trees so quickly I don't trust myself to stand. We travel thirty minutes away today. We arrive in eighteen minutes. I feel like my insides have been scrambled.

After showing him how to hold a pencil, Elite Navigator has been writing furiously on the paper.

Slightly woozy as I step onto the platform, I feel him before I see him. He comes out to meet me the moment my foot touches the ground.

He scoops me up, crushing me into his massive chest.

"Ronan, what's the matter? Is that device only used in an emergency?"

"No, but Macsen should not have used it while out with you." His hand runs through my hair. "I believed for a moment that you were injured or in danger."

"I'm fine. I'm sorry you were worried," my voice trails off as he pulls me toward the door quickly.

Halfway to his room, he picks me up, holding me in his arms so that he can kiss me while we walk.

"Ronan," I breathe against his lips, "I'm fine, I'm safe."

"You are very small. You have no shields or defenses. Your life is fragile."

"I'll be careful, I promise."

His swirling eyes feel like hands holding my heart. At all times, I am treated with tenderness, with gentle regard. It makes me feel fluttery and ridiculous but also cared for. Like I'm some precious thing. Like how my father cared for my mother.

As soon as we reach the room, he takes me straight to the shower. Smirking as I undress, I can feel his eyes on my skin.

"Are you sure you want me to get in? You seemed to think it was gross to *bathe* with someone else..." My arms fold over my chest.

"I have never been more wrong about anything," he holds his open hand out.

That was easier than I thought.

The water is perfect, cascading over me as Ronan's arms wrap me up tight. With gentle hands, he massages my scalp, carefully washing my hair with such a tender touch that it makes my heart ache. The kind of feeling that you get at Christmas when you see the wonder on a small child's face. The kind of ache you get when you happen to see a proposal. Two people, in love, happy and excited, choosing one another.

After my hair is cleaned and rinsed, he lathers soap and, with excruciating slowness, washes my body.

When his hand dips down between my legs, I kiss his parted lips eagerly. This acts as a spark to the flame. In a rush of move-ment, he hoists me up into his arms and brings me to the bed, wet and slippery.

The moment I touch the cool sheets, there is a knock.

"Shit," I whisper, sitting up.

Ronan shouts, but no one responds. After a moment, a quiet shuffle outside lets us know that there is still someone there.

Grabbing for my clothes and tossing a very irritated Ronan his, I take a few steps toward the door.

"N-Nicole?" Santi's voice makes me cringe.

"One second."

Ronan scowls as we pull and tug at our clothes until we're dressed.

"Go sit on the terrace," he kisses my temple. "If he angers me, I will throw him over the side."

I'm pretty sure he's kidding, but the thought makes me nervous.

Santi looks understandably nervous as he wheels a cart into the room.

"I, uh, I brought coffee," he gestures.

Perking up instantly, I jump to my feet.

"The bean water?" Ronan is still scowling.

"Y-Yeah," Santi shrinks back. "I came to apologize to you. To both of you. I didn't mean to insult you, I just... I can disagree with something that you're doing without being hurtful or disrespectful."

"Now that we're calm and the shock has worn off, can you explain to me why you feel this way?" I take the cup from his hand.

"Be careful. They don't drink hot beverages, they don't have mugs or cups with handles..."

"It is consumed hot?" Ronan is temporarily distracted from the conversation at hand.

"Yes, do you want to try mine?"

His scowl deepens, "I do not."

We sit facing each other on the terrace. Ronan's arm is comfortably over my shoulders, my back slightly angled into his chest.

Santi sighs and his eyes bounce between us for a moment. "I am a scientist first and foremost, a doctor. I believe in science, that it holds the answers to everything as long as we can find them. I have a moral prejudice toward sex within your own species. I guess this whole situation just caught me by surprise. I haven't fully come to terms with the fact that we are the whole of humanity left on earth, just the three of us. You deserve happiness and we have to find a way to forge forward," he sighs, rubbing his hands on his pants nervously. "I want to be clear that I do not, nor have I ever thought that I have some kind of ownership over your body or choices. I'm sorry that I spoke to you like that."

Ronan's arm tenses around my shoulder and he lets out a slow breath. He is not moved to forgive based on this conversation.

Sitting quietly for a moment, I consider how I feel about this. I appreciate his apology and I can understand his initial shock, but some of the things that he said play over again in my head.

"Thank you for apologizing. I know you were surprised, but I still can't understand why you said some of the things you said. We're the last humans left. We've got to stick together. I want to move past this, but for a while, I think it's probably best if we keep a bit of distance between us."

He nods, "I understand. I just had to speak with you. I truly am sorry."

When he slides, the door closed behind him, I turn back to Ronan, watching the thoughtful crease between his eyes. "You're still upset."

"I am." He pulls me up into his arms. "I will not tolerate anyone speaking of our relationship with disdain." There is biting anger in his voice that takes me by surprise.

"H-Has anyone else spoken about our relationship with disdain?" I hadn't even considered that his people could be upset. Maybe they have the same view as Santi. "Ronan?"

"I will not tolerate it."

"I heard you. But you're not answering my question. Are

other people saying-" he shuts me up with a kiss that makes my hair curl.

"Ronan, I'm serious," I pant, pushing him back.

"I do not wish to waste one precious second discussing others and what they might say. Sa'nu," his thumb swipes over my lower lip as he cups my face in his hands.

"O-ok," I want to protest, to talk about this, but that word, it hypnotizes me.

"I need to speak with you," his tone suddenly more serious. "Olexa is insistent that we have this conversation, she is convinced that I am incorrect. I would like you to be present during the challenge. I have made arrangements for you."

"What?" My voice comes out like a cough.

He looks caught off guard. Next time I see Olexa, I'll have to thank her. I don't want to watch the challenge!

Swallowing the sand in my throat, I take a deep breath. "Do you think it's a good idea? I won't distract you?"

"I will be reassured by your presence."

Well, shit.

"If you want me there, I'll be there." I fake calm, cool confidence, even though my knees are trembling and I'm completely nauseated.

"Do not worry," he smiles and my knees wobble again, "I will win."

CHAPTER 28

Rinsing the disgusting taste of vomit from my mouth, I exit the bathroom to find that Olexa has joined Clarisse in my room. Wonderful.

"That is very unpleasant." Her lips tip down into a repulsed frown.

"Yeah, tell me about it. I'm just so nervous. Ronan is completely calm. He doesn't seem nervous at all. In less than an hour, he'll be fighting someone who hopes to kill him." I press my fingers into my temple. "Please, can one of you distract me? If I think about this for too long it makes my stomach twist in knots."

"Macsen and I had sex," Clarisse blurts out, then claps her hand over her mouth.

I knew it. I could tell from the moment I saw her this morning. She's been dying to tell me, but I'm sure a sense of decency and decorum held her back.

"What?" Olexa looks completely stunned.

My brows quirk, arching up as I wait for her to gush about the details. "I thought that he didn't want me. We've started to talk about it a few times, but he always looks so freaked out that I end up running away! So, he wrote me a letter discussing his concerns. Nic, he had concerns about me. He was worried he was going to hurt me or that I would get pregnant." Her eyes look glassy. "Not in an- 'I don't want a baby with you way. In an- 'I'm afraid for your health and safety way.' He was so sweet and gentle." She looks smitten.

"I did not realize that you had become so close." Olexa smiles once the shock wears off.

"I did," I finally feel the nervous tremble in my chest calming. I just need to think about something else, anything else. Even if that something is gossiping about someone's sex life.

"He has been very pleasant recently," Olexa muses quietly. "This explains it."

"If it makes you feel better, Nic, Macsen isn't worried either. He is sure the Commander will win."

"He will win. I have watched him in training. You appear to strengthen him, he is not distracted in the way I assumed he would be." Olexa looks genuine but her words don't really help.

I've never watched anyone fight before, human or otherwise. "Can you tell me exactly what is going to happen? What should I do?"

"Of course." She crosses the room to sit beside me, taking my hand in hers.

Time always seems to move at lightning speed when you're desperate to avoid something. Before I'm ready, we're sitting in the arena.

My fingers tremble in my lap as I sit, watching everyone else come into the room and take their seats. I don't miss the way each of their faces morph into shock as they notice me. So far there haven't been any surprises. Everything is exactly as she said it would be.

I am grateful that they've pulled back the roof to allow open air to circulate. The cool breeze is the only thing keeping me from passing out. I know I need to get it together. I can't react, I can't panic, I can't tremble or scream or cry. I can't do anything that will distract Ronan.

He needs composure, alien logic, and steadiness, not human emotion.

When the ten regional heads are seated across the large training room, the room goes silent. A door off to the side opens and three An'eo walk in. One I recognize, the angry one from the meeting, and two that I don't.

This is her family. I can see it in their posture. I can see it in the emotion on their faces. They're furious. They're here for blood… for Ronan's blood.

Olexa sits up straighter—taller—tipping her chin up slightly. Showing no fear, no emotion, no guilt. She knows that what happened isn't her fault and she's not going to cower.

They walk together toward two seats at the far end of the room, staring us down and blinking as they pass.

The one that I recognize bows slightly before the others and returns to the center of the arena. He shouts something into the silence, his voice booming so loudly that it vibrates in my chest. I don't understand a single word, yet somehow I do. Rage and pain. His voice cracks as he wails toward the sky, his arm reaching out to point toward Olexa.

With each angry word, he takes a step forward. Why is he coming toward us? Looking past him, I meet the eyes of Caelum. I hold contact, narrowing my eyes slightly. He looks surprised as I scowl at him.

I don't want to break first, but I have to when one of the long silver bars flies through the air, landing in the challenger's open hand. He takes one more menacing step toward us when Ronan's voice, calm and smooth, echoes off the walls.

My eyes jerk to see him standing just inside the arena, Elite Navigator walking behind him.

I watch him, mesmerized. It feels like I'm seeing him for the very first time. No one, including the challenger, moves or even breathes. He looks bigger, taller, and like his muscles have somehow grown. He's not yelling but his voice carries, hanging over our heads like a weight. He's in control of everything.

It's Ronan, but it's not. This version of him is different. He's not the man that holds me against his chest while I sleep. This man doesn't have any softness in him. Only absolute raw power and authority. It's in the air. I can feel it like when he gave me his strength, only this time, it's pressing down on my head, not flowing through me.

Each step he takes deepens the pit in my stomach. When he's only a few steps away from the center of the arena, he pulls his shirt over his head and holds out his hand. A silver spear whistles through the air before landing in his open palm.

Ronan tips his head to the challenger. When he doesn't reciprocate the action, Olexa's breath hitches. The disrespect.

Sweat rolls down my back as both men take their places, standing before the regional heads.

Ronan speaks, then the challenger.

One of the regional heads opens his mouth, ready to call the challenge to start when everything changes. Before he can speak the words, the challenger jumps. This is not how she explained this to me. He shouldn't be attacking already.

In a blur of motion, he's above Ronan, coming down on top of him.

Olexa jerks beside me but forces herself to stay seated. On instinct, my hand comes up to cover my mouth, physically holding is closed. The scream that I force down burns my throat like acid.

The sound of the silver bars clanging together echoes loudly in my head, each hit making me dizzy. My body jerks and tenses with each swing, waiting for a piercing cry, for blood and gore.

They move like a choreographed dance, graceful and elegant in their violence. If they weren't trying to kill each other, it would be beautiful. The challenger pulls the ends of his weapon, the single bar opening into two smaller bars in his hand. The points on the end look sharp enough to pierce through anything they are pressed against.

It was explained that they are forbidden to use their body

armor during a challenge, but it keeps coming into my mind. I want to scream out, to beg him to protect himself.

When he pulls his weapon apart, the already unbearable tension gets worse.

Each strike is met by a waiting block from the other man. They go back and forth like this, hitting and blocking, striking out and deflecting.

Olexa reaches out and grabs my arm, holding me down in the seat as we both see the challenger move a second before Ronan does. The sharp end of the blade drags across the skin of his shoulder. Blood pours from the slit covering his chest and arm in only a second.

His face is calm as he jumps back before lunging forward and spinning, both of his blades catching in the middle of his challenger's chest. I can tell, even from this distance, he didn't cut him as deeply as he was cut. It's like he's going easy on this guy.

Ronan hasn't shown any emotion, he's not screaming or growling, his face is neutral, never showing the same rage his opponent shows.

"He is fighting from his heart, not his head," Olexa whispers. "That is his mistake. Ronan will beat him."

No sooner have the words left her mouth when he jumps up, forcing Ronan to the ground. I'm momentarily stunned as his fist comes down against his face. Luckily, he only hits him once before Ronan swings the blunt end of his weapon, hitting him so hard that he falls to the side. The sound of metal bouncing off bone vibrates in my chest.

Ronan stands, his blood dripping down onto his challenger. When he stretches out his arm, pressing the pointed tip of his weapon into his neck, his voice, calm as always, silences the arena.

"He is demanding surrender," Olexa translates, though I somehow already knew. He is offering his challenger a way out, a peaceful end to this ridiculous conflict.

Some of the tension in my body releases but I'm still holding my breath, waiting for the end.

The challenger yells angrily before pulling down on Ronan's weapon as if he's trying to yank it away from him. When he's cleared enough space between the point and his neck, he slides his legs across the floor, kicking into Ronan, hard. He doesn't fall, but the impact shifts his balance enough to give the other man enough space to roll out from under him.

With his weapon secured in his grip, he runs forward, jumping into the air again. For the first time since this began, Ronan's composure cracks only slightly, but I see it. I'm sure everyone does. He sprints forward before jumping to the side. Instead of colliding, Ronan swings his silver weapon like a bat, knocking his opponent down.

When they hit the ground, Ronan has the upper hand quickly. Laying his weapon across his throat and pressing down, he demands submission that the challenger refuses to give.

Commotion from the end of the arena momentarily pulls my attention away from Ronan. The woman, I assume his mother, has jumped up and is running toward them. A small silver glint in her hand makes my blood run cold. She has a weapon.

"Ronan!" My scream is raw, filled with the fear that is choking me.

He must see her coming because he ducks, rolling across the ground, away from them before she can plant her knife.

"Why isn't anyone stopping this?" I grip Olexa's hand in mine.

Aren't there rules here?

The thunderous boom of his voice stops everything. My body slumps back in the chair. He has to be putting a stop to this madness.

When they both approach him, walking side by side slowly, like hunters that have found their prey, my mouth drops open. I make eye contact with Caelum across the arena as a tear drips down my face. Why isn't anyone doing anything?

"Ronan has demanded we not interfere." Olexa sounds completely bewildered.

My hands tremble as I force them down in my lap. He's going to fight the two of them?

When they advance forward, attacking from opposite sides, I have to close my eyes. I can't watch it anymore. The clanging of their weapons is sickening.

Clearing my mind, I focus on the silence. Aside from the sound of fighting, the room is deadly quiet. If I try hard enough, I can block everything out, and the only sound I can hear is the loud beating of my own heart.

Minutes, hours, days. I don't know how much time has passed as they rage with seemingly unending energy. When I finally force my eyes open, there is blood everywhere. The three of them are covered in it. It runs down their bodies onto the floor. Thick pools dripped and splattered.

Ronan says something that only they can hear, and the woman screams, falling to her knees. She looks like she's begging. Her hands reach out for his feet, her head bowed down.

"What is she saying?"

"She wants her daughter back." Olexa's voice is strained.

"What?" I don't understand, but I don't have time to ask any more questions. The man looks like he's boiling from the inside out. His rage is so hot I can feel it from here.

Surrender, please. I beg any merciful deity that may be listening to put an end to this.

The man lunges forward, but Ronan moves to the side, sliding one of his legs out to kick the challenger's leg out from under him. When he's on his knees, Ronan speaks again.

Whatever he's saying seems to be angering the challenger even further. His body shakes, his bloody skin trembling over each tense muscle. With his arm outstretched, he points to Olexa, speaking quietly to Ronan.

He lets out a long, slow breath. When he turns to address the others, the challenger jumps up to his feet, but before he can run forward, Ronan stops him with the sharp end of his weapon. I watch in horror as the silver tip comes through his chest completely before he falls to the ground, presumably dead.

The woman wails, her wretched sobs making my eyes sting with tears.

The deep, low sound of Ronan's voice is like a blanket, thick and heavy, covering everything. I'm comforted slightly, but my legs itch, desperate to stand and leave this arena.

After a moment, amid obvious protests, he turns, walking toward me with his hand held out. I jump up, scrambling to his side. With his large, bloody hand engulfing mine, we leave the arena, ignoring the chaos behind us.

" am unharmed," he repeats again.

"This is hardly 'unharmed,' Ronan. This is a pretty deep laceration." I gently wipe away the blood from his shoulder. He's so bloody I can't tell where any of the wounds are.

His fingers catch my chin, tipping my head back. I can't look at him yet. The tight, fluttering feeling of fear is still coursing through me. Once I know that he's alright, I might be able to relax but not before then.

"Nicole," his soft voice makes me shutter, a wave of emotion clapping down on top of me.

Biting into my lip, I shake my head 'no' and continue to busy myself with his injuries. I was able to hold everything in, to keep it together during the challenge but now I feel completely over-whelmed. Every nerve is exposed and vulnerable.

It's like every emotion possible is weighing down on my chest. The fear that simmered below the surface through the entire challenge has switched now and I am angry. I'm angry at the challenger and his family. I am angry at everyone who was present for allowing the fight to go on for so long. I am angry at

Ronan for asking me to be there. He should have known that watching that would be too much for me.

When he whispers something softly in his language with his voice so sweet and gentle, I lose it.

"Stop it!" I can't hide my clipped anger. "You said that everything would be fine."

"I said I would win, and I did."

"I—" I'm completely lost for words for a moment, then a tidal wave of words hits me all at once. "That was an absolute shit show. Why was this allowed to go on for so long? Why didn't someone, anyone, put a stop to it? He cheated from the start, then he wouldn't fucking surrender, then he was allowed to have a partner? What is this tag-team challenge where anyone can join in?"

"It will never be said that I backed down from a challenge or that I used my position to cut short a grieving family's need for revenge. I was in control the whole time. They needed to let out their rage."

"You were in control the whole time?" My anger is growing. "Maybe it felt different watching from the sidelines, but from where I was sitting, you won by a hair." I hold my thumb and finger up with no space between them to emphasize my point. "If you hadn't killed him, he never would have stopped fighting."

The smile that tugs at his split lips is like a crack in the dam holding back my emotions. I feel everything all at once.

"God damnit, Ronan, why are you smiling? That was so awful to watch! I'm glad my distress is so amusing to you!"

He grabs me as I turn to walk away. Lifting me into his arms he walks toward the bathroom.

"These are superficial wounds. I will be healed by morning," he kisses my chin before I tuck my face down. "Nicole, look at me."

When I don't look up, he sets me down and takes my face in his hands. "Your distress is far from amusing to me. I did not kill him. I only disabled him temporarily. I suspected he would not surrender easily, but I needed your presence. You kept me calm and level-headed, in control. I am sorry for your discomfort and worry."

"Come on," I sigh, the exhaustion of today feeling heavy on my shoulders. "I'll wash your hair."

"I hardly deserve the honor," he stops, pulling me back to him to kiss me. It's soft but needy. I can feel it on his lips, in his hands as they run over my skin. "I am sorry. If there is ever another challenge issued, I will not ask you to watch."

"Ronan," I sigh, craning my neck to look at him, "I just don't want you to let it go on for so long while you're outnumbered. I understand, I think, why you did it. You were letting them fight out their anger, but you were hurt! Look at all of these cuts!"

Pulling him into the shower, I peel back the blood-soaked clothes and begin to wash his skin. With painstaking care, I clean every inch of him, save one place. That can wait until last. That can wait until I'm less upset.

"Nicole," he groans as I purposely skip over it again.

"It doesn't look like you're actively bleeding anymore. All of this is from before."

"This one hurts."

I jerk my face up to see which injury he's talking about.

"Right here," he points to the cut on his lip.

Narrowing my eyes, I inspect the broken skin. "It looks fine."

"It is not. It hurts more than any of the others. Look closely." He looks completely serious, but I know what he's doing.

Cupping his face in my hands, I bring him closer to look at his lips again.

"Yeah, it looks fine."

"Nicole," the way he says my name makes my insides flutter. "Let me apologize."

"Apologize how?" That desperate, needy feeling between my legs is back with a vengeance.

Running my fingers along the smooth muscles of his lower abdomen, he takes a shuddering breath.

"My need for you grows each day," he says, pressing his hips forward and letting his cock nudge between my legs. "I am sorry," he falls to his knees while lifting my thighs up.

"Ronan," I yelp, feeling flushed. There is something so vulnerable about sitting on his face like this. It's hard to feel self-conscious when he moans like that, though.

No human being could move his tongue like this. He's vibrating against my clit like he's battery-operated. When I reach down to grab a fistful of his hair, I feel him jerk, thrusting his hips forward shamelessly.

Tipping my head back against the wall of the shower, I let the water run down over my face. His manic tongue has me squirming in mere seconds.

The ache between my legs grows. He's only fanning the flames. The pleasure is overwhelming, but I'm still so profoundly empty. My body clenches on instinct, searching for something to grip onto. The only thing that can satiate the heart-beat hammering between my legs is his cock. It's the only thing that reaches it.

"Please, more, I need more," I beg, my body trembling.

After taking one last lick, he slides me down his body as he stands. With my hips resting against his, he carries me to bed. When I'm spread out, open, waiting, he stops. His hands hold my knees, pushing them open.

"Watch," he groans, leaning forward to drag the head of his cock through the wetness between my legs. His eyes are fixated on his cock as it slowly disappears. The deep, full feeling makes my toes curl.

Each thrust builds pressure in my stomach, like adding gaso-line to a fire. When his hand comes up to my neck, gently holding me, I know the end is circling around me. I can't fight it or prolong it. He moans every time our hips meet.

"Can you take more?"

My eyes jerk up to meet his. "More? There's more?" I'm not sure what he means. More, what exactly?

"Do you trust me?"

My head nods before I even have a chance to consider it. I do. Deep in my bones, I trust him.

He bends down, his elbow supporting his weight. Our lips meet, soft and warm. He kisses me for a moment keeping his body completely still. As his tongue glides into my mouth, I feel it. I gasp, my mouth dropping open.

He's bigger. Thicker, wider, longer, however, you want to measure it, he just grew inside of me.

"Holy fucking shit," my voice is a high-pitched mixture of shock and strain.

The pained sound that heaves from his chest makes my body shiver. How is this possible?

Opening my legs wider, I try to accommodate what this bigger size demands. He starts slowly, pulling out, leaving me painfully empty then pressing forward, filling me beyond what I can handle. Each thrust is an assault of pleasure on my body.

"Relax," he whispers, before adding speed. His hands roam over my skin, his fingertips leaving trails of goosebumps behind. I feel myself melting into him, his pleasure and mine fusing so that I can't tell what is what and who is who.

"Oh- god," my voice is lost in my throat, drowned out by the moans that force themselves out. "How are you doing this?"

The thunderous pounding of our hearts, beating in unison, drums in my ears. When I open my eyes, I'm lost in the dark, silky black night with stars swirling in purples, blues, and greens, Ronan's eyes.

With wet, sloppy, eager lips, I pull his face to mine. Holding tightly to his hair, I anchor myself to the bed. Everything feels too intense. It feels like I'm losing touch with reality.

"Let go, Nicole. I will catch you." He pants against my lips.

Choosing to trust, I let my eyes flutter closed. I'm a million miles up, floating above the earth, gently cradled in the arms of the universe. A hoarse cry spills past my lips as my body is submerged in bliss so thick I can't breathe. He roars above me, warmth spreading from deep in my belly out to my limbs.

Still inside of me, he drops, pressing his face into my chest. I can hardly breathe under his weight, but I don't want him to move. Wrapping my arms around him tightly, holding him to me, I drift off to sleep.

CHAPTER 30

"You do this every other month?"

"Yes," he gives me a stern look. I've asked him several times, but I just can't believe they do this so often. It seems a bit… excessive.

"Why?"

"It's necessary for preparedness. Everyone does training modules every six weeks. It keeps us in a constant state of readiness."

"Readiness for what?"

Every six weeks, everyone gathers in the arena for training. I was expecting some sit-ups and push-ups, maybe a bit of running. This is not that. They are training for war. This is training for the apocalypse. Everyone is working through various exercises. They spar and use several weapons, most of which look too large or heavy for me to even lift. Men and women fight each other with no holds barred.

It's been three hours of grueling, rigorous work. Sitting beside Clarisse and Santi, we're mostly silent, watching in awe as they fly through the air, slamming into each other with such force it should be breaking bones.

Their physical abilities are incredible. Each of them appears to have extensive training in gymnastics, martial arts, and combat. The skills that they display here, in training exercises, would be fatal to any human.

Clarisse mumbles under her breath, biting into her lip as she watches Elite Navigator and Ronan sparring.

Crossing my legs in my seat, I watch the muscles in his back tense beneath his skin. God damn. He reminds me of a dancer, graceful and in control of every movement in his body. This dance is lethal, their weapons clashing loudly, like cymbals. There is no sweat, no exhausted sighs or breaks to catch their breath. They fight tirelessly, endlessly, anticipating each other's movements before they even make them.

Watching his body move fills me with liquid heat.

I try to distract myself by looking over at Olexa and Gaia, but my gaze always finds its way back to him.

He drops down, ducking to miss the swinging silver bar and suddenly everything slows down. The tension on his face, his muscles flexing as he brings his arm forward to throw a punch. I'm suddenly all too aware of his body. Hard and hot and towering over me.

He turns suddenly, dropping his weapon. Our eyes lock as he takes a deep, lust filled breath.

Without a word, he walks away from his training.

I'm out of my seat before he reaches me. We need to leave before I embarrass myself. I recognize this hallway. For once, I actually know where I am and I'm going to use it to my advantage.

Sliding the door open to the library of human books, I pull him into the room.

"Nicole?" He looks confused as I attack him, pulling myself up on my toes while yanking him down by the shoulders. When our lips meet, he groans into my mouth.

"I'm not going to make it all the way up. Does this door lock?"

"You want to fuck here?" He is completely shocked.

"Yes." Lifting my shirt over my head, I let the material fall to the ground at my feet. His surprise vanishes as soon as my pants hit the floor. Pulling him by the shoulders, I walk backward until my legs hit the table. Breaking my lips away from his, I spin around letting my ass rub against him before laying my face down on the table.

A loud, throaty sound and shuffling from behind me makes me wiggle in anticipation. He's pulling off his pants.

Taking a deep breath, I prepare myself for him to slam forward, filling me completely, but he doesn't. He moves slowly, rubbing his tip through my dripping wet skin. Nudging forward slowly, he slides into me in a controlled, unhurried stroke. With white knuckles, I grip the edge of the table, waiting for more.

I want him to slam into me, to beat the pulsating ache away. At this point, I truly believe that he could fuck me to death and it wouldn't be enough.

"Is this normal? I've never been so out of control and completely insatiable."

"This is normal. Our bodies belong together, joined like this," he slides into me. He leans forward, gripping my shoulders, using them to hold me still while he fucks me so hard I'm sure the table is going to shatter beneath us.

My thighs burn as they press into the tabletop with enough force to bruise, but I still want more.

"Harder, Ronan, please-"

He doesn't waste a single second before he picks up speed.

"I need you," his voice is lower, rough and filthy. It makes my heart beat somehow faster and slower.

I open my mouth to respond but only moans and whining, begging sounds come out. He leans forward and clamps his hand over my mouth, muffling my shameless loudness. I know we're not in the privacy of our room, but I can't stop myself.

The strained grunting sounds spilling out of his mouth hit the back of my neck as his face presses into my skin.

My eyes roll back, every thrust beats against the hot coil of frustration in my stomach.

"Ronan, more," I scream against his hand. The sound that comes out of him is so loud and low, my body is tipped over the edge. He roars above me, growing painfully harder, bigger. My orgasm rages on for unending minutes. Over and over again my body shakes, reverberations from an earthquake with a magnitude that cannot be measured.

He stills, burying his face in my hair as he grunts words in An'eoc.

With each deep twitch, he moans softly.

"Holy shit," I pant as he pulls out of me, a hot gush of fluid following behind him.

"Woman," he sounds bewildered.

"Sorry about that, watching you fight, shirtless…" I hum and bite into my lip, the memory warming my belly again. Turning to sit on the table, I watch him.

"You may need to skip the next training module." His brows are furrowed. I think he might be upset that he let himself be distracted.

"Yeah, maybe." My legs swing, dangling above the ground. "It's really cool, actually. I still think it's kind of crazy that you train like that so often, but I liked watching."

"It's cool?" He looks confused. I've explained 'cool' to him before. "Why is it cool?"

"I mean, all of you are pretty incredible. The things you can do… The way that your women participate. The women do everything along with the men. It didn't look like they were being treated differently or like anyone was doubting their abilities."

"Why would anyone doubt their abilities? Everyone in the arena today is a warrior."

My lips pull down into a frown. Of course, he wouldn't understand this.

"There were a lot of gender issues in our world. Men, for a

long time, sort of dominated everything. Things were getting better, but there was still a long way to go. Physically, our men and women have more differences than An'eo but they ruled over everything. I was seventeen when women were finally allowed to get a credit card separate from their husbands." I shrug. "Women would not have been allowed to train with men. They probably wouldn't have been allowed to be warriors, period."

He huffs out a breath. Almost like a laugh, but not quite.

I quirk my brow, waiting for him to explain that reaction.

"It is amusing that they could think such a thing."

Amusing?

"Because of how wrong they were to think that women were inferior to them?" I don't know why I feel the need to clarify this, but something about his reaction is off.

"Human men believing that they were superior to anything is amusing. They were still human…"

I'm taken aback for a moment. "What do you mean by that?"

I'm starting to get nervous and I'm hoping he can fix it by elaborating.

"It is comical that any human would assume that they were superior in any way to anything."

"Ronan, what the fuck does that mean?"

"I have traveled the universe as far as Netula. Humans are obviously not a superior species. You may have been dominant here on Earth but within the solar system, no."

I blink at him, not believing I'm hearing what he's actually saying. He called me physically weak, but this…

"Do you think we are inferior to you?" My lips tremble. The sinking feeling in my chest should be enough of a warning not to ask that question, because I don't want to know the answer.

"Of course." There's no humor in his voice. Clearly, he believes what he is saying. There's no taunting or malice. He's calm and logical. His face is passive. He truly doesn't see that what he's saying is crushing me. In his brain, these are just facts.

"You think I am inferior to you?" I roll my trembling lips into my mouth, blinking back tears.

The silence screams. Five seconds pass between my question and the step he takes toward me, but it's enough. When a tear slips down my cheek, he looks confused. "This hurts you?"

"Yes, this hurts me. I never realized how poorly you thought of me." I grab my pants from the floor and jerk them up my legs.

"Nicole." He has the audacity to look confused. "You said it yourself, Earth had sexual assaults and racial and gender inequalities. You persecuted people based on religion and orientation. You forget I have read your history. You conquered and colonized on your own planet. Taking from your own species. Apart from that, we are also superior in our biology. We are bigger, faster, and stronger. Our skin is not affected by the sun. We have built-in body armor to protect us. I have read your medical texts. We do not have the same maladies that your race often succumbs to."

For a moment, I'm speechless, and I hate myself for it. He's right about everything he listed, but I still can't wrap my head around this.

"We're different. Different isn't better or worse, it's just... different. We don't have armor that protects us but we made it for ourselves. We yearned for knowledge. We did everything we could to learn, to create, to advance. We traveled and explored. We climbed every mountain and explored the arctic tundra. We sent a man to the moon! We weren't perfect and there were things that needed to be improved, but... I just... I don't even know what to say. I don't understand why you would want someone that you think is so far beneath you."

"Nicole," his voice is soft.

Pulling my shirt over my head, we make brief eye contact, but I drop it to the ground before another tear spills from my eye. My mom was in a marriage with a man who believed he was superior to her. Her life was sad and lonely. I grew up watching the example of my parents—partners in every way. My dad valued her. She was his equal, and he supported her in everything. I can't accept less than that.

"I think very highly of you, you are-"

"I'm a human. You think that humans are inferior. I'll tell you a little something about that. When you think someone is less than you, you make justifications in your mind for why it's alright to treat them badly, to take away their freedoms, to hurt them." I don't try to hide the hurt in my voice.

"Nicole, I would never allow any harm to come to you."

"What about Clarisse and Santi? They aren't your Sa'nu so who cares what happens to them, right?"

"I did not say that." His frustration is growing.

"You think highly of me in spite of my unfortunate origins. How can you be alright with binding yourself to someone that you freely admit is deficient? How could you want me?"

His jaw clenches.

Santi's comment about a cat, and a worm flashes in my mind. I'm the worm.

"What if we had a baby? Would you think it was inferior because it was partially human?" My voice cracks painfully. The thought is like a jab to my heart.

His face changes completely. "My offspring will be inferior to no one." He growls in the back of his throat. Thinking of his child in the same way he thinks of me makes him angry. Got it.

A humorless laugh bubbles up from my chest. "You're so superior that your supreme DNA would cancel out any of the shitty weak stuff that I contribute, huh?" I swallow down the painful lump in my throat.

"Nicole," he reaches for me, but I pivot back out of his reach.

"I need to leave. Please don't follow me." My voice cracks as I stumble out of the room and run down the hallway. When I'm sure he's not behind me, I let my tears fall freely. My lungs burn as I rush toward the only place I know I will have some privacy.

I shouldn't have let him wiggle his way under my skin like

this. I let my guard down completely. I was ready to learn everything he wanted to teach me, but the fact remains that I will always be human. We can't move forward if he thinks that I'm lesser. It won't be long before it becomes an issue. If he feels this way, they all do.

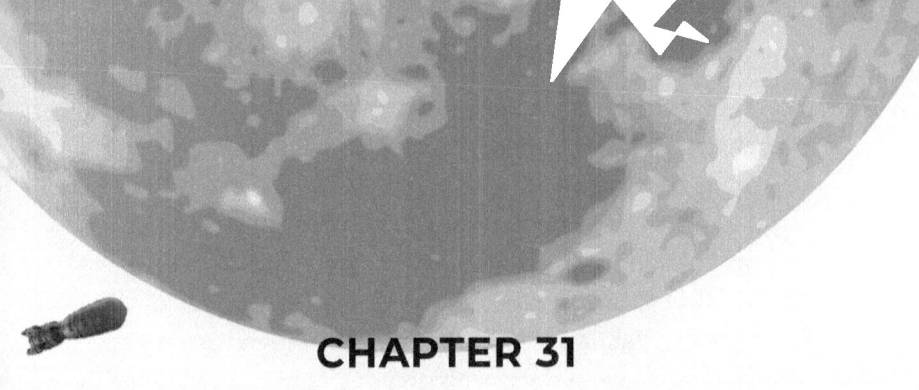

CHAPTER 31

My eyes hurt. Wrapping the blanket around my body, I walk out to sit on the terrace. As the sunrise looms far away on the horizon, the lavender sky begins to fade to blue.

Blinking away the sting in my eyes, I take a deep breath and stare up at An'eo. It's beautiful. It looks like it glows from the inside; the light bursting out of small open pockets like sunlight beaming through thick clouds.

He hasn't told me much about his parents, but I know they live there. Ronan is a third-generation earth fleet commander. When he took over the command position, they went back. It's probably for the best, as they would likely have been very against our relationship. A cat and a worm...

My parents would have loved Ronan. After getting over the initial shock of their daughter, bringing an alien home, of course.

I thought I had cried all the tears I could cry, but they burn in my eyes again. My sore, puffy eyes are exhausted but powerless to stop the fresh tears.

It's difficult to blame him for his feelings after he listed all of the horrible things that humans have done. He is only focusing on the bad. Humanity also had so much good. People who cared for others, who gave and sacrificed, people who tried to help. Humans are flawed, imperfect creatures with fragile lives, but he's got us all wrong.

It's rare for someone to change their opinion. I saw it on his face last night; he believes that we are inferior to him. Not just to him, to all of them. The thought never occurred to me that one day an issue might arise where we would be pitted against each other. Not just an argument with differing opinions, but where it would be human against An'eo.

I have no plans or desires to change the An'eo way of life. I haven't given a single thought to asking for more human accommodations. Last night, it was made very clear to me that if I ever did, even for a valid reason, it would be rejected, on principle. Why would they ever want to do anything the inferior way, the human way?

The door slides open behind me and I wrap the blanket around myself more snuggly, protecting my chest, my heart.

A deep frown pulls at his lips when he sees my face.

"Nicole, I stayed away as long as I could. I did not follow you." His fists clench by his side.

"Thank you." My voice is raw, the result of exhaustion from a sleepless night spent crying. The dull ache in my chest intensifies as I look at him. His face is still as flawless as it always is, but he looks tired. Not puffy and red as I'm sure I am, but tired all the same.

With quick steps, he's in front of me, pulling me up into his arms. His nose inhales against my hair and his arms squeeze me into him. The comfort and warmth from his skin is instant, like a salve on a burn. I want to melt into him, to let him heal the painful fissures in my heart, but I know I can't.

"Put me down, Ronan." My voice doesn't betray me. I'm stern, serious. The conversation from yesterday cannot and will not be swept under the rug to be forgotten.

He places me down and as soon as my feet are on solid

ground; I move away. I need to be out of reach. I can't allow him to lull me into a passive state.

"Nicole, you are my Sa'nu. You are precious to me, a rare gift from the universe."

"But, I'm human." I force myself not to liquefy at his words. I can't melt at his feet, not this time. "Ronan, you can't want a life with someone that you feel is beneath you. Those two ideas can't exist together."

"I do not believe that you are inferior to me. You are strong and smart. Your biology cannot be helped, but I know you are not capable of the same atrocious thinking as the rest of your species."

He thinks he's helping. I know he does.

"I don't want you to actually answer this." I'm not sure my heart can take it. "Just think about it. If you could change me, would you?"

A strange expression takes over his face, as if he's considering it for the first time.

"Last night you were adamant that your child would not be inferior to anyone, but if we had a child, do you actually believe that? I don't really care about the rest of the world, only about you. Would you look at our baby and see its inferiority?"

"My child will be perfect in my eyes." He takes a cautious step forward, then another. When my back is pressed against the thin safety rail, he steps in front of me. "I do not want to talk about children during an argument. When we speak of our child together, it should not be used as a weapon."

"I'm not using it as leverage. I just don't see how you can look at me and see something lesser than turn around and consider having a child together, even a hypothetical one."

"Just leave it-"

"Just leave it? No." I feel anger swelling beneath the hurt. "I'm not just going to forget about this. I won't be in a relationship with someone who doesn't think of me as an equal partner! I'm not the exception to the lowly human condition. I am human. If you think humans are corrupt and worthless, you think I am."

He scowls. "You are being unreasonable."

"I'm not."

The silence is painful. I feel myself begging him, as a woman standing before a man. I'm begging him to see me.

"Clarisse asked about eating animals. Did you consume animals for sustenance?"

"Occasionally, I did."

"Then you agree that there are lifeforms that are less than others."

I'm taken aback by his question.

"I- well…"

"By that logic, given your physical limitations and the baser intellect that your history has shown the human species capable of, you must also agree that overall humans are an inferior species."

"Baser intellect?" Is he comparing me to a chicken right now?

"You are very intelligent. I know this to be true, but as a species, humans made unintelligent decisions often."

He steps toward me again, reaching for me to pull me toward him.

"Ronan, we were flawed, and we made enough mistakes to fill our history books, but…" I yank at my hair. "We tried. We got it wrong, then we tried again. That is the beauty of it all."

"I see no evidence of redemption."

I recoil at his words as if he slapped me across the face.

"No evidence of redemption?" Hot, heavy tears burn a trail down my cheek. "Everyone is dead, everything we tried to build and be was wiped out. I would give anything to have them back, to give everyone a second chance."

"What makes humans worthy of a second chance?" It's like a switch being flipped. I can see him shifting, a coldness taking over his face. He's shutting down. He doesn't want to argue this with me just as much as I don't want to argue this with him.

I could argue that people like Clarisse and Santi are worthy. All the scientists that were willing to sacrifice themselves in the hope that we could help the world. I could argue that throughout our history, even during our ugliest moments, there were people willing to stand up, to help, to fight back, even at great personal cost. I could argue that his opinion doesn't matter. He's not the master of the universe. What he thinks doesn't really matter. We were here; we existed on this planet and it's not up to him to decide if we mattered or not.

Instead, I roll my trembling lips into my mouth. It doesn't matter what I say.

"I would like a room, please. If there is one near Clarisse, I would appreciate it, but I want my own room. Anywhere will do as long as it's not with you."

He lets out an irritated huff before turning on his heels and stomping toward the door. "Olexa will come for you shortly." He doesn't even look at me before he slides the door open and walks out.

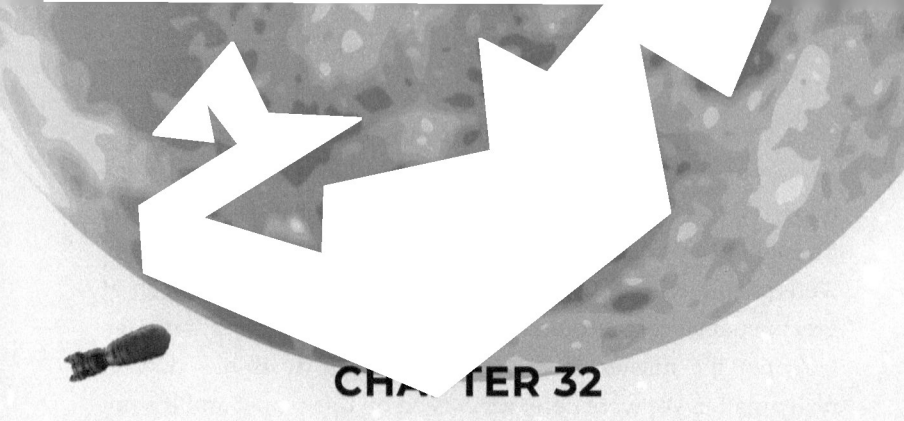

CHAPTER 32

"**N**icole," his voice is soft, silky, and warm as it wraps around my cool skin.

It's been two weeks since I last saw him. I know that during the first week, we were both actively avoiding each other. Then he left, traveling to the northern city. I've felt empty, like a hole was punched through me. Heat radiates from him, bringing life back into my limbs.

I'm frozen in bed. Just the sound of his voice makes tears prick in my eyes. I've missed him.

"I have been consumed by thoughts of you." The bed dips beside me, and I'm flooded with relief. I just want him to hold me, to tell me that everything is going to be alright.

His powerful arms curl around me and pull me into his chest. For the first time in days, I can breathe again. In an instant, the weight that has settled into my chest is lifted. I was starting to get used to the dull ache just behind my heart. It didn't hurt less. I just adjusted to life with it. A new version of normal.

The notion of star-crossed lovers, destined by fate to find one another, is all well and good until you break up. Then it's shit. This is the kind of heartbreak that takes you out for weeks.

Just one touch, and the hole starts to fill. The painful sting of an open wound finally subsides as he pulls me into his arms. I'm weightless.

The soft thump of his heart is like a magic eraser that dissolves all the pain and sadness from the last two weeks and makes it vanish. His fingertips fill and spackle all the cracks in my chest.

"You invaded my dreams; even in sleep, I found no peace without you." His voice is low, dipping down in a way that awakens a fire in my bones.

"Just kiss me," I beg against his lips.

His hands move through my hair, a gesture that I now know is more than just a sweet touch; it's intimate. The kiss starts slowly, timid lips caressing, but it builds into an aggressive aching mess of moans and need. He's breathing the air right out of my lungs, pulling it from my body, and using it to sustain his.

Pushing myself up, I roll over so that my hips are over his. Spreading my hands out across his warm chest, I feel the rise and fall of his breath.

"Take off your pants." The tremble in my voice is embarrassingly apparent, but I don't have time to care. Right now, I'm on a mission. Two weeks without him has made me ravenous. I've been fed; all the food and water in the world is at my fingertips, but it's not enough. I'm never satisfied. I crave him, a deep, endless longing in my stomach.

"Pull them down." His tongue wets his lower lip as he watches me, waiting.

Shuffling back, my hands shake with nervous anticipation as I tug his pants down past his hips.

"These weeks have felt like years." He groans, taking his cock in his hand. "I'm aching for you."

"I've missed you so much." I stare down at him, letting my eyes roam over everything that I've so longed for. His mouth, his chest, his hands... I want it all.

With movements so quick, I don't register them until I'm

already on my back. He rolls us. My body is pressed into the mattress by his.

"Tell me that you want me," his tongue trails softly over my neck.

"I want you." I'm breathless and panting, my body trembling with excitement.

"Tell me that you missed me." His voice sounds like sin. Dark and low, promising dirty, vile things.

"God-" I choke as he grinds his cock into me. "I missed you. I missed you so much."

"I am going to fuck you until your body gives out, until the pleasure is so intense that it turns to pain. I want to pump you so full of my cum that it drips from your cunt for days." He slams forward, and a strangled moan claws its way up from my throat.

"Ronan," I rock my hips up to meet his thrusts.

He feels so good. Why did we ever separate in the first place? How could I give this up?

"You're the worm, remember?" He grunts as he speeds up.

"What?" I moan. I don't understand.

"You're inferior, insignificant. Humans were wiped out because they weren't smart enough to save themselves," he presses his lips to mine.

Gasping, I jolt forward. Sitting alone in the dark with sweat dripping down my neck.

"What the fuck was that?" I hold my head in my hands. My temple throbs, and a shiver runs down my spine. I wish he would at least do me the favor of staying out of my dreams.

Groaning, I fall back in bed, blushing and embarrassed by my own unconscious thoughts. What is wrong with me?

The complete silence is broken by the door sliding loudly open. By the way, it slammed; I'm sure it was broken.

"Nicole." Ronan's voice is like a knife in my chest. I know this is real. I wish I was still dreaming, that I could wake up and have it be just another nightmare, but I know it's not.

"You're back," my voice shakes.

Blinking against the unwelcome lights, I gasp and gather my blankets around me like they will save me. His bare chest heaves, loud, hoarse breaths that rattle my bones. Sweat drips down his skin, sliding down toward the one place I should not look.

The fabric of his pants strains against his massive erection.

"What are you doing?" His burning gaze scorches my skin.

"N-Nothing."

"Nicole," he growls, and steps forward. His tense, hunched shoulders look ready to attack, like he might strike out and grab me.

"I'm sorry, I was asleep," my trembling whisper is barely audible.

He makes a tortured sound. A low growl so full of pain and longing that it makes my skin prick. I know that sound, it's echoed in my head every day since I last saw him.

"How long must this torment continue? Will you see reason?" He paces at the foot of the bed. "End this. We are both miserable."

"You end it, Ronan. Understand why your beliefs are causing this and do something about it!" I sit up, my voice is stronger than I was expecting it to be.

"I think of you without reprieve. I am in agony. My body searches for yours. I know you feel it; that is why your dreams caused the release of enough pheromones to bring me to my knees." He groans and inhales.

"Of course, I miss you. I hate this! But I can't just pretend that I don't know your true feelings. You like me in spite of what I am. You said humans, me... that I essentially don't deserve to live... You're not as smart as you think you are if you can't understand why that breaks my heart."

"Read your own history! Humans allowed their greed to consume them; their lust for power led to atrocities that date all the way back to your beginnings." His voice has taken on a chilling calm.

"Please, leave," my voice wobbles. I don't want him to see me cry. It's been two weeks, I should be stronger than this by now.

"Nicole." He moves faster than me. Before I can get away, he's pulling me forward, crushing me into his chest.

Pushing with both hands against his chest, I stumbled backward. "Get out, Ronan!"

"The pain in your chest that radiates with every breath will only worsen. The gnawing, burning pit in your stomach will grow. You will be driven mad by the tormented sleep, your body calling to mine. You are my home. You belong in my arms as I belong between your legs. See reason, put an end to this suffering." His chest heaves with each rapid, shallow breath.

"How is it even possible that you want me?" I swallow the growing lump in my throat. "If I wasn't your Sa'nu, you wouldn't care if I lived or died."

"That is untrue. I was intrigued by you the moment our eyes met. Despite everything, I wanted to speak with you. Each time I saw you, your small body, your curiosity, the quiet strength of your will, everything drew me to you."

"Please, you have to leave," my voice cracks as I beg.

He sucks in a sharp breath, his calm exterior finally cracking. "This is foolish. You are being emotional about factual truths. Look objectively at the-"

"Get out!" I scream, clutching my chest. I don't want him here. I don't want to be so close to him, to see him. I need space. I can't think straight.

"Commander," Elite Navigator is standing in the doorway beside a wide-eyed Clarisse.

Ronan roars something in An'eoc and walks out of the room without giving me another glance.

"What happened?" Clarisse is by my side in a second. "Please, tell me, Nicole."

Everyone knows that something is wrong. Clarisse, Santi,

Olexa, they have all asked, but I won't talk about it. I don't even know where to begin.

Sitting down on my bed, I bring my knees up to my chest, hugging myself. "Everything is fine. Thank you for coming to check on me."

She rolls her lips into her mouth and nods. "We'll let you sleep. I'm just across the hall if you need me."

CHAPTER 33

Pouting beneath my blankets, the events of last night play over and over in my mind. It's a reel I can't stop replaying.

The dream was bad enough, but to have him come here, like that, hard and sweating and so irritatingly good-looking. I'll never get over the embarrassment. He knew I was dreaming about him? Humiliating.

Rolling in the bed until I'm wrapped in the blankets several times, I wait, hoping that all the oxygen will turn to carbon dioxide and I'll pass out.

A quiet knock on the door startles me. Sitting up, I close my eyes, searching for any Sa'nu, heartbeat, or shared blood bullshit. When everything feels normal, just the same familiar gnawing pit in my stomach and ache in my chest, I answer the door.

"Nicole," Gaia looks cautious.

"Good morning." I smooth my hair down.

"Will you come with me?"

"Sure," I say, eyeing her suspiciously. "Give me a second."

Running to the bathroom, I do the best that I can to make myself look less like someone who just fell out of a truck full of hot garbage.

She leads me down a hallway and into what I'm fairly certain is her office. When we step inside, a woman is already waiting.

"Nicole, this is Operational Director," Gaia introduces us. "I am here to translate for you."

"O-Ok, translate what, exactly?" I'm so lost.

While she opens her mouth, a faint squeak from beside the desk draws my attention to a white dome floating in the air. It looks like an egg the size of a pillow.

Operational Director speaks and the egg floats toward us. As it approaches, I can see that it's open on one side and hollow. My heart pounds in my chest as the retaliation of what it is hits me.

"This is Stark. He will be two weeks only tomorrow." Gaia translates.

"Oh, my-" I gasp as a huge, stupid smile that hurts my cheeks spreads over my face. My eyes feel wet, and I can't stop the giggle that bursts forward. "Oh, my god."

My hand reaches forward on its own, but I pull it back, holding them together against my chest to keep them from trying to touch him.

His hair. He has a full head of thick, silver hair that looks so soft I want to nuzzle my face into it.

He looks slightly larger than a two-week-old human, but only by a few pounds. I study his tiny nose and lips, the slight movements of his chest when he breathes. He is a perfect baby.

"He is so beautiful," I gush, meeting his mother's smiling face.

She says something and reaches into his carrier.

"Do you wish to hold him?" Gaia asks as Operational Director brings his little sleeping body into her arms.

"Oh, my- of course, I want to hold him! If she's alright with it, yes, please!" I feel giddy. The heaviness that has been weighing down my chest for weeks is lifting. As soon as his soft, warm body is placed in my arms, I know that everything is going to be alright. I stare in awe at the minute changes in his facial expression and the tiny cooing sounds he makes.

So, this is an alien baby.

He looks... so human.

Without the muscles and staggering height, with his eyes closed, he looks like any other baby. But he's not. He's a miracle. A baby born here, on Earth, years after the end of the world.

As the minutes pass, I feel a fragile peace bloom in my chest. I don't know what the future holds or what will happen with us but I need to get my shit together.

"Gaia, is Olexa here? Can you ask her to come find me when she has a few minutes?" I smile down at Stark as he starts to move and stretch in my arms.

Reluctantly, I pass the baby back to his waiting mother. "Thank you so much. I can't explain to you how much it means to me to meet him. Thank you." I blink back the mistiness in my eyes.

"Olexa will be here momentarily." Gaia sits behind her desk after Operational Director leaves us alone.

I nod, awkwardly staring at my hands. I don't really know how to act anymore. Does everyone know why Ronan and I are fighting? Do they all think I'm completely unreasonable? He sees his statements as fact, not opinion. My objections are emotional and ridiculous. Do they feel the same way?

She makes a small, hesitant sound, like clearing her throat. When I look up, she's looking at me.

"This is not my place, I am aware, but," she pauses, "you and the Commander-" she sighs. I can tell she's torn. Whatever she wants to say, she's not sure she should. "What happened?" The words finally spill out.

"We had a fight, a big one." I chew my lip. If he's not telling them, I probably shouldn't either.

My internal debate, tell her or not, is interrupted by the door sliding open. Olexa gives me an excited smile.

"Would you like me to take you to Ronan?" Her enthusiasm is obvious, and it makes my heart sting.

"Um, no," I clear my throat.

"Oh," the disappointment in her face and voice is making me regret asking to speak to her.

"I want to learn An'eoc."

The change in the room is immediate. They both light up, pleasantly surprised.

"I will teach you!" Olexa volunteers immediately.

"Really?" I didn't expect her to be so willing to add more to her already busy days.

"Of course, we should begin now," she jumps up and starts touching the wall, pulling up different screens.

"I wish to help, as well," Gaia speaks into the room, and the chairs move themselves to face the screens.

"Um, before we start, I was also wondering if there is someone I can talk to about work. I'm not sure where I would be useful, but I know I can be somewhere. I want to help, to pull my weight."

"I have a position that you can fill." Gaia taps the screen and pulls up a picture that comes out of the screen, another hologram.

"You're the Chief Engineer. Would I be qualified for the position?"

"My team specializes in the stabilization of Ulaar, our energy source," she starts to explain.

"I know a little bit about it."

"I will explain the details. If you want the position, you can have it."

In just a few hours, everything is looking much less gloomy. Regardless of where I stand with Ronan, I can still be useful, I can still learn and grow and use the life that I have. I want to add value, even in the smallest increment.

"First lesson, our alphabet." Olexa points to a symbol on the screen.

Taking a deep breath, I set my mind to the task at hand. I

can't let him creep in and distract me. Pulling in the same laser focus that I had after my parents died, I'm ready in an instant. I'll stay up every night studying if it keeps him from absorbing all of my energy and attention.

"Let's do this," I nod with a smile, renewed purpose settling in my chest. I'll make myself useful, no matter what.

CHAPTER 34

aking a breath, I force back the urge to blush and apologize for my measured response. With painstaking slowness, I translate his question in my head and respond with what I hope is perfect An'eoc.

In the last thirty days, I have made the language my sole mission. I eat, sleep, and breathe it. Olexa, Gaia, and Elite Navigator speak to me exclusively in An'eoc and only speak English when I'm struggling.

'Do you remember my given name?' I'm almost positive that's what he asked.

"I do."

"You may address me as such."

"Macsen." I smile at his serious expression. This is a gesture of friendship, but he still looks stiff and uncomfortable. This is just his way.

"Your An'eoc is getting better every day. I am impressed with your pronunciation."

His compliments mean much more than Olexa and Gaias. I appreciate their praise, but Macsen is much less likely to give an undeserved pat on the back.

"Thank you." My smile falters when his expression changes.

He's doing it. The thing. All of them do it. I can spot it from a mile away now. He wants to talk about Ronan or to ask what happened between us. They all get the same weary expression, a specific kind of hesitation.

"We should eat before the kitchen is closed."

Nodding, I follow him down the hallway toward the cafeteria. He is the only one who doesn't mention him at all. He looks like he wants to, but he always stops himself. I appreciate that.

I don't like coming here. I was told that word spread quickly about our relationship. I'm not sure how much people know, but they heard about me touching his hair and living to tell the tale.

It's impossible to ignore the way they stare at me.

As I learn the language, I'm able to catch bits and pieces, phrases here and there. I've gathered that they do not like me.

Today, something is off. The air is different. I can't put my finger on it, but I can feel it.

Halfway through my assortment of fruit, a woman walks toward us up the center aisle. She's bee-lining right for us, with purpose in her steps and quick stride.

Stopping just short of our table, she growls something angrily while making eye contact with me.

Her rushed, angry words are too emotional and rambling for me to fully understand. I catch the words 'human, worthy' and 'challenge.' Turning to Macsen, I hope for some backup. He's staring at her with wide, shocked eyes.

I jerk back to look at her again when her fists slam down on the table. The echo rings out in the otherwise quiet dining hall. There were a few people not watching this interaction, but now we have the attention of everyone. Great.

With hunched shoulders and disgust etched into her face, she stands above me, waiting.

I open my mouth to fumble through a response, when my throat goes dry. I feel him. I can't see him, but I know he's here.

When his thunderous voice vibrates in my bones, I freeze. My spine shudders violently at the sudden close proximity.

When the stupefied shock wears off, I realize that he's threatening to kill her.

"Stop!" I feel myself jumping out of my seat before I can stop my body. When I turn to face him, it's like a punch to the gut. He doesn't look like my Ronan. An expression of hideous, frightening rage is twisted into his face. I hardly recognize him. A look like this has no place on a face like his.

I've never seen him like this. Even in the middle of the arena, with two people trying to kill him, he was calm. The heat radiating from his body hits me in palpable waves.

It's been twenty-eight days since our last face-off.

I thought I was cured of my broken heart.

I thought that I had made myself strong again.

I thought I could handle seeing him.

I thought wrong.

I gasp, my lungs burning as I heave for air like a fish out of water. Clutching my chest, I take an involuntary step toward him, my body reacting to being in his presence again after so long. It feels like my ribs have been cracked open, ripped apart to expose my barely beating heart.

"Nicole." His voice is distorted as he steps toward me, his arm outstretched, ready to grab my swaying body.

"Get her out of here," he growls before turning his attention back to the woman behind me.

Hands pull me back, leading me away by my shoulders.

I can't stop myself from looking back, watching him as I'm guided out of the dining hall. Our eyes meet for a moment before I'm pulled into the hallway.

Turning, I'm surprised to see Olexa, not Macsen, gently taking me away.

"I understood him." An irrational smile tugs at my lips. He spoke An'eoc, and I understood it. There is so much chaos swirling around, and this is what I'm focusing on.

"Did you understand her?" Her voice wavers.

"Not all of it. She was talking so fast…"

"She issued you a challenge."

"What?" I stop walking. I heard the word mixed in there, but I didn't understand the context. I know this is serious, though. She's speaking English. She hasn't done that in weeks.

"She wishes to challenge you on the grounds of disrespect."

"Disrespect to who? I've never done anything to her!" My head is spinning.

"Ronan." She gets quiet. "She believes you are disrespecting Ronan, the commander of Earth fleet."

"W-Why does she think that?"

"He will not speak of you. I do not know what happened between you but-" she sighs. "Since you stopped speaking to him, he has become unapproachable. He rarely sleeps or leaves the vehicle bay. The woman, Defense Coordinator, works closely with him. She is distressed by his behavior."

"Why didn't you tell me this sooner? I didn't know that he's been neglecting his duties."

"He has not neglected his duties, he is just withdrawn. He is… different." The sadness on her face is like a weight in the pit of my stomach. Guilt and regret swirl nauseatingly together to create doubt and self-condemnation.

Am I handling this wrong?

"A challenge must be accepted. That is law, but he will not allow you to face her." She looks as bewildered as I feel.

'A challenge must be accepted?' What the hell does that mean?

"Do not panic. He is overriding her."

"He's breaking the law for me?" I'm about to throw up. If they didn't hate me before, they most certainly will now.

"Well," she considers for a moment. "Yes, and no. You are not An'eo. The law applies to An'eo. He is denying her challenge on those grounds."

When we reach my room, she hesitates. "I know it is not my place. He has been clear that he will not discuss it. As his sister and your friend, I beg you, speak to him. Whatever the transgression, it cannot be so great as all this."

I give her a small smile. If I explained it, she probably wouldn't understand, or more likely, she would agree with him.

"I'll talk to him," the words slip out of my mouth completely against my will.

After seeing him, I'm back at square one, anyway. I might as well make this worse and go see him. What's one more gaping crack in my heart?

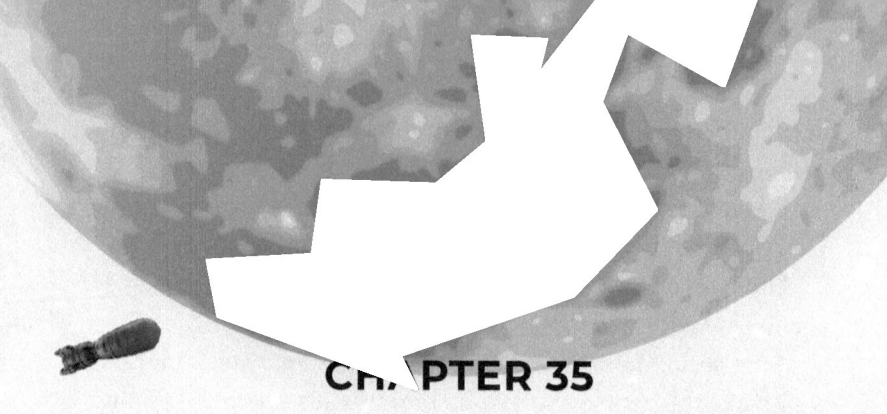

CHAPTER 35

My hand trembles as I knock on his door. With each second that passes, my nerves grow. After a minute ticks by, I sigh, relieved that he's not here. The looming sense of dread is still hanging over my head. I'm only prolonging the inevitable, but I welcome the extra time.

I know I should just ask someone to call him, but I don't want anyone to know I'm coming to talk to him. I waited until the sun sank down to creep through the hallways like a burglar in the night.

Olexa mentioned the vehicle bay before. I have a general idea where that is.

We need to talk about the challenge. We both exist in this place now, two people with complicated feelings and connections. I don't want his people to see me as disrespectful.

The whole situation is so absurd that it's actually funny. Not in a comical way, but in a laughing because it's preposterous way.

They think I'm disrespecting their commander. Obviously, the blame lies with me, it's out of the realm of possibility that he is the wrongdoer. I respect him. He is worthy of admiration in every way I can possibly count.

Our issues stem from him not respecting me. Oh, the irony.

Passing through long, silent hallways, down the stairs, and onto the terrace, I'm finally outside. From the terrace, I can see the warehouse garage where they store the airbridge. Light glows from inside. He must be there.

The chill in the air makes my skin prick and shiver as I walk through the grass, cutting through the gardens. It's not late enough to completely avoid people, but I'm determined to try. The last thing I need is to meet another angry An'eo that wants to crush me like a bug.

As I get closer, my hands sweat. I'm so focused on the anxiety I feel that it takes me longer than it should to notice it. Stopping dead in my tracks, I'm shocked when it registers.

The soft hum of music floats on the cool breeze. It's coming from the hangar.

Jogging toward the open door, I forget my nerves completely.

I'm not sure what I was expecting to see, but this is not it. My breath catches as my eyes find him immediately. I watch him, shirtless, hair pulled back, leaning against a table. He's so focused on the screen in front of him that he doesn't notice me.

His back is tense, hunched over whatever he's studying. Tools and parts are spread across the floor and scattered on tables. When I tear my eyes away from him, I see it, and my knees wobble.

Taking a step forward, I can't stop myself. Standing just inside the huge garage, hot tears well up in my eyes. It's like time is standing still as my eyes frantically take in everything.

"Ronan," my shaky voice calls over the music.

He spins around, locking eyes with me. For several seconds, we stand, frozen, staring at each other. The song playing, slow and sad, makes me feel dizzy. Just as before, I feel overwhelmed. My body reacts to his physically. My heart rate skyrockets, and the rest of the world seems slightly out of focus. It's just him and me here.

My throat feels tight, so I don't speak. Instead, I point. My shaking hand hangs in the air.

The music stops, and he takes a few cautious steps toward me.

"Ronan, what is that?" I choke out. I know what it looks like, but I'm struggling with believing if it's real or not.

"I-" his hand comes up to grip the back of his neck. He actually looks nervous. "A car."

"Where did it come from?"

"I built it."

"You built it?" I swallow down the burning lump in my throat.

"Yes."

"Why?"

"For you. To drive it…" he shrugs and stares at the ground.

Taking another step forward, I'm not sure why, but a giggle unexpectedly bubbles up in my throat.

He is building me a car. An actual, real, full-sized vehicle. It looks like a strange mixture of alien technology and an old military-style truck. It's a boxy, square shape with no roof and small half doors.

"Can I look closer?" I bounce on my toes slightly. I wonder if it works.

"Yes, it belongs to you."

As I run my fingers over the cool, buffed metal hood, excitement courses through me. He built me a fucking car.

"Does it run?" I turn back, expecting him to be where I left him. Instead, he's right behind me, close enough to touch.

"It does."

"Ronan, how?" I'm flabbergasted.

"Research, trial, and error." He points to a table with mechanical parts spread all over it. A page ripped from a book, a picture of soldiers, probably from World War One, standing in front of a truck hangs on the wall.

I feel warm, heat radiating from my chest outward. Crossing

my arms around myself, I discreetly pinch my skin. This can't be real. He *built* me a car, as in, made one, out of nothing. He didn't buy one or fix one up, he built it.

Walking around to the side, I pull the handle, and the door clicks open. It's the strangest sensation, the sound of the door opening. It's comforting. It's a small, meaningless sound that I never cared about before. Right now, it's everything.

"You built this for me?" Everything I came here with the intention of talking about is lost. All the emotions I've felt over the last month and a half are simmering below the surface. Everything is bubbling, threatening to overflow. I'm a gentle breeze away from melting down completely. One body isn't meant to contain every emotion all at once. I feel anger and hurt, guilt and heartbreak, excitement and sadness. It's a rolling, turbulent current, hell-bent on sweeping me away.

"My presence is requested in the northern city. It will take four days to drive. Will you accompany me?"

"Wait, you want to take a road trip?" I'm sure that's not a good idea. I'm struggling to just stand in his presence for a few minutes. I doubt I will be able to sit in a car with him for days. My body is betraying me, longing for him even though my head is saying 'no.'

"It was my intention to find you tomorrow after the route is finalized." The look on his face makes my chest ache. He's nervous.

"Do you think it's a good idea for us?"

"Before you decide, will you look at something?" I freeze as he steps toward me, walking past me to the back of the truck. He pulls several textbooks from the seat and holds them out to me.

I look at the top book on the heavy stack, and it appears to be French.

"I have marked several pages for you. You will find them." He steps away from me, his fists clenching by his sides.

"O-Okay," I whisper, clutching the books tightly, as I hurry out of the hangar before my body decides to revolt against me. I didn't ask about the challenge. I didn't even sit in my car or thank him for all the work he obviously put into it. My brain isn't functioning at full capacity. I blame the sleepless nights.

By the time I make it to my room, I'm out of breath and huffing for air, but I don't care. Sitting on the floor at the foot of the bed, I spread the textbooks out. French, Spanish, Arabic... seven textbooks total.

Taking the first book, I flip through it to find a plastic-looking tab on one page. Tucked into the book is a loose piece of paper or a flexible paper-like sheet. Taking it out and unfolding it, I blink down at the immaculate handwriting.

The handwritten passage is about Anne Frank.

> "...The family was helped into hiding by a number of people who had worked for Otto Frank, including Miep Gies, for two years and thirty-five days. During that time, Gies visited frequently with food and other supplies. Any of the helpers could have been sentenced to death for their participation..."

Flipping through the next textbook, the marked page has another handwritten passage.

> "... between May 26, 1940, and June 3, 1940, more than 300,000 troops were evacuated from the beaches of Dunkirk. Civilians with leisure and small fishing crafts sailed back and forth, rescuing sailors unable to escape the war-torn beaches. At great personal risk, men and women, old and young, traversed the seas to bring their soldiers home."

My heart thumps in my chest as I open the next book, frantically turning the pages to find the passage he wants me to read.

My conversation with Macsen echoes in my mind. 'We do not write.' That's what he said, yet here are pages of translated history. Not only did he read and research, he translated them into English for me.

> "On the eighth of October 1871, a fire broke out in a barn on the southwest side of Chicago, Illinois. For more than a day, the fire burned through the heart of the city. Queen Victoria donated more than 8,000 books, establishing the city's first free, public library."

With tears streaming down my face, I read about floods, famines, diseases, and wars. He translated passages from every book that showed the good in people. He searched for acts of kindness and humanity during the worst times in our history.

The last book has a picture that I recognize. It's a cryopod.

> "In April of 1983 scientists from around the world were put to sleep in LevenCorps research facilities. Each scientist volunteered, hoping to be a part of true medical change for all citizens of the world."

My lungs burn as I bite back sobs.

Jumping to my feet, I don't even take the time to put my shoes on. I don't care that I'm barefooted or that my face is red and blotchy from crying. I don't care that I'll be winded and ready to pass out when I get there. I run with as much speed as I am able back to the vehicle bay.

The lights are still on as I cut through the freezing cold grass. The temperature has dropped since I was last here. Maybe shoes would have been a good idea.

Bursting through the door, I stop mid-stride, our eyes meeting across the room.

"Ronan," my voice cracks, partially from my emotions but also from all the running. His face is serious as he makes several long strides until we're toe-to-toe.

"Where are the coverings for your feet?" He looks upset.

"I wanted to get here as fast as I could. I just ran out without them. I couldn't wait one more second." I feel like an idiot.

"It is cold."

"I-I know," I feel like I'm being scolded. "I've missed you so much, and I read the passages. Thank you for translating them for me. I-" My ranting is cut off by his arms scooping me up. The warmth from his chest is only partially responsible for the sudden heat in my body. His hand grasps the back of my head and pulls my face toward his.

He slams his mouth down against mine, and it's like all the sadness disappears. I can't even remember what it felt like to miss him.

The kiss jumps from zero to one hundred with one swipe of his tongue. My body melts into his. I surrender my mouth, giving him the access he demands, and he doesn't disappoint. He takes charge, pulling the life from my body. If he wasn't already holding me up, I would fall over.

He breaks the kiss, his nose almost touching mine as he studies my face. "Humans were fragile and often made mistakes, but they were quick to help and sacrifice not just for the greater good, but sometimes just for a small group. Even in the bleakest times, they thought of others and showed kindness and compassion."

"Thank you," I whisper in An'eoc.

He laughs softly under his breath. "Your accent is very good."

My heart flutters just listening to him in his native tongue. I understood him.

"Do you forgive me? I am sorry for my harsh judgment of your species."

"I forgive you," I ghost my lips over his cheek. Every fiber of my body is calling out to him. I know we have more to discuss, but I'm suddenly profoundly aware of how exhausted I feel. A month and a half of restless sleep has me ready to pass out in his arms.

As I press my face into his neck, I feel him walking, carrying me across the hangar.

"Will you visit the northern city with me?" He holds me in his lap after sliding into the car.

"Yes," I press quick, light kisses across his jawline. "I can't believe you made me a car."

"Do you like it?"

"I love it."

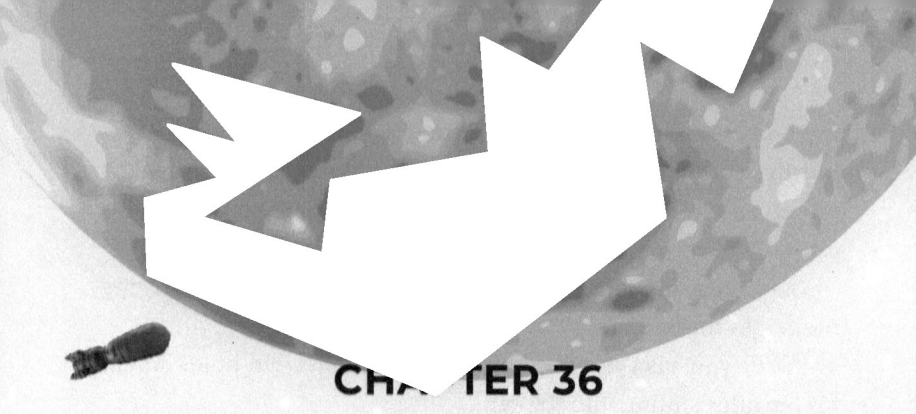

CHAPTER 36

Blinking against the bright sunlight, I am thrown into a state of panic. Sitting straight up, my foggy sleep brain tries to make sense of what is happening around me.

I'm in the hangar, in Ronan's arms. We're crammed into the passenger seat of the car. The large door to the warehouse is open, letting the crisp morning air in.

Most jarringly, we're not alone. There are at least fifteen An'eo trying desperately to avoid making eye contact with me.

"Ronan," I frantically whisper, turning to find him sleeping beneath me. The sun is bright, the air is cold, we're surrounded by people quietly working, but he's completely peaceful. For a moment, everything around us is forgotten. I've missed waking up beside him. We spent the night in a cramped car seat, crushed together with no space to move or stretch out. Yet, somehow, I'm more rested than I've felt in weeks.

Cupping his chin, I press gentle kisses to his lips. Last night, we talked until we fell asleep. I hadn't realized it was happening. We sat, holding each other. My body curled into his, and I drifted away slowly.

The sound of his voice whispering in the dark and the

rhythmic thump of his heart made it happen so slowly that I didn't feel it coming.

He hums, and his eyes flutter open. The way he looks at me makes me feel like the only thing in the world that matters. He doesn't notice how squished together we are or that we have an audience. His eyes never leave mine as he takes my face in his hands.

"I have never rested so well." He doesn't kiss me, instead, he runs his thumb over my lip. Leaning in, I watch his eyes, waiting for him to move. We didn't kiss last night. The tiny kisses I gave him were the first in over a month. My lips are desperate for his. My mouth craves the taste of his tongue.

"Can I kiss you?" He has never asked me that before. We have to adjust to this again—to us. After a fight like the one we had, everything feels fragile and unstable. He doesn't want to mess it up. Neither do I.

"Please kiss me." My voice is raspy and low.

His lip twitches, tugging up at the corners as he tips my chin up. The world fades away, and we're floating, alone, in a wide open void. Nothing exists but his lips. There is no one else; there never was. What started off sweet, quickly grows. Heated flames lick at my skin as he starts to demand more. The tight grip of his hands moves down my back to slide into the back of my pants, gripping my skin. He's not holding back anymore. The trepidation from just a moment ago is forgotten, washed away by the wetness of our mouths.

He groans, sucking the air from my lungs as he uses his grip to pull me closer to him. My hands fist through his hair, pressing myself into him as hard as I can. My chest is molded into mine, and my hips are open, holding him between my legs. It's still not close enough.

I want to crawl beneath his skin, to flow through his veins. I want to be the air that he breathes.

"I missed you."

The sounds that spill into my mouth from his, the raspy sigh, make my blood burn.

"Apologies for the interruption, Commander. There is a message from Secondary Commander." A voice rings out, and we both stop.

I let out a whimper, frustrated, before I notice his smile.

"You understand."

"Yeah, I do." A smile creeps onto my face despite my disappointment.

He wraps his arms around me, pulling me into his chest as he calls out to start the video message from his brother. His angry face appears on the wall just across from the garage. His gravelly voice barks out angrily in An'eo, I would probably be able to understand him if I was able to pay attention, but I can't. For the first time in several minutes, I realize we are not alone.

Was I moaning while he kissed me? Was I grinding my body down against his? We're in the car, but there's no roof.

Looking around the room, I see no one will make eye contact with me. Oh, my god.

A rush of heat covers my cheeks as I press my face into his shoulder. He chuckles quietly and runs his hand over the back of my head, combing through my hair with his fingers.

Closing my eyes, I focus on his arms. They feel so comfortable wrapped around my body. When the message ends, I have to ask him what several words are.

'Destabilized' isn't a word I've had to use in conversation yet.

"Is everything alright?"

"They have run into an unexpected problem. That is the nature of my visit. We need to leave earlier than expected." He lifts me, setting me on my feet so that he can climb out of the car. "This is the route we will take." He pulls up a hologram that maps out the journey.

"Wait, is that California?"

"I believe it was, yes." He nods.

Looking at the route he has planned out, I don't even have to wonder whether the car can make the trip. If he planned it, I know it will work. There are not any roads anymore, but I don't doubt that he has accounted for that.

"Do you want to go for a drive?"

"Yes!" I answer too quickly and much too loudly.

I'm practically jumping up and down as we walk back to the car. As I sit down in front of the steering wheel, I start to panic. Is this a car or an airplane? I feel like I'm sitting in the cockpit of a jet. I was so wrapped up in him last night that I didn't study the console.

"Um, is there a key?"

"A key?" He slides into the seat beside me.

"H-How do I start this?" My excitement from just two seconds ago has been replaced by anxiety. I'm supposed to know how to do this.

"Push here," he points to a button. "I found a picture that partially showed the inside of a car. I believe it should be similar."

The brakes and acceleration look the same...

"When it's on, how do I put it in drive?"

"How do you move forward?" He looks confused by my questions.

"Yes."

"Here," he points to a row of buttons. "Forward and reverse," he touches each one.

After pressing the button to start the engine, the car comes on with a roaring hum. This engine sounds powerful.

"Is there a shifter? Does the car automatically shift gears?" I stop myself from putting the car in drive.

"Press the button and go, that is all."

Taking a deep breath, I press the button to drive forward.

Three things happen at once. The car lurches forward, hard and fast. I scream. Everyone around us stops to watch.

The wheels screech against the floor of the garage as I stomp down on the brake. Ronan and I jerk forward, then fall back hard into our seats. Clearing my throat and avoiding eye contact with everyone, I stare at the steering wheel.

"So, the brake and the acceleration pedals are reversed in this car. Good to know." I look at Ronan sheepishly. His hand slowly moves toward the door, gripping it tightly.

Taking another slow, deep breath, I slowly lift my foot off the brake and press down on the acceleration. The car lurches a little bit but rolls forward. The pedals are extremely sensitive. I'm about to give us both whiplash.

Easing out of the garage, I'm horrified to find several people outside. Macsen and Clarisse are watching with smiles on their faces as we pass by.

"I swear, I'm not a bad driver," I fumble. "I'm just nervous." The less-than-smooth ride would probably give anyone else motion sickness.

Following his directions, I steer the car toward the wide open world.

Once the nerves wear off and I feel more comfortable behind the wheel, my cheeks hurt from smiling so much. This car has a bit of oomph to it. Picking up speed, I whip through an endless field.

"Oh my god, Ronan!" I squeal, my head tipping back to laugh.

He looks more relaxed now, smiling at my uncontrollable laughter.

This is such a strange moment. I'm driving around in a car with a boy. So typical, an ordinary moment. Except that it's not. I've got the nervous jitters, like a teenager on her first date. We're miles away from the capitol. We're the only people around, in every direction.

"There is a ridge ahead," he cautions.

"I'm going to park there so we can talk." I swallow nervously.

He nods. It actually makes me feel less nervous that he's nervous, too.

Stopping the car, my breath quickens. The valley below us stretches out as far as I can see. It's a perfect, cloudless day. The kind of day with crisp air and clear blue skies.

Turning toward him, my body feels tense.

"What is all of this?" I put off talking about the important things to ask about the console in front of us.

Without a word, he reaches forward and touches the screen. The dashboard appears to be embedded with the same type of navigation system as the airbridge. He presses a few buttons, and music starts to play.

I jump at the sound, meeting his gaze with wide eyes.

"There's a radio?" I can't believe it. Clapping my hands over my mouth, my eyes water, and a giggle rips through my chest.

"You are crying?"

"No, no, my eyes are just watering. I'm excited."

He looks confused but accepts it.

I don't know this song, but I don't care. When we drive back, I'm going to blast whatever this is at full volume.

"You've been listening to music lately?" I watch him squirm in the seat.

"It began as a way to understand humans better. It seems that through the words in a song, people were reaching out to others, to humanity, and the human experience. Music is about connection with others. The more I listened, the more I began to enjoy it."

For a split second, I hesitate, unsure if I should do what my natural instinct is telling me to do. Throwing caution to the wind, I pull myself up, climbing out of my seat and into his lap. With my legs on either side of his and our noses practically touching, I settle into the warmth that always radiates from him.

"I want to be closer to you. Is this alright?"

His hands wrap around my hips, holding me. "This is alright."

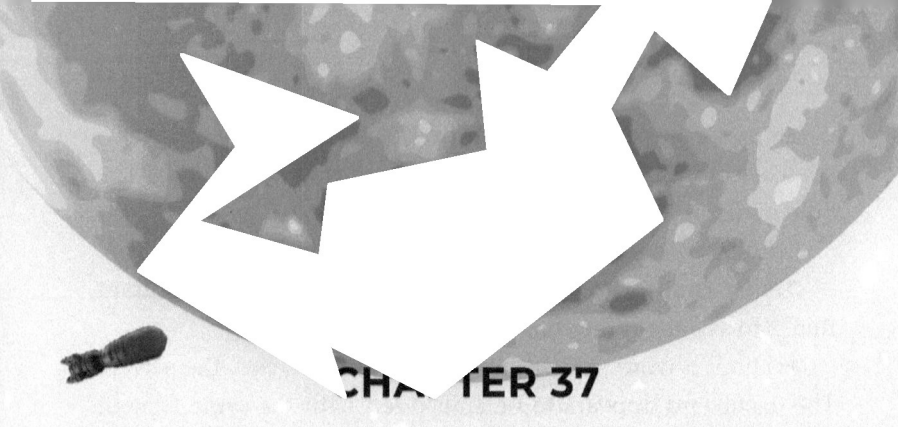

CHAPTER 37

"It was critical to me that the car be built quickly. I did not neglect my duties, I just dedicated all my extra time and resources to this project." He explains. "She was out of line. The rules of a challenge are clear. You are not An'eo and cannot be held to that."

"Obviously, I know I can't fight her. I'm grateful that you stepped in and shut it down but..." I'm struggling to articulate my feelings. "Is it going to be a problem? Will people see it as favoritism or unfair? If someone had challenged Santi or Clarisse, would you have done the same?"

He tilts his head and wets his lower lip, thinking for a moment.

"Yes," he eventually nods earnestly. "The laws of a challenge do not apply to humans. It could not be a fair fight." I can feel his nervousness in answering this.

"Ronan, you're bigger and stronger. I know that is factual. Our differences can be acknowledged without creating a situation where one is less than the other." I sigh, leaning my forehead against his. "I can feel that you're hesitating to answer. I know we're different."

I don't want there to be barriers between us. I value open,

honest communication *and* respect. I don't want either of us to feel uncertain of our footing with one another.

"How much of what she said did you understand?"

"Not all of it. I got the gist, though."

"I have made sure that everyone is aware that humans are not to be challenged. Any issues will be brought to my attention directly."

"I've missed you," I find myself staring at his lips. I've missed them too. We kissed this morning, but it wasn't enough.

Instead of kissing me, he leans back, creating more distance between our mouths, not less.

"Nicole," his tone is so serious that it concerns me. "Are you happy with your life?"

"What do you mean?" I am completely unprepared to answer that.

"Would you change it?"

"Would I change my life?" I huff out a nervous laugh. "That's a loaded question. Do I wish I could just snap my fingers and bring everyone back? Sure, of course. But I think that for whatever reason, we were supposed to meet. Call it fate or Sa'nu. I can't ignore the fact that we have come together under some pretty incredible circumstances."

I feel self-conscious under his gaze. The weight of his stare is more than I'm used to. He's always intense, but right now, this is different. His face is completely serious, a deep scowling crease in his brows.

"I wouldn't change things for me, for us." I try to elaborate. Mom always said, 'The past can't be changed. Regrets and what-ifs waste the present.' I can't focus on impossibilities I wish were true. There are three humans left, and I found an extraterrestrial soulmate. I'm choosing to put my efforts and attention there.

He studies my face with that same seriousness, searching for anything I'm trying to hide beneath the surface.

"All the choices I made in my life brought me right here to you. Some things were completely out of my control, but there were more decisions that I made. I don't regret my decisions. I'm happy with my life, and I'm happy to be here, right now, with you."

He lets out a slow breath, and the intensity of his expression softens. It still feels like I'm being studied — like he's observing me. Tilting my head down to stare at my lap. The quiet music catches my attention— I know this song.

"Can I ask you a question?"

He nods, cupping my chin.

"The research you did, reading our history. Why did you do it?"

"The passages I translated for you were my favorites, but there were others. I was searching for the goodness, the sacrifice that you spoke of. You are a credible source," he finally smiles. "But I needed to understand. Before we met, I read texts, but not extensively. I had an idea what humans were like, but then you came. I was intrigued by you instantly. When we spoke about humanity, it further cemented the ideas I had previously believed. You are a direct contradiction to everything. I knew you were different the first time we spoke."

"The day you told me about the end of humanity and I cried on the floor for an hour?"

"That is the second time we spoke." A lopsided grin plays on his lips.

"Wait, what? We never talked before that morning!"

"No, I carried you to my quarters-"

"Oh my god," I cover my face with my hands. "When I was drunk on A'shuur? We talked?"

"We did. You were incredibly forthcoming."

My face is so warm. I don't know what I said, but I know by the look on his face that it's embarrassing. "What did I say?"

"Well," he tucks my hair behind my ear. "You told me that you think I am the prettiest man you have ever seen."

"Oh, god," I cringe.

"And you asked if I was about to kill you."

"Hey, that was a valid concern."

His thumb runs across my lower lip, and I shiver. "Then, you asked if I wanted to make out."

"No, I didn't!" I clap my hand over my mouth.

"I did not know what that meant, but after you explained it, it was all I could think about."

My breath catches. "Really?"

His eyes flick down to my mouth. When his hands drop down to my thighs, I feel myself growing warmer. The air around us changes in an instant. We were laughing not one second ago. Now the air is heavy, full of anticipation.

"Your lips are-" he shutters, and I lunge forward, diving into him. He sighs against my mouth, the kind of soft, content sound that makes me feel anything but content. I'm growing more riled up by the second. Our kisses don't match. I'm harsh and aggressive against his tenderness.

His hands gently rest on my legs, squeezing softly. The subtle touch is like a tease. I want more. I want the desperation that we both seemed to share this morning in the garage.

Frustration grows with each passing second. I've completely skipped the simmer and jumped straight to a full, rolling boil in ten seconds flat.

Sliding my tongue forward, tasting and lapping at his. His mouth is so soft and warm, wet. He tastes slightly sweet and soft like the fruit we eat.

Gripping his shirt in my fists, I pull him forward. Nothing I'm doing seems to be adding to his need at all. He's the picture of calm. I am chaos. Everything in my body buzzes. My skin tingles and burns. My muscles jerk and flex. My blood churns, thrashing in my veins. Worst of all, I ache everywhere, but mostly between my legs. Two layers of clothes, his pants and mine. That's all that separates me from sweet relief. Knowing that is killing me.

"I have missed your mouth," the low rumble of his voice making it almost impossible for me to breathe. "Not just your lips, but the words, the sighs…" The only indication that he's struggling at all is the slight tightening of his fingers around my thighs.

"I've missed you too, everything about you," I pant. My voice is breathy and low, my sex-deprived brain struggling to think of anything beyond that.

"Nicole," he groans when I press my hips down, grinding against him.

I hum, leaving a trail of kisses down his jaw and onto his neck.

"We need to return to prepare for tomorrow. I want to leave at sunrise."

Pulling away, I blink back my shock.

"I… yeah, alright. Good idea." I barely recognize the sound of my own voice. This is a terrible idea. The worst idea. I don't want to go back. I want him to slam me into the hood of this car he built and kill me with his cock.

"Do you want to drive?"

"Oh, uh, you can." I'm too distracted. I'll probably drive us straight into a tree.

He slides out of the car, walking around to the driver's side.

What the fuck just happened? I'm still as desperate for him as I always have been, but he seems to have cooled off completely. He doesn't even look like he's struggling.

With ease, he starts the engine and reverses the car away from the cliff. When he turns his head, reaching his arm over the back of my seat to watch behind him, I nearly choke on my spit.

When did driving become so sexy?

As he accelerates, he suddenly jerks the car to a stop. Jerking his widening eyes toward mine, I can see it. Gulping, he shakes his head slightly and accelerates again. Stupid pheromones. He knows I'm over her, drowning in lust.

Watching the road, I listen to the songs that play as I try to calm myself down. I shouldn't look at him. It's too much.

Against my better judgment, I sneak occasional glances in his direction. Casually peeking over at him, I can't help myself.

He's slightly reclined, relaxed against his seat. With one hand on the wheel—effortless and smooth—he steers us toward home. God, how is it so attractive?

"Oh!" The thought suddenly occurs to me. "I need to talk to Gaia. I can't just leave. I have to make sure she knows so she can have someone else record the Ulaar expenditures."

His lips turn slightly upward. "She has praised you as efficient and timely with your reports."

"I-I mean, it's not that difficult. I just have to read numbers and record them in a log three times a day. I'm not doing anything."

"Nicole, accept the compliment. Three times a day, you stop what you are doing, go to the engineering bay, and record several sets of numbers in the records. You are on time, and you are scrupulous."

"I just want to make sure I'm doing everything correctly." I smile down at my hands as my fingers knot together in my lap.

"I will alert Gaia that you need to speak to her when we arrive."

"Thank you."

Several songs play as we sit in silence again. As the city appears in the distance, I know that our quiet time alone is coming to an end, at least until tomorrow morning.

"Ronan," I clear my throat, trying to sound more assured and less nervous. I want to ask him if I can come back to his room. I don't want to sleep alone anymore. "T-Thank you for this. I can't even put into words how much this means to me."

I lost my nerve.

"I would do anything for you." His eyes, full of sincerity, meet mine, and my heart aches. We aren't fighting anymore. He asked for forgiveness, and I gave it, but something still feels off. After this morning's kiss, I had hoped that we would fall into our old rhythm immediately.

I guess not.

CHAPTER 38

tossed and turned all night long, no matter what I did. I just couldn't get comfortable when we got back from our drive. Ronan disappeared. He was calm and casual. He didn't seem like he was rushing away, but it just feels off.

While we were apart, I dreamed of our reunion. I played out scenario after scenario in my head. The real thing turned out to be more incredible than any of the ideas I thought up.

Even the wildest stretches of my imagination couldn't conjure up a scenario where he scoured history books to find passages to show the goodness of humanity. I never could have imagined that he would spend a month and a half building a car from the ground up just because she knew I missed driving.

As far as apologies are concerned, he kind of crushed it.

Now I forgive him, but we didn't fall into each other's arms the way that my daydreams made me believe we would.

Standing under the warm spray of the shower, I roll my stiff neck. It's almost time to meet him in the vehicle bay.

My emotions are all over the place. I'm excited and nervous. Butterflies flutter in my stomach with excitement at the thought of being alone with him, and at the thought of going on the adventure with him, but there's also this underlying fear that it will be awkward, that it won't be him and I.

With my backpack and the small bag that was delivered to my room, I make my way down the quiet hallways.

As I step outside, I am surprised to be met with busyness and people. The car has already been loaded with supplies and parked in front of the steps of the capitol building.

I don't see Ronan anywhere, so I walk down to the bottom of the steps and sit on the last one.

Quiet mumbled chatter draws my attention to the area behind the car. When I look up, I recognize the woman that challenged me standing with a man that I don't recognize. They're trying to be inconspicuous, but I notice the way their eyes flit in my direction.

When she starts to walk towards me, I sit up straight, feeling nervous about the altercation that is probably about to take place.

"Medic." She nods her head, tipping it down. "After speaking with the Commander, I have come to realize the error of my ways. I apologize for the way I spoke to you and for assuming in a situation where my opinion was unnecessary and uninformed."

"Oh," I am sure she can see my shock. This is not what I was expecting at all. "Thank you."

She nods her head and turns to walk away just as Ronan sits on the step beside me. I notice her eyes, the way they drop down to the ground in front of him.

"Ready?" His hand inches toward mine, resting on the ground as close as he can be without actually touching me.

"Yes."

He doesn't say anything, he just touches his pinky to mine for the most fleeting second before standing and holding his hand out to me.

He barks final orders at the group as we leave, each of them nodding at his list of demands.

I slide into the driver seat, double-checking the foot pedals to make sure I am stepping on the brake as I press the button to bring the engine to life.

When Ronan has settled into his seat, I press the car into Drive, and we officially start our journey.

The route is displayed on the screen in the center of the console.

"This is so weird," I giggle, adjusting the wheel to keep the car following the course.

"I believe humans had this technology after you were asleep."

"Really?" I can't even imagine it. "How did you know that cars had radios?"

"Santi."

The car veers slightly left before I jerk the wheel to bring us back on course.

"What?"

"He works in the vehicle bay."

"Right, I know that. He helps with maintenance on the airbridge."

"He saw me working every day. Eventually, he approached me, and we spoke about the car. He mentioned the radio."

I'm shocked. He never mentioned it!

"I asked him to allow me the time to complete the project without speaking to you about it." It's like he can read my mind.

"How many songs are there?" I haven't noticed any repeating yet. Not that I would notice; I've only recognized a handful of the songs or artists.

"There are just over five hundred files."

I drive until lunch. When we stop to eat and stretch, he pulls out a small metal container filled with sliced fruit. An An'eo lunchbox.

We've been mostly silent, listening to music while the wind blows through our hair.

"Unless you object, I should drive the remainder of today's

journey. We will be coming to water that might be difficult to navigate."

"I have no objections."

It feels like we've reverted to the beginning, reset. The comfort and ease we had has been replaced with the awkwardness of two strangers traveling together.

The next five hours pass slowly. We discuss my job, the scenery, and the northern city. He explains how he built the car, the vial of Ulaar that powers it, and how he made wheels that cover all terrain.

It's interesting, but I want him to stop the car, yank me over into his lap, and kiss me.

But he doesn't.

When we stop for the night, he pulls out a thin mat, unfolding it into a large sheet. When he spreads it over the ground, he gestures for me to lie down.

"Would you like to bathe?"

"How?" I look around. There is no lake or water anywhere that I can see.

"I can set up a shower if you would like."

Staring up at him, I'm not sure what I'm waiting for. Of course, he will not elaborate; they never do.

"Sure, if it's not too much trouble, a shower would be great." A shower sounds nice, but I'm most interested in seeing how he pulls this off.

He pulls a silver pole out of the trunk. Extending it in his hands, it pulls until it is as long as he is. One end has a spike, and he screws a small round piece of metal to the other end. Pointing the spike to the ground, he raises it up and slams it down with so much force that most of it disappears into the ground.

He then pulls out another silver pole with a dome on the end. He screws it into the first pole and extends it until the dome stands just above his head.

"Come," he holds his hand out to me. "Push this button, and the water will come."

From start to finish, the construction of this outdoor shower took him about fifty seconds.

"Thank you," I try to smile so that he can't tell that I'm panicking. Am I expected to strip down naked and shower out in the open? I know he's seen me, he's seen… everything. Things are different now.

Standing naked in front of him feels too vulnerable.

Hesitating, I turn around to face away from him. If I don't shower, he'll know I'm freaking out.

Taking a deep breath, I slowly kick off my shoes. I know I'm undressing in slow motion as I pull my shirt up over my head before slipping my pants down. The grass is cold beneath my feet as I press the button. The water starts slowly, trickling out before the water pressure improves. It's slightly colder than I would like, but it's warmer than I was expecting it to be.

Pinching my eyes closed, I try to pretend I'm alone. I don't have the guts to check to see if he's looking.

"Nicole," his voice from right beside me makes me yelp.

"What?" I clutch my chest.

Even as the sun sets and the purplish sky gets darker, I can see that his pupils are blown out. His eyes are laser-focused on mine.

He holds out a handful of iridescent balls. They look like pearls.

"What is it?"

"Soap," he clears his throat.

"Oh, ok, thank you," I step forward, and when our hands touch, it's like a static electric shock. His chest rises and falls rapidly with each breath.

The little pearls are squishy. When I squeeze one between my fingers, it bursts open in my hand.

I wash as quickly as humanly possible. I need to put clothes on. Aside from the fact that he's watching me, it's freezing.

The tiny towel he gave me unfolds to be much larger than I was expecting. The An'eo really nailed travel size and portability.

When I'm dressed, I still feel jittery, but I sit down on the edge of the mat.

"Better?" He pulls himself up.

"Yes, thank you, I needed th-"The words die in my throat as he drops his pants.

"I will bathe quickly before we sleep."

"Mmhm, yeah, great."

The temperature of my cheeks has spiked by about a thousand degrees. I've seen him naked so many times. That's more of a problem than a comfort. His body is so…goosebumps roll across my skin at the sight of him.

Dripping wet skin stretched over hard, chiseled muscles.

So many muscles.

Pulling my blanket up around my shoulders, I focus on the little puffs of white that linger in the air as I breathe.

I hardly notice when he comes to lie on the mat beside me. I've been so focused on not watching him that I've zoned out.

"Come," he holds his arms open. Scrambling without a second of hesitation, I curl into his warm body. "You are cold," his hand rubs quickly up and down over my arm.

"Are we going to freeze out here?"

"Our bed is heated," he speaks, and the mat almost instantly warms beneath us.

The exhaustion of the day and the warmth of his body zap the consciousness right out of me. In what felt like a blink, the sun is rising, and Ronan is pulling away from me.

Day two of driving passed in a strange sort of haze. Everything is almost the same as yesterday, only the view has changed. We drive in almost total silence, hour after hour, passing with the music and nothing else.

When we stop for the night, we eat, we set up camp, and we shower.

My frustration is like a mosquito bite. I'm trying to ignore it but the more I try to pretend it's not there, the itchier it feels. Rolling so that my back is to him, I force my eyes closed.

When my eyes blink open in the early morning light, I can feel him behind me. Biting into my lip to keep from screaming, I pull my eyes closed again.

I was having the best dream. It was more like a memory from before everything fell apart. It's not that he's being cold he's just holding himself back from me. I want him to suffocate me in his affection. I want his hands on me constantly. I want him to make me feel the way he used to, like he wants me like I want him.

When he groans behind me, I freeze. The sound is so low and rumbling, I feel it in my stomach.

He moves, the mat shifting as he presses his body against mine.

"Nicole," his deep, tired voice makes me shiver.

When he rubs against me, long and hard as a rock, I whimper. I tried to hold it but it slipped out.

"What were you dreaming of?" He grinds himself against me.

"You."

"What about me?" His fingers bite into my hip as he sucks in a sharp breath.

"Do you remember when you came home from the northern city? It was after the accident when you had to leave, right after…" I'm fumbling around trying to find the words.

"I remember."

"It was late when you returned. Middle of the night late and raining."

He hums and shifts forward again.

"You picked me up and carried me out to the terrace…"

An obscene sound claws its way out of his throat. His composure is cracking. I can feel it in my chest like it was mine.

"You peeled my clothes off in the rain and fucked me. Do you remember?"

His hand slides down, rubbing against my skin as he slips into my pants. When his fingers brush over the wetness there, he chokes.

"Ronan, please," I whisper in An'eoc.

I hoped this would elicit a reaction. It did. Just not the one I was expecting.

A tortured roar vibrates in the low light. He rolls away from me and stands up so quickly that by the time I can turn around, he has already walked away.

"Ronan!" I jump up and run after him, the cold, wet grass sending a chill through my body. The cold air is no match for the bitter cold I feel in my chest. "Why are you running from me? Are you mad at me?" I don't understand this back and forth. He asked me to come on this trip with him. We kissed. His distance doesn't make sense.

"I am not." He runs his hands through his hair.

"Could have fooled me! Explain this, please. Every time we get close, you pull away. Why?"

"There are things that you do not know. Things that would change your mind. I am trying to do what is best for you." He growls through clenched teeth.

"Just tell me what I don't know. Problem solved. Why ask me to come with you if you're going to keep me at a distance the whole time?"

"I fear my selfishness will overtake my logical mind. If I have you…" He takes a step forward. "If I hold you, if I taste you," our bodies shudder in unison. "I will not be able to do what is right."

"You're not making sense."

"Everything will make sense."

"When?"

"Eventually."

Frustrated and rejected, I turn on my heels and go back to the mat. Why did he build the car and write the passages? Why fix everything only to be distant?

Packing my belongings, I slide into the passenger's seat, waiting for him.

Not even the music can ease the uncomfortable tension between us.

A song starts to play through the speakers that I know. I hum along with the lyrics. I don't feel lighter or less irritated, but the song helps.

When it ends, he starts it again.

I quirk my brow, but sing along.

"I like this one," he whispers quietly.

"Me too. It's called Right Down the Line. My mom would have liked this song. It came out just after she died." I don't know why I'm telling him this. I guess I'm just grasping for anything. Hoping to bring him back to me.

He hums but doesn't respond.

So much for that.

The hours and miles slowly pass. When we stop for the night, I'm exhausted from the emotional weight on my shoulders.

He turns toward me, but I get out of the car, slamming the door behind me. I need to put some distance between us.

"Nicole!" I hear his door slam, but I don't stop.

Curse his long legs. He covers the distance I put between us in no time. Grabbing my arm, he pulls me back.

"If you had the choice, would you choose me?" The look on his face is like a knife twisting in my heart. It's mostly vulnerability, fear, and hope, but there is something else there, too. Something hidden.

"Why are you asking me this?" I fucking hate hypotheticals. "We are here right now. We're connected by more than mere attraction. All the little, inconsequential things that had to happen to bring us both here... this is more than a lucky coincidence. I- I love you."

Booming thunder cracks in the sky above us as soon as the forbidden words leave my lips. I meant them; I meant them with every fiber of my being, but I didn't mean to say them.

Lighting sparks across the sky as he reaches me. The light flashes, illuminating his face.

When he grabs me and lifts me, pulling my thighs around his waist. I'm flooded with relief and apprehension. He's holding me, but is he going to pull away again?

"What have you done to me?" His voice is gravelly. Before I can answer, he slams his mouth against mine.

"Finally." I smile against his lips.

Another loud clap of thunder rolls above us, and just like that, a downpour unlike any that I've ever seen rains down on us.

By the time he's walked us back to the car, we're soaked to the skin. Heavy drops of rain splash against us, but I don't care. Ronan doesn't seem to notice the rain at all as he sets me down on the hood of the car.

"I would choose you on any planet, in any universe, no matter the cost." He tugs the hem of his shirt up.

I run my hands over his chest. There is no turning back this time.

While he watches me, I pull my shirt over my head, letting the water-heavy material fall to the ground. His eyes are piercing into my skin. The rain is freezing, but I'm burning up. I need him, not just physically. I need the wide open, vulnerable state that he brings me to. I need to feel the inseparable closeness that I've never felt with anyone but him. I'm never more alive than when his consciousness joins mine, when I see through his eyes.

"Put your hands on me."

CHAPTER 39

With a gentleness I wasn't expecting, he pulls my pants off. They hit the ground with a loud, wet plop.

Weeks of emotions are barely contained in my skin. When he finally touches me, I might burst into tears, or it could go the other way. I might laugh. The only thing I know with any certainty is that I will go crazy if he doesn't hurry.

He's moving too slowly. It's like he's not experiencing the same frenzy that I am. Everything I need is right in front of me. I just need to convince him to take what I'm willingly offering.

Resting my back against the hood, I spread my legs wide, placing my feet flat.

He freezes, looking between my legs. He's close enough to touch me, but he doesn't. The rain slows, scattered drops falling here and there. Unmoving, our eyes are locked together. I'm begging him to step forward, to sink himself into me. He's looking at me as if it's the first time.

Impatient and throbbing, I slide my hand down my stomach, letting it dip down between my legs.

His body jerks forward slightly, like every muscle in his body just tensed at once.

Pressing my heels into the cool metal beneath me, I slowly push my middle finger into my wet center. Groaning in frustration, I slide in and out, desperate to ease the tight, burning feeling coiling inside me.

This feels...fine. It's not what I want. I could have had my own fingers every day for the last month and a half. I want the real thing. I want him.

With slightly parted lips, he watches me. When my back arches up, leaning into the agonizing pressure, he finally wakes up. His pants hit the ground, the soaked material hitting the ground loudly.

Anticipating his touch, his body between my legs, I spread them wider. All he has to do is step forward.

Instead, he takes his cock in his hand, closing his fist around it.

"Keep going." His voice is different in An'eoc. It's deeper, heavier, it drips with authority.

The cool breeze against my wet skin sends shivers down my spine and goosebumps everywhere. I can't find it in me to care about the cold. Watching him is all that matters.

Pressing my fingertips down, circling my clit, I moan into the air. Short, stuttering breaths slip past my parted lips.

I want to pinch my eyes shut, but I can't. I have to see him. I don't want to miss anything. His hand moves slowly, and the muscles in his chest and abdomen flutter under his skin.

I move my fingers faster. My thighs tense, and my hips shift and squirm. I'm going to come. The pressure is excruciating, tingling in my stomach. Wordlessly, he watches, his eyes glued to the gleaming wet skin between my wide open legs.

His fist pumps faster, grunts and harsh breathing sounds wrap around my body. A strangled, broken cry shakes my chest as my hips buck forward. I'm so close, I'm almost there, I just need a little bit more.

I want to reach out and grab him, to pull him toward me. I

want to wrap my lips around him and suck the pleasure from his body.

I'm afraid that if he isn't the initiator in this, he will back away again. For whatever reason, he has put a barrier between us. If it's going to come crashing down, I need him to stop pulling back.

"Ronan, I'm lonely," I whisper.

His head tips down, but his eyes never leave mine. For a moment, it looks like he's about to fight this. "Move your hand."

I pull my hand away, squirming at the unreleased tension.

When he steps between my legs, I'm hesitant to get too excited. He could still run.

"Are you certain that you want this?"

"I want you, I always want you," I'm begging now, my body burning, aching, and throbbing everywhere. Why is he having such a hard time understanding? How many times, how many ways must he ask?

He takes my thighs tightly in his hands, holding me open and pulling me toward him. A shameless, desperate moan echoes in the silent field as he drops down, suctioning his mouth on the horrible aching spot.

It only takes a few flicks of his tongue to give me exactly what I was missing. Him. That's all I need to fall into the abyss of an orgasm so intense it makes my muscles tense and shake so hard that they hurt.

His mouth is hot as he devours me, licking and sucking me into a bundle of exposed nerves.

My fingers knot through his hair, gripping him tightly. When my nails scrape over his scalp, he makes a sound so tortured and loud that I'm thrown into another whirlwind of rippling pleasure. My thighs spasm in his tight grip. I fight against it, trying to close my legs, to protect my oversensitive clit.

He looks up from between my legs, a deep scowl on his face. "Stop trying to close your legs. I have been deprived of this for weeks. No food or drink would satisfy my ravenous appetite. I longed for you. I will bring you to orgasm until the ache is forgotten. Then I will fuck you until the sun rises."

A stammering, incoherent mixture of An'eo, English, and moans is all I can manage when he attaches his lips to me again.

It feels like he gives me an orgasm for every day that we were apart. I'm barely clinging to life when he finally stands. I know he's not done with me. He told me his intentions but I still gasp when I see his cock.

I only get a glance before he pulls me to the edge and presses the leaking tip against me.

He looks like he could fuck me for days, weeks maybe, and he would still be hard.

He slacks his jaw and his head falls back as he inches into me. Although he made me come more times than is medically safe, and my body is now a worn-out rag doll, I still moan at the feeling. My pussy suctions around him, pulling him in.

He draws himself back, looking down between us.

"The sight of my cock covered in your wetness..." he groans and his voice fades away.

"I thought about you all day, every day," I whisper, leaving a trail of kisses across his chest.

His thrusts are leisurely, he's in no rush. It's like he's set on prolonging my demise. My body is worn out and tender, but it's more than physical. I've missed this closeness, the feeling of being complete. He's going to wreck me tonight, and I'm ready for it.

"Can I show you something?" He presses his forehead to mine.

"Yes," my voice wobbles. I'm too tired to speak or to try to think of anything beyond the slow rhythm of his hips.

"Close your eyes," he grits through his teeth. His damp breath fanning across my skin.

Letting my eyes flutter closed, I grip his shoulders tightly as he kisses me. Deep and gentle.

It starts slowly, the subtle beat of our hearts. It's so soft at first

I don't even notice it. It spreads through my body, warm tingles that bubble under my skin.

When he brings his hand to the side of my neck, holding me, deepening the kiss, it starts to become more powerful.

He's connecting with me, joining his consciousness to mine.

My eyes are closed, but a hazy light is growing. Soft at first, then brighter and brighter until I'm squinting. There, in the middle of the shiny emptiness, is me. Only, I look different. As my body comes into focus, I can't stop watching myself. I'm dancing, my head thrown back, a wide, open smile on my lips as I laugh and sing.

I look… beautiful.

I can't quite put my finger on it. It's me, exactly as I am, only… better. The little things that make me insecure, my short, thick legs, my slightly crooked bottom teeth, or the cowlick in my hair, are all still there. I just don't notice them for some reason.

When I realize what I'm looking at, tears swell in my eyes.

"This is how you see me?" My chin trembles as I blink my eyes open.

"Yes," he sweeps one hand down my body, hooking it under my knee. With my leg up, he can stretch me open even more. With a shuttering breath, I feel everything building, ready to boil over. "Look at me, Ya'abe."

"I don't know that word." I meet his gaze. He smiles before tightening his grip on my leg and picking up speed.

My head falls back as the pulsing length of his cock slides in and out so quickly it forces the air out of my lungs.

He hums, his free hand cradling the back of my head. "Look at me, Nicole. I want you to see what you do to me. I want you to watch me as I fill you with cum."

My hands come up to grip his hair, holding on for dear life. The sound of our wet skin as he forces our bodies together makes me delirious.

"Ronan," I choke as he hits the spot inside of me that makes my back arch up. With a breathless cry, my body tightens around him. Forcing my eyes open, I watch as he stares down at me. I see lust and determination on his face as he fucks me through aftershocks that seize and wreck my muscles.

With a raspy groan, he shudders and twitches, emptying himself inside me. His face drops down into the curve of my neck. He pants against my skin.

"Fuck," I groan as he lifts me up, his cock still firmly planted between my legs.

He slides into the passenger seat of the truck, my legs tucked on either side of his. Gently rolling himself upward, he somehow awakens my unending desire for him. Even after everything, I want more.

"What does 'Ya'abe' mean?" I whimper before sliding my tongue into his mouth for a brief, but fiery kiss.

"The one I most adore." His hands find my hips, lifting and lowering me onto him.

Slamming our lips together, I lean into the warmth of his chest. "Show me. Let me see how much you love me."

"After tonight, you will never doubt it."

CHAPTER 40

Every bump in the road sends a jolt of pain to my tender, ravaged body.

When we untangled our limbs this morning, I winced, and he carried me to the car. I couldn't help but notice the way his chin tipped up slightly. He's proud of his work. I may never sit right again, but it was worth it.

I'm exhausted, sore, and swollen, but so content. He's my Ronan again. We've been talking and laughing all morning. In the quiet moments when we let the music play, it's not uncomfortable. He's back. The wall he built to keep me out is now in ruins.

"Repeat the words," he asks as the car comes to a stop in the middle of a wide-open desert.

"Sex."

He hums. "Good pronunciation. Continue."

"Pussy, cock, fucking…"

"Do you remember the sentence?"

"Ronan," I whine. No, I don't want to say it. If his hope is that I will use this during sex, he will be waiting for a long time, forever. I'm never going to say this to him.

He just lifts his brow, waiting for me to repeat the sentence with my newly learned dirty vocabulary from our lesson earlier.

As flatly as I can, I whisper, "Ronan, I need you; never stop fucking me.".

"You lack enthusiasm, but your pronunciation is excellent."

Chuckling, I slide out of the car with a groan, stretching my tight muscles. We're almost in the northern city, and I'm getting excited. I'm not expecting tourist attractions or vacation-type activities, but it's still fun to travel.

His arm snakes around my waist from behind as he pulls me into his chest. His other hand comes up, holding fruit to my lips.

Leaning back, letting him support most of my weight, I eat, letting my eyes drift closed. Lunch is quiet, neither of us feeling the need to speak. Being in his arms again feels so good that I don't want to ruin it with words. I just want him to hold me.

"How is your pussy?"

I choke, looking up at him with a grimace etched into my face. "It's beaten to shit, thank you very much."

"Does this mean that I will have to hold myself back from you?"

"Yes."

He groans and holds me tighter.

"You should have thought about that before you tried to kill me with your cock last night."

"You were not complaining last night."

I don't turn to look at him, but I know if I did, there would be a smirk on his face. Smug bastard. "I didn't complain because I was too busy gasping for air." I pout.

He hums, his chest rumbling against my back. "I do love the sound of you gasping for air."

Oh no. My stomach clenches, my painfully overworked muscles reacting to the low timber of his voice against my wishes. Am I really about to let this man anywhere near my sore, overworked body?

His hand presses flat against my stomach, holding me in place as his lips touch my neck.

A dry, cracked, desperate sound comes from the back of my throat. My head rolls against his shoulder as his tongue traces the dip between my jaw and neck.

"We should go. It is supposed to rain again. If we leave now, we will arrive before it starts."

My eyes snap open as I spin around in his grip. "What?"

His lips twitch as he points upward. "Rain."

Scowling, I untangle myself from his arms. I will remember this. He chuckles behind me, and I hobble to the car. As the door opens, the ground begins to shake beneath my feet. The tremor is so violent it almost knocks me off my feet. It takes a moment to recognize what it is. Growing up in Georgia, we don't get earthquakes, but I know enough to understand, after a moment of disoriented shock, that it's happening now.

Before I can turn, he's behind me, wrapping me in his arms again.

We're out in the middle of nowhere. There isn't anything to fall on top of us, but it's frightening to have the world shifting beneath your feet.

When the shaking stops, it takes a moment for the wobble in my knees to subside as well.

"Are you alright?" The concern in his voice makes me nervous.

"I'm fine. What's wrong?"

"Come," he holds my door. "We need to leave."

We're silent as he speeds through the desert, sand flying up behind us as he drives faster than he has on the whole trip.

"My brother scouted locations for another settlement for two years." He reaches over and grips my thigh with one hand. "Land surveys were done, and weather conditions were recorded for a year. We studied everything. Movements of tectonic plates within the earth cause these tremors. I was assured that it would not be a problem. Caelum and his team found a solution to this. Now, it seems, it is a problem, and their solution has failed. The tremors are becoming more frequent. I was led to believe that they were minor and still not worthy of much concern." He growls and starts pressing buttons on the console.

After a moment, Macsen's face appears on the screen. In rapid-fire An'eoc, Ronan rips into him. I know he's not angry at Macsen; he's just angry, and unfortunately for him, he's getting the brunt end of his rage.

"Caelum called in the event." Macsen is completely calm.

"We will arrive soon. I want the reports in hand the moment I arrive."

"Yes, Commander."

The call ends, and Ronan sighs. His irritation blooms in my chest as he rests his hand on my leg again.

"Olexa told me that there were tremors, but they were minor and insignificant enough to cause no damage. What we just felt was not minor."

"Definitely not; that would have had a high Richter scale rating."

He looks surprised, and we spend the rest of the drive discussing earthquake magnitudes and what we humans knew about them. To say he was stunned to find out that we actually knew about them pretty extensively would be an understatement. I am no earth scientist, but I know enough.

"I apologize for over-explaining before," he smiles as he maneuvers the truck up a large hill.

"It's fine, just don't let it happen again." I take his hand in mine. I open my mouth to say something snarky, but we reach the top of the hill before I can say it. Once I see the view of the valley below, the words are forgotten.

The expanse below us is breathtaking. It looks nothing like the Capitol. It looks like it was designed by Gaudi or Salvador Dali. The shape of the buildings, almost like wet sand that was dripped to form a castle. It's beautiful and strange.

The closer we get, the more it looks like sand. I wonder what it's made of. From a closer distance, it looks like it has a rough, bumpy texture. Each building is impossibly shaped.

His fingers bite into my skin with a bit of tension as he steers us down into the valley and eventually into the vehicle bay. A woman is standing by the door. She's holding one of the little screens that I use to check the Ulaar expenditures at home.

All eyes are on us as we walk toward the woman. Feeling slightly uncomfortable under the scrutiny of so many eyes, I reach out and take Ronan's hand. I immediately pull back, but he holds tight, interlocking his fingers with mine.

The woman greets us both respectfully and hands him the screen. He reads over the information, then hands it to me.

For all of the language that I can understand and speak, my reading and writing skills are undeniably lacking. Looking over the screen, I can piece together that there has only been one other earthquake of the magnitude that they have recorded to date.

When I hand him the screen, I don't miss the astounded faces of our audience.

"Where is Caelum?"

"The control tower." The woman has been staring at our linked fingers.

"Come," he pulls me beside him. As we walk through the courtyards and toward the capitol building here, every An'eo watches us, fascinated.

I'm tempted to reach up and touch his hair, just to give them something to talk about. Our handholding will probably keep them busy for this visit, at least.

The control tower is high up, overlooking the whole city. The panoramic view is incredible and I'm immediately drawn to the lookout.

"Ronan."

"Caelum."

They greet each other coldly. I don't have any siblings, so I never had to deal with that dynamic. I suppose if my own brother challenged me, talked someone else into challenging me, then built a city on a fault line, I might be a bit icy, too.

"Have you read the reports?"

Ronan stops, staring at his brother with a passive expression for several seconds.

Caelum sighs, clearly irritated. "Hello, Doctor." So, he doesn't speak English. The last time we met, he refused to say a single word to me.

"Hello, Secondary Commander, nice to see you again."

His attention falls back on Ronan.

"I have seen the reports. Why is the failsafe you created malfunctioning?"

"A team is inspecting the drill. They began yesterday. I will have an answer by tomorrow."

Ronan accepts this answer. "Now what about the training modules?" He must feel me tense beside him because he turns to make eye contact. "They have been developing weapons simulators. We are not here to participate in warrior training."

"She understands An'eoc?" He cuts off our conversation.

"I speak some, too." I snap before turning back to Ronan. "Weapon simulators?"

His lip twitches as he nods. "I will take you to see them."

Caelum studies us closely as we walk toward the training arena. In a smaller dome off to the side, we enter their weapons' training facility. I have to bite back a laugh. It looks like an arcade. It's incredibly sophisticated and much cleaner than any arcade I've ever been to, but it's basically the same thing.

"What is this?" I point to a large screen with a control panel in front of it.

"It is a simulator for a device that shoots infrared beams that cause the molecules of the target to scramble."

"Can I try it?"

"You wish to use the simulator?" Caelum is looking at me like I've sprouted a second head.

"Yeah, I do."

As he sets up the screen, several An'eo gather from around the room to watch.

Stepping in front of the panel, I look it over. "This is the trigger?"

He nods, stepping back with the others to watch me.

Taking a deep breath, the lights fade, and the screen glows in the darkness. From the corner of the screen, a flicker of light grows larger as it moves toward me. Moving across the screen, I push the trigger button. Over the next several minutes, I shoot down every 'enemy' that approaches, either blowing their ship up completely or by rendering it immovable. The simulation goes on much longer than I was expecting it to, and by the end, my arm hurts from holding up my 'gun.' When I turn around, everyone is wide-eyed and silent.

"Nicole," Ronan whispers. "How?"

"I mean, it's not a big deal," I shrug.

"Not a big deal?" Caelum steps forward almost angrily.

"You're looking at the Pennymill Arcade *Space Invaders* and *Asteroids* high scorer. Looks like the whiz kid's still got it." I smile when the realization hits me. "Weird that they all have to do with alien invasion," I laugh.

They aren't laughing. I think I've broken everyone here.

"You have experience in alien weaponry?" Ronan asks quietly, stepping forward. I'm not sure if I should be offended here. They didn't think I could, essentially, play a video game?

"That was the easiest setting," Caelum's snarky voice cuts in from behind us.

"Then turn the settings up," I snap back before I can stop myself.

Stepping away from Ronan, I roll my neck and step in front of the controller. The lights dim again, restarting the simulation. The 'enemies' are noticeably faster and come in groups of three and four this time.

By the end of the round, I missed one shot, and a sheen of sweat has formed on my forehead.

Turning triumphantly on my heels, I bite back the urge to giggle when I see their shocked faces.

Ronan steps forward and takes my hand, pulling me quickly away from everyone. Blinking against the sudden bright sunlight, I jog beside him.

"Slow down!" My thighs burn.

"How did you do that?"

"Were you expecting me not to hit anything?"

He looks like he's carefully considering his answer. "I did not expect you to hit everything." He responds with honesty. "How did you do that? There would have been no reason for you to have artillery training…" He's flabbergasted, and I love it.

"Like I said, I'm the arcade top scorer," I shrug.

"What does that mean?"

"Wow, the tables have turned," my serious tone cracks. "I'm always trying to get more detail from you. It's frustrating, isn't it, asking someone something and they give you the vaguest answer possible?"

A deep crease forms between his brows as we walk out into the courtyard.

He's so impressed that I don't want to ruin it by explaining video games, but it's time to put him out of his misery.

"Video game arcades." I squeeze his hand. "They were games, electronic games that were almost exactly like that simulation. The graphics on yours were much better, and your controls have better precision, but it's basically the same thing."

"Games?"

"Yeah, kids played them for fun."

"And you were the champion?"

I'm still not sure if he understands, but I'll take the compliment. He reaches out, grabbing me in his arms, crushing me into his chest. There are several people in this courtyard, but he doesn't seem to care.

His mouth comes down on mine hard, bringing the ache back with full force. Suddenly, I don't care about the people here either. With my hands in his hair, I hold him against me, deepening the kiss with my tongue.

He groans and begins walking blindly toward the nearest building.

An evil, brilliant, wicked idea pops into my head. I wonder how much torture he can take.

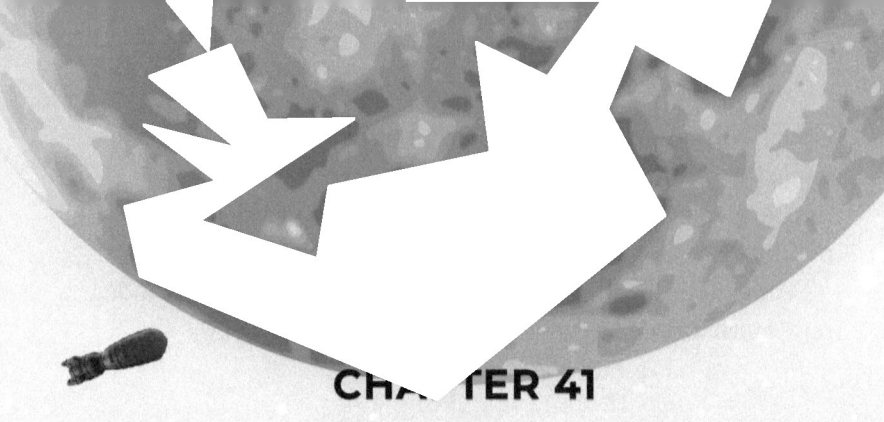
"Sit down," I point toward one of the very odd chairs on our small terrace. They are narrow and armless, like a snake when it comes up into the air, with a small curve to sit on. I guess they are well suited to the interesting architectural choices of the city.

Shaking my head, I force my focus away from the chairs and toward Ronan.

He quirks his eyebrow, watching me as he sits.

I always melt into his arms. He only has to look at me or groan lowly in his chest, and I'm putty in his hands. Today, I'm in charge. He had his way with me last night, over and over again, for hours.

He teased me earlier, and he underestimated me. Use that. I force those thoughts into my head.

"What are you doing, Ya'abe?" His voice is raspy, lust swirling around in his eyes.

Damn him. He's pulling out the big guns. Ya'abe. How dare he.

"I'm so sore," I pout innocently as I slide into his lap. My feet dangle above the floor as I straddle his hips.

This seems to sober him up, quickly. His fingers grip my hips softly. "I will fill the bathing pool with hot water."

"Bathing pool?" Please, please don't tell me they have bathtubs all this time, and I'm only just now hearing about it. When we were brought to the alien jail spa, they washed us in large whirlpools. I asked Gaia about bathtubs later, and she didn't seem to understand what I was talking about.

"Come," he stands from the chair, all of my plans suddenly abandoned. So much for that.

He leads me up several floors and into a room marked 'medical unit' on the door.

"Medical unit?"

When we enter, three An'eo freeze, watching us nervously.

"Leave," is all Ronan has to say to have them scrambling for the door.

This room looks exactly like the jail spa! Were we in the medical unit? Ronan moves around the room, gathering vials and powders. He fills one of the enormous tubs with water. It's so warm that the air starts to feel thicker. I can't wait to soak my body.

With scientific precision, I watch him measure out exact quantities of the different items he collected. When they mix with the water, the scent memory of our first bath here fills me with déjà vu.

Portable travel showers in the middle of a field were nice and all but this is going to be amazing.

Stripping my clothes, I wait with giddy anticipation.

"I will help you-" his voice fades away as he turns and finds me already naked. His jaw clenches as he picks me up and gently places me over the edge of the tub.

"Oh my god," I groan, letting myself sink to my shoulders. The slight sting of the heat melts the pain away from my body almost instantly. Pushing away from the seat on the edge, I tread water in the center of the pool. Swirling around, I turn to face him.

"Are you going to come in?"

"I am not in need of medical care." His head tilts slightly to one side.

"Jesus Christ, Ronan. Will this water make you sick or hurt you if you get in without medical need?" I thought we were past this already.

"No," he's still trying to work it out.

"Ronan, get in."

"This is a medical treatment, Nicole."

"Get in."

He huffs but pulls his shirt over his head. I watch his muscles move, tensing and flexing as he steps out of his pants. Breaking my gaze, I glide back, making sure that I'm on the opposite side of the pool when he climbs in.

"Doesn't it feel nice?" I dip down, tipping my head back to wet my hair.

"It does," he looks wary, like I'm pulling him into a trap.

Slipping below the surface, I push my arms through the water. When I resurface, I'm in the center of the pool again.

"Why are you so far away?" His eyes are glued to my wet chest.

"I'm not, I'm right here." I smile sweetly.

"Come," he holds his hand out.

"Uh-huh." I fall below the surface again for a moment. "It's not going to be that easy."

His jaw ticks. "You demanded I enter the water to toy with me?"

"Yeah, basically." I bat my lashes and swim backward, putting more distance between us.

He hums, a deep, low grumbling moan full of irritation. He moves back, sitting on the edge of the pool. Watching the water roll in droplets down his skin makes me incredibly thirsty. I wonder if all the stuff he put in here would poison me if I licked it off him?

The familiar tugging in my belly as I let my eyes wander down starts to get stronger as I set my eyes on his cock.

He's always ready.

Biting into my lower lip, I paddle closer, but still out of reach. I'm not foolish enough to think he couldn't reach out and grab me if he wanted to, but he's letting me play my game, at least for now.

"I'm curious." I tilt my head to emphasize my thoughtfulness. "Is this water safe to consume?"

"Are you thirsty?"

"I am."

"Do not drink from this pool!" His eyes are wide and completely disgusted. "I will get you a drink."

"I don't plan to drink from the pool; some of the water might get into my mouth, though." Swimming closer and looking up at him, I wonder how long it will take him to get it.

A single second, apparently. He groans, and his head falls back. His cock twitches, standing up against his stomach. "You are teasing me again."

"Yes."

Lowering himself down into the water, he grabs my arm as I try to back away. Pulling me forward, he pushes me back into the wall of the pool. I'm caged between the wall and his body, his cock pressing into my stomach.

"Would you like a drink, Ya'abe?"

Letting the tips of my fingers graze his thighs, I move upward until I can grip him tightly in my hand. His hips buck forward, and he groans, leaning into my touch. Feeling bold and free from pain and soreness, I lean forward to kiss his chest just above the water.

"Sit back down."

He spins, pulling himself out of the water to sit on the edge again. Standing on the bench in the water, I put my hands on his knees, moving slowly toward my intended target.

He tortured me with his mouth last night. I want to return the favor.

Licking a long, wet strip with my tongue flat against the underside of his shaft, I jump right in. Licking, sucking, kissing. I take my time, giving him a little bit, then taking it away. Opening wide, I carefully pull him in.

When I look up at him, I keep eye contact as I pull him as far as I can without actually choking. He slides his fingers into my wet hair, holding tight at the roots. I can feel his thighs tensing. If it's because he's trying to keep his hips still, I'm grateful. Nothing would ruin this quite like his cock killing me before we even get started.

Hollowing out my cheeks, I move my mouth up and down over him. The sounds— they get me every time. He never tries to hold back his moans, the deep, rumbling groans that start in his chest and burst through him.

"Nicole," he pants, "I will be gentle. I will not enter you if you do not want that, but…"

I ignore him, slowly moving my mouth and my hand in sync. His cock is leaking, light, salty, sweet. It's delicious.

"I can not-" A loud growl cuts off his voice as I lightly twist my hands. "Not without you."

He doesn't like to come without me, I know that, and I usually really appreciate it. But right now, I want to make him come.

Doubling down on my efforts, I move faster, letting my mouth make him slippery for my hands.

His feet are starting to move, shaking and flexing next to my calves. He's fighting it, but he will lose this battle today. There is a certain spot on the underside of his shaft, right below his tip, the frenulum. When I flick my tongue against it, his body jerks and he moans.

After several minutes, with an aching jaw, I close my mouth around him and suck, hard.

"Nic—" He sobs my name—desperate and needy.

A thick, warm spurt of cum pumps from his pulsating head. I swallow as much as I can, letting the rest leak out of my mouth and back down onto him.

With a satiated groan, he pulls himself back and grabs me. "Your turn." The fire in his eyes should intimidate me. Now that I know about this healing bathtub, nothing is off-limits.

"My turn." I nod before kissing him. I want him to taste himself on my tongue.

"We should stay here." He slides into the water with my thighs around his hips. "You will need another dip when I finish with you."

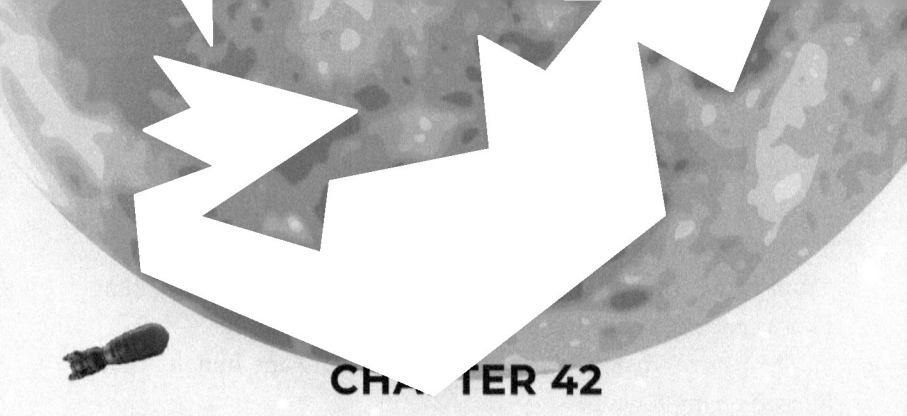

can't stop fidgeting as we eat breakfast. Olexa will be here any minute with Santi and Clarisse. We're going to tour the city. My mom would have been crawling out of her skin to be able to explore this place. Seeing new places was always her favorite, but an alien city? Forget it, she would have been unable to contain her excitement.

"You are wiggly this morning." Ronan watches me with a mixture of amusement and confusion.

"I'm really looking forward to touring the city."

Caelum's face bunches up, his mouth tipping down and his forehead puckering.

"If I had known how much you enjoy tours, I would have taken you yesterday." Ronan still looks like he's trying to figure out why I want to see the city.

"It's not just tours, it's seeing a new place, traveling, learning something new."

His lip twitches, and he nods, looking down at his plate. "Always very curious."

I feel a heated blush creep over my cheeks as the door slides open.

Jumping up, I greet everyone. Caelum isn't exactly a warm

host, but he does say a quick greeting before leaving.

"We are on the airbridge, we're ready to go when you are." Santi cranes his neck to look out the window. I can see that he's excited about the tour as well.

"I'm ready!" I answer enthusiastically.

Gaia smiles. "I am happy to show you around."

As we walk down the hallway, Clarisse pulls me aside. "How was the road trip? Things look better?"

"Things are better." I sigh, relieved. Grabbing her hand, I squeeze it gently. "I need to say thank you. You were there for me every time I needed you, no questions asked. I can't even begin to tell you how much that means to me."

"Oh, stop," she blushes and swats my hand away. "You would have done the same for me."

"That doesn't mean I can't thank you for it."

Hearing Santi's laughter from behind us, we both turn. Things have been much better between us recently. I half expected an 'I told you so' attitude from him when Ronan and I fell out, but he was only supportive. That said, it's still strange to see them together, walking and talking, even laughing. I'll have to thank him for the radio tip later.

We walk until lunch, taking in everything the city has to offer. The buildings themselves are architecturally different from home, but everything is also very similar. While Capitol City is beautiful, it's not as inviting. This city is visually fascinating and lush with gardens and trees.

"It's really beautiful here," I lean into him as we walk.

"An'eo began to build earth's first fleet twenty-nine earth years before I was born. Our father designed the Capitol City himself. This city is our mark, our contribution to An'eo and the future." I can see that he's proud.

"You said your dad designed the Capitol. Who designed this city?"

"I did."

I stop walking and jerk my body to face him. "You did?"

"Yes, I made the building plans."

"Ronan," I gape at his nonchalant demeanor. "That's amazing!"

"I would not go so far as to say 'amazing.' It is not a big deal."

"Look around you! You designed a whole city, and now we're standing in the middle of it! That's really cool!" I nudge his arm.

"Alright, alright," he rubs his hand over the back of his neck. The light blush that creeps over his cheeks and the way he's hiding his half-smile make me want to pull him back inside.

As we pass the weapons training center, I have an idea.

"Can we stop and see the weapon simulator?" I smile innocently, but he's not buying it.

"We can," his mouth twists slightly.

After Clarisse and Santi have come down from their shock at the sight of this place, I pull them aside.

"Are either of you any good at arcade games?"

"I was shit," Clarisse shrugs.

"I'm pretty good," Santi smiles. He's underselling it. I can tell, just by the glimmer in his eyes, he was more than *pretty good.*

"Do you want to run the simulation? That one," I point out, "is almost exactly like Galaxian."

His smile spreads, stretching across his face with excitement.

"I did it yesterday, and everyone was completely floored. To them, it's not a game, it's training for their weapons systems. The controls are just like old arcade games, though. They were ready to laugh at me until I aced it."

He rubs his hands together. "I'm in."

As he steps up to the controls, I notice everyone slowly, casually, making their way over to watch. Ronan tugs me to stand in front of him, his arms wrapping around me as we wait for the game simulation' to start.

"If you could put it on the hardest level," he smiles at the technician running the simulation.

When the lights dim and the enemy ships come, Santi is completely calm as he shoots them out of the sky. He's better than me.

When the last ship falls, he turns around with a passive, nonchalant look. "You want next?" He tips his chin at Ronan.

Everyone looks suddenly terrified. With their eyes fixed forward, they awkwardly stand, waiting for Ronan to react to his challenge.

His chest rumbles against my back, a laugh instantly releasing the tension in the room.

"That is the simulation that I enjoy," he points across the room to a huge, broken chunk of an airbridge.

"What is that?" I crane my neck to look at him.

"Would you like to see it?"

"I don't want to do it, I wouldn't even know where to begin."

"I will do it." The cocky grin on his face is very telling.

Everyone follows him toward the broken ship. I still haven't quite worked out how this is going to be a simulation. He steps inside of the broken piece of ship, and it raises in the air, way high up. The screen in front of it turns on to chaos. Enemy ships are everywhere. Loud, exploding sounds make the floor buzz beneath my feet. Ronan holds onto the opening in the airbridge, leaning out to shoot at the screen.

The airbridge violently shakes and starts to fall to the ground.

Ronan's silver skin gleams against the fiery explosions on the screen as he plummets toward the ground. He's so focused, he doesn't miss a single shot. Biting into my lip, I wonder if we can come back tonight. Maybe I can talk him into doing this shirtless...

The ship is connected to a lever. This is all controlled, but I can't help but to hold my breath. When he is slammed to the ground, he jumps right before impact, landing on his feet beside the heap of metal. He takes cover and continues to shoot at ships.

This is intense. I know it's not real, but it's so realistic that it's frightening. When the last enemy ship explodes, the silver on his skin fades away.

"Want to try?" He holds the gun out to me.

"Absolutely not!"

His eyes go wide, the smile slipping from his face a second before I feel it.

The ground rumbles and shakes. It's not the same as the simulation. It's deep, the earth swaying beneath us. In an instant, I'm in his arms. He holds me tightly to his chest and rushes toward the door.

"Follow me to the arena." He shouts through the creaking sound of metal. "Go!"

Several others are already gathered in the center of the open stadium. It feels like minutes pass as the ground trembles. By the time the ground finally stills, there are at least one hundred people gathered here. Everyone, human and An'eo alike, share the same fearful expression.

This is bad.

Caelum's voice booms through the air. "Ronan, I am in the control tower. Come, now."

He doesn't sound worried, he's got the same irritated growl in his voice that he always does. Maybe that's a positive sign.

"Come," he takes my hand and pushes through the crowd.

CHAPTER 43

Aside from a single crack in the walkway outside, everything looks normal. The buildings appear sturdy. A tiny glimmer of hope blooms in my chest. I was expecting catastrophic damage, rubble, and ruin. This looks manageable. This looks like everything might be alright.

From the corner of my eye, I notice a flash of movement. Olexa is sprinting at full speed across the courtyard toward the control tower. The glimmer of hope quickly fades away.

Turning to look at Ronan, he makes eye contact and gives me an encouraging nod, but it does nothing to ease the knot forming in my stomach. This is bad. Something is very wrong. His expression is closed up, completely poker-faced. He's trying to hide from me. Whether or not he realizes it, that is just as telling as if he let me see what he is really feeling.

"I will take you to your rooms," he suddenly turns, guiding me in the opposite direction.

"No, no way!" I press my heels into the ground. "I'm staying with you."

His chest moves rapidly with each breath. He doesn't have time to argue right now. He knows it. I know it. Narrowing my eyes, I wait for him to decide if it is worth wasting the time.

A gruff, angry sigh escapes from his lips before he turns and continues toward our original destination.

"We're staying together." My voice is softer now than it was just a moment ago.

The scowl on his face softens, not completely, but some.

When we reach the control tower, the cracks in the side of the building make my heart stop.

"Stay by my side," he grips my arm tightly as we make our way up. It's obvious that the building is damaged. We haven't seen anything yet, but there are times the ground feels uneven. The floor is slanting beneath our feet.

Inside the control room, I expect panic. I brace myself as we step inside. What we're met with is more frightening. No one is panicking. Everyone is pale-faced and silent—absorbed in the screens in front of them. There is no disorder, no frantic hysteria. This is too serious for that. There is no time for it. Everyone has buckled down, swallowed down their fear, and is working, as quickly as possible, to fix it.

Santi and Clarisse immediately join the others in looking at the screens. I'm overwhelmed by the sheer amount of moving parts. The screens are flashing, changing every second to reflect a new development or different set of data. I don't know where to look.

Caelum is using a strange laser tool, like a sander, to fix a deep crack in the glass that keeps the Ulaar contained.

"There are two layers." Ronan dips down slightly to speak quietly to me. "The Ulaar is behind a polymer shield that contains the radiation. The glass is a secondary layer of protection that is meant to hold in the event that the polymer is damaged."

"What happens if a person were to come into contact with Ulaar, like, what if it touches your skin?"

"Notice that Caelum is not wearing his skin armor. To date, Ulaar is the only substance that can penetrate it. If it touched you, death would be instantaneous."

"The polymer sustained no damage." Caelum looks over his shoulder. "The door is broken, the glass is cracked, and the steel track is bent. The door cannot open more than a sliver."

The glass wall surrounding the tank of swirling pinkish electricity is cracked in several places. I can see where the track for the sliding door is slightly turned inward.

"How long will it take you to have the door fixed? We need access." Ronan's voice is not soft when he addresses Caelum. The concern he had a moment ago has vanished, replaced by seething animosity.

"After this crack is sealed, I can bend the steel back without breaking it completely."

"I will go in," Ronan volunteers.

"Go in?" I turn to face him.

"Inside is a panel, a switch that suppresses the Ulaar into a cylinder below ground. We need to repair and stabilize the building without the Ulaar.

"Oh," I'm not sure why a sinking, nervous feeling tugs at my stomach. Clutching his arm, I follow his gaze to the screens. Numbers, rows, and rows of numbers scroll across the page faster than anyone would ever be able to read them. Another screen of landscape scans brings up pictures, placing them in rows, searching for damage. One row is undamaged land and structures, the other row is displaying changes in the scan. My heart sinks every time an image moves into the row, indicating changes. This earthquake did damage, by the looks of it, a fair amount.

"Nicole." Ronan steps in front of the screens, blocking my view of anything but him. His fingertips, my chin upward. His other hand is tightly wrapped around my upper arm. He doesn't speak, but he doesn't have to. I feel it. He is giving me strength.

The fear I felt a moment ago is still there, but it's like a muffled voice in the background.

"How can I help?" I look around at the screens. "Is that the Ulaar output? I can do a quick check of the numbers."

Caelum stops working to give me a quick once-over.

"Yes." Ronan moves so that I can step closer to the wall.

"Here," Olexa hands me a handheld screen to input the data into.

For a moment, everything is fine. I wish I could have known how truly fleeting it would be.

"Whoa," I turn to find Ronan as I come across a number that is higher than any I've ever seen in weeks of data entry. "This is-"

A deep cracking sound and the feeling of the world crumbling beneath my feet cut me off.

"Aftershocks," Santi yells, but it's too late.

The glass cracks, and a huge fissure runs through the entire length of the panel. Olexa and Caelum push against the door, forcing it open enough for her to slip inside. Without her weight supporting the door, it slams closed, pushing Caelum away.

Olexa runs to the panel to shut off the Ulaar but before she can reach it, the polymer cracks.

The sharp clink echoes in my head. The sound makes the whole room freeze. Ronan grabs me, pulling me down to the ground hard enough to rattle my bones.

A beam of pink light, like the sun breaking through the clouds, pierces through the broken tank. The vertical crack grows, moving the shaft of light across the room. The quiet tinkling sound of the fracture spreading is the only sound in the room. I barely notice that the shaking has stopped.

It happens so fast that I can hardly see it, but so slowly that it will be imprinted in my brain forever. Ronan jumps forward, but Santi is closer. He lunges toward the door just as the glass shatters completely. As Ronan reaches the place where the door was, he drags Olexa out by the arm. He pulls his sister out of the way of the moving beam, falling backward.

For a moment, it doesn't register; a scream echoes through the room, shrill and full of terror. It isn't until the sound stops that I realize it was coming from me.

When Ronan was grabbing his sister, Santi was slipping behind them into the room.

"Santi!" Ronan scrambles behind him.

The beam of light pierces through his neck as he smacks his hand down on the override. The damage is instantaneous. The Ulaar immediately turns dark, the fluorescent glowing light dims like a light switch being flipped.

He crumples, falling to the ground as if he doesn't have bones. I don't even have to get close to know that he's gone. In the blink of an eye, everything that he was, everything he accomplished and lived for, faded away.

The punched-out wail that comes from Clarisse stops my heart in my chest. I'm stuck, I can't move. My eyes won't leave his body. I can feel myself being lifted and carried away, but it doesn't feel real. I'm not sure if my eyes are open or closed or if I'm even conscious. Through the darkness and the pain, the only thing I know is real is Ronan. So, I lean into that.

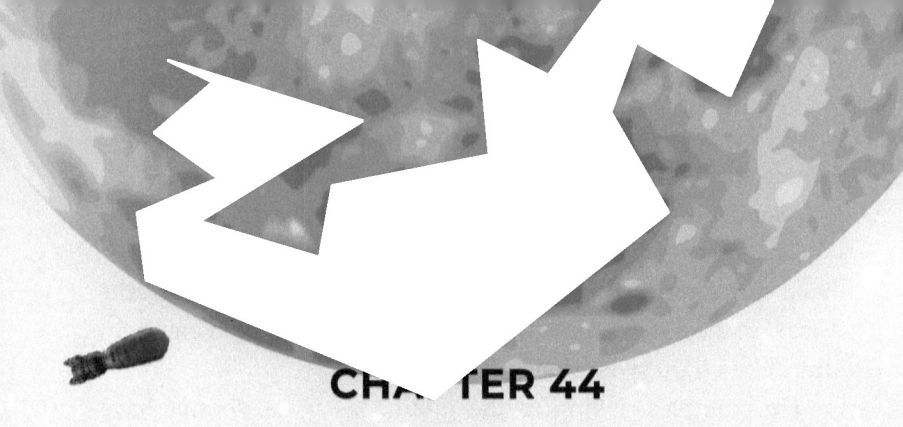

CHAPTER 44

The cold air coming in from the open terrace door makes the whole room chilly. Huddled under the mass of blankets, tucked into Ronan's body, I get flashes of memories. All of it seems so far away now.

"When I was a little girl," I don't bother to open my eyes, I know he's still awake. "I used to ask my dad to open my bedroom window in December. This is my favorite type of sleep. The air being so cold makes the bed feel warmer, doesn't it?"

"It does," he hums, letting his fingertips graze my shoulder beneath the blankets. He's so still and quiet. He's afraid of me. Afraid that if he touches or kisses the wrong place, if he says the wrong thing, I'll break.

In the hours since 'it', I have circled through the different stages of grief. Moving in and out of each emotion with rapid speed, then feeling it again. The only one I haven't felt and probably never will is acceptance. I will never accept this.

He's right to be cautious. A storm is swirling just below the surface, ready to break open, messy and violent with the slightest cause.

Bolting upright, I turn to look at him, my chin trembling. He watches me with wide eyes, frozen, waiting to be impaled by the shrapnel of this explosion.

"I never talked to him about the radio." My voice crackles and wobbles. "I wanted to thank him for telling you that cars had radios, but I never got around to it."

"I told him," he whispers so quietly I barely hear it.

"But I didn't. I didn't tell him. I should have! He should have known how much I appreciated it. Now I'll never get the chance!" I jump up from the warmth of the bed and feel the cold air hit me. A wave of emotions is rolling toward me. I can see it, but I'm powerless to stop it. I can't outrun it. I can't do anything but watch it come.

It crashes down on my head, sweeping me up in the current. I'm rolling and tumbling below the surface, but I can't reach it to take a breath.

"This is the end for us," I choke, staring at him as the new realization punches a hole in my chest.

"No, Nicole, it is not. I will always protect you-"

"No!" A mangled scream rips from my throat." "You don't understand. This is the end! He was the last human man. With his death, that's it, we're extinct! Another human child will never be born."

He reaches for me, but I step away.

"You wanted this, didn't you?" I hear the things I'm saying, but I can't stop them. Nicole—the rational, thinking Nicole— is hiding in the corner, watching this, powerless to stop it. Even as the hate-filled words spew from my mouth, I know I'm being irrational. "You don't care about what happened to him because you think he's not deserving of life. So lowly and insignificant that it's better that he's dead!"

"Nicole," his voice is still soft, even with the pain in his eyes.

"No!" I'm hysterical, screaming. "Admit that you are happy he's gone because now, no more weak, greedy, worthless humans to muck up your planet!"

I didn't want to have a child with him. To my knowledge,

neither did Clarisse. I can't pinpoint what it is about the idea that makes me cling to it. Even if he had lived, the likelihood of a human child being born is extremely low.

Taking a cautious step forward, he puts his hands out in front of him. He approaches me the way one would approach an injured, feral animal.

"Nicole, Dr. Santiago sacrificed himself and, in doing so, possibly saved your life. I have never held anyone, human or An'eo, in such high regard. I know that I do not understand your pain." His voice is so gentle it makes me hurt more. "We are not in the same situation. However, I can say with certainty that I would feel profound sorrow. I realize that my previous judgments have caused you to believe that I do not care about his death or the survival of your race, but you are wrong, Ya'abe."

When he finishes speaking, I just stare at him. I'm trembling, my body vibrating with the overwhelming intensity of everything I feel.

Deep down, in the lowest, darkest part of my brain, I hear what he's saying, and I want to kiss him for it. I want to jump into his arms and beg him to hold me and never let me go. He's so sweet and understanding. I'm throwing my worst at him, and he's calm. He's taking it on the chin and being loving to me in return.

Unfortunately, all of my other emotions are burying that feeling alive.

I also want to scream at the top of my lungs. I want to cry. I want to break things. I want to hide under the covers and never come out. I want to fight him. I need to let out the rage I feel.

"He was a hero. He died saving everyone else! He didn't deserve it! He lived through everything I lived through. His pod didn't break. He survived being unfrozen and reanimated. He deserved a chance to live!" I am weeping.

"He did deserve to live."

"They all did! Humans should have had a chance. Why didn't anyone come to help them? There was so much left for us to do and to learn. We could have been so much more if we had just been given the chance..." I start to fall to my knees, but he catches me. He cradles me in his arms.

He doesn't speak. We sit until I pass out from exhaustion.

It doesn't feel like any time has passed when I wake up, blinking in the dark room all alone.

"Roman?" My voice is almost completely lost.

Normally, I would sit and wait for him to return, but tonight, I'm out of sorts.

As I wander aimlessly through the hallways, I'm comforted by the cold, dark emptiness. I haven't seen a single person. I'm starting to think I'm the only one left here. With each step, I feel stronger and more sure of myself. I need to find Ronan and hug him. He was so sweet while I accused him of being happy that Santi died. Now, on top of all of the sadness and grief, I have guilt.

Ronan's voice cuts through the silence as I walk past a closed door.

He's asking Caelum to back him. It's obviously out of context but I don't like the sound of it. It's like he's begging. Any situation where Ronan has to beg Caelum for something can't be good.

"Ronan, please." Olexa is there, too. "Think about this." She's begging him. The fear in her voice sends a shiver down my spine.

"I have, it must be done. It is the only way, the right way."

I can't listen anymore. This is obviously a private conversation. Taking a deep breath, I knock lightly and wait.

With wide eyes, Ronan slides the door open. "What are you doing awake?"

"You were gone." My cracked voice wobbles.

"Nic-"

I launch myself at him, holding him as tightly as my arms will allow.

"I'm sorry. I'm sorry. I didn't mean it. I was a horrible, mean bitch. I know you aren't happy he died."

"Do not apologize."

Without turning around, he leaves the room, carrying me in his arms. Despite everything- the world shaking at any given moment and buildings crumbling- I feel safe in his arms.

"The airbridge is prepared for departure when Clarisse wakes. Macsen will accompany me at the controls. A mourning dinner will be prepared when we arrive."

"You planned a mourning meal for Santi?" My eyes well up with tears.

"Of course. He deserves the honor."

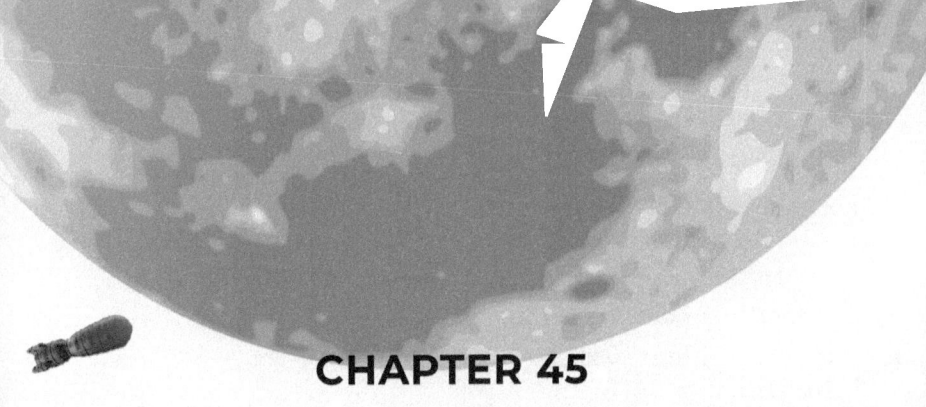

CHAPTER 45

The six-hour silence on the way back to Capitol City feels like a weight on my shoulders. I will myself to sleep, to let my eyes drift closed, but I can't.

Memories of the day Gaia and Macsen saved us, of the first time we rode in a sairbridge, keep flashing in my mind. I was terrified. I'm sure Santi was, too. He didn't seem afraid, though. If he was, he didn't show it.

My heart is in my throat as we touchdown. There are flowers everywhere. Flowers and thousands of An'eo in the courtyards and lining the walkways to the Capitol building. With blurry, tear-filled eyes, I clutch Clarisse's hand.

Even surrounded by thousands of people, the walk into the building is silent, eerily so. No one speaks, moves, or even breathes.

The dining room is set with a beautiful spread of exotic fruit and flowers. It looks too beautiful to eat. The vibrant colors and soft, sweet smells feel too cheerful for a mourning meal.

Sant's chair is flipped upside down, making it unusable for anyone else.

When everyone has gathered around the table, Ronan begins to speak just as he did at the last mourning meal.

"You are lost for now.

May the universe hold you,

We will not forget.

May the sun enfold you."

He looks up to make eye contact with me and Clarisse. "Speak your dead."

"Dr. Arturo Santiago." We say together in raspy, shaky voices.

Forcing down a few bites of food under Ronan's watchful gaze, I try to focus on anything other than the pounding in my head. I've cried too much in the past twenty-four hours. My brain feels swollen, and my eyes burn.

"Eat one more piece of fruit." Ronan leans in and whispers as he scowls at my nearly full plate.

I turn, ready to reply with some snarky response about not being a child. When our eyes meet, the look on his face stops me. He's not being bossy, he's worried about me. Acting like a child about someone who is treating you like a child won't help.

Taking another piece of fruit, I swallow it, ignoring the nausea.

When the meal is over, I still feel heavy. This is it. We've had his mourning meal, and we've honored his memory. Now, it's time to move on, but it doesn't seem like enough. He deserves more for what he did for us. He deserves more for being the last of his kind. The very last human male.

"Come," he whispers, taking my hand.

"Where are we going?"

"You will see." His face is somber as he leads me outside. The sun is just starting to set, the purple streaks in the sky reflecting off his hair. He never looks human. He's always something more. Right now, he looks like a god walking on earth, gently leading me away.

Past the gardens and the human museum, to the garage.

"Ronan, where are we going?"

"Patience."

Pouting, I sit in the passenger seat as he loads a few things into the back of the truck. I'm not in the mood to be surprised right now.

He puts on a specific song, one I don't recognize, and drives us away from the city. I want to climb into his lap, to force him to look into my eyes. I know he's holding himself back. Instead, I sit, silently, missing him even though he's right beside me.

He takes us about thirty minutes up a rocky but fairly low hill slope. At the top, he stops the car at the edge of a vista over-looking a lake. Climbing out of the truck, I'm completely mesmerized. I can't tear my eyes away from the water. Against the purple sky, the bright turquoise color seems to glow.

"I've never seen water that color before." I'm not even sure if he can hear me. He's busy unloading whatever he packed into the back of the truck earlier.

The creaking sound of the truck momentarily pulls my atten-tion back. Looking over my shoulder, I smile. Maybe for the first time in days. He's lying with his back against the windshield, his legs stretched out across the hood, with a blanket over him.

As I turn to walk back to him, a strange beeping sound and then a flash of light startles me.

"What was that?"

He smiles and holds up… a thing. It's a small, flat, silver rectangle. There isn't anything on it, it doesn't look like it opens. I have no idea what it is.

"What is it?" I climb up to lie beside him on the truck's hood.

"I built it with Gaia and Macsen. It is a camera."

"Wait, you made a car and a camera?"

"Yes."

"And you just took my picture?"

"Yes, I want to have it, to remember whenever I look at it." He pulls me close to him. Showing me how to use the very inter-esting camera he made. It's so small and flat. I don't know how a camera works, but it's hard to believe that this thing is doing the same job as the rectangular box my parents had.

Leaning into his chest, I hold it up, taking a picture of the sky. The purple and blue with An'eo in the distance.

"I will print them when we return."

"We converted a scanner to make a paper image like the one you have of your parents."

I blink back at the tears welling up in my eyes. "You thought of everything."

"I have one more thing to show you." He sits up, pulling something from his pocket.

The tiny silver disk sits in the palm of his hand. In the center of it, a pink, swirling bead of Ulaar is embedded on one side. When he holds it out to me, I'm almost nervous to take it. I don't have much faith in Ulaar right now. After hesitating, I open my palm, and he places it in the center. It's so much heavier than I was expecting; I almost drop it.

"This is a port key. Press this." He points to an almost imperceptible indentation. "It opens, and a beam of light will surround it. If you stand within the light, it will take you to An'eo."

"Are you giving this to me?"

"I am showing you. In case of an emergency, I want you to be aware."

"Ronan, do you think there is going to be another earthquake? Is this failsafe failing here, too? IS something going to happen here? Are you-"

"Nicole," he stops me by pressing a kiss to my frantically moving mouth. "The failsafe is functioning. It was tested and retested immediately after the first tremor. I am showing you, in case. That is all."

Nibbling on my lip, I force back the barrage of questions I still have. I want to ask about the bit of conversation I overheard. He was asking Caelum for a favor, and Olexa didn't seem to like the idea.

Curling back into his chest, I stare up at the stars.

"You are tired." He pulls the blanket up around my shoulders.

"It's been a long day."

I feel his lips against my temple as he holds me tightly.

"Can you tell me about your history on earth?"

He hums, his lips still gently pressed against my skin. "On An'eo, when sovereign descendants reach maturity, they are given the chance to move to a new planet to begin a new fleet. My father came to earth from An'eo the day after his fifteenth year. Forty-four earth years later, I was born. My father continued to command the Earth fleet until my twentieth year. That is when he chose me to replace him. He now rules as Commander of An'eo..."

I feel myself nodding off even though I don't want to. I want to listen to everything he's saying.

"Sleep, Nicole," his chest rumbles beneath my head. It feels like he's rocking me to sleep, and before I know it, I'm waking up in his arms as he carries me into our room.

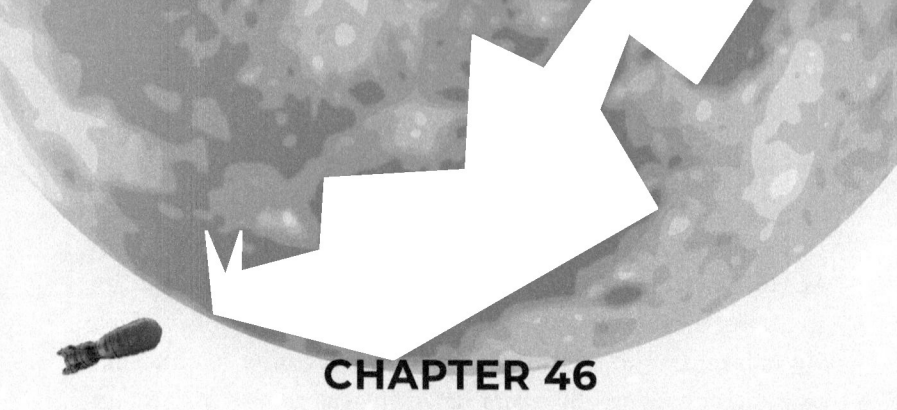

CHAPTER 46

I t's been seven days since our night under the stars.

Things are weird.

Ronan has been so distracted and distant. Everyone seems busy, rushing here and there frantically. I'm running over and over everything in my mind. What happened?

The investigators in the northern city sent back their report yesterday. Apparently, the pump malfunctioned, allowing water to build up that got hot enough to create steam. The steam pressure caused the earthquakes.

So, there you have it, I guess.

I hoped that this information would bring Ronan back to me. It didn't. I've asked him repeatedly if something is wrong or if I've somehow done something. His answer is always the same.

"No, Ya'abe." Then he kisses me softly. He holds me, kissing my forehead and running his fingers through my hair until I fall asleep each night. Then, once I'm asleep, he leaves again.

Maybe he doesn't know how to handle this sexless dynamic we've had since Santi's death. It's not that I don't want him; I always want him. I've just been so tired, I wake up exhausted.

He doesn't seem sexually frustrated. He hasn't even attempted anything. I don't think that's it...

He told me that everything here is in working order. It's been inspected more than once. That is what he said. Then, he showed me how to use a port key. Things just aren't adding up.

I don't understand why everything feels so off. Clarisse feels it, too. I can see it in people's eyes when they look at me, or rather, how they avoid looking at me. It's in the way they stop talking when we enter a room. Even Olexa and Gaia are distant.

After showering and getting ready for the day, I decide that I've had enough. I am going to go find Ronan. I'm going to make him tell me what the hell is happening. I'm not stupid or blind. He can't just 'Ya'abe' me. Not this time.

As I stomp toward the door, it slides open.

"R-Ronan?" The look on his face killed all the confidence I had built up during my shower.

He looks hurt, not physically, but it's in his eyes and his posture. I can feel it in my own chest. A deep, burning ache. He grabs me, pulling me up so that my body is crushed against his and my feet dangle above the ground.

"What's the matter? Please stop shutting me out."

"Nicole," he sounds like he hurting so badly, I pull away from his chest to look at him. Surely, there must be an injury somewhere.

"I miss you. Come back to me. Tell me what's going on. I promise, if it's bad, I can take it. I won't freak out. I'll help you!"

He doesn't say anything; he just stares, his piercing cosmic eyes searing into my skin. "I am struggling."

"Why? Tell me, let me help."

"I need you..."

"I'm right here."

The pain that flashes in his eyes is crushing.

When our lips touch, it's like a burst of pressure in my chest. I must have somehow adapted to not being able to fully take a breath because until he kissed me, I didn't even realize I couldn't. His mouth on mine lifted the invisible weight.

My emotions roll and bubble in my veins, hot like lava

oozing from my chest down through the rest of me. I've seen him every day, but I've missed him so much it hurts.

He takes a few staggering steps toward the bed as I cling to him. With my legs wrapped tightly around his waist, he tips me backward, pushing me onto the mattress below him.

With rushed, shaky hands, I pull the hem of his shirt up. I want his skin against mine. When he steps back to undress, I watch as each new inch of his skin is exposed. The world outside has faded away. Nothing and no one outside of this room exist anymore. He's taken over my senses so completely, I can't see past him.

"I love you," I gasp, my body heating up at the sight of him naked. With his clothes discarded on the floor, he comes for mine. With greedy hands that rub and squeeze, he pulls my clothes away.

When I'm naked, he looks down at me, a shiver runs through my body. His heavy, darkened eyes are full of lust as his tongue runs over his lip, hungry. There is something else there, too, something soft and sad. It's like he's seeing me for the first time, or he's trying to memorize every inch of me.

He comes back between my legs, standing at the foot of the bed. When his fingers graze my ankles, then run up my legs as he sinks down to his knees on the mattress. The trail of hot, wet kisses he leaves from my stomach up to my chest makes me dizzy.

It's like I'm hyperaware of every nerve ending. Each touch is searing and too hot, but I don't want him to ever stop.

He moves my legs, holding them behind my knees, pushing them open. My mouth falls open as I watch him inch forward. Our chests rise and fall in time, both of us gasping for air together.

His eyes never leave mine as he presses into me. Dropping one of my legs, he keeps the other pulled up over his arm. With his elbow holding his body from crushing me, he slides in completely.

He groans, and I gasp, my eyes fluttering closed.

"Tell me what love feels like. Tell me how I make you feel."

"It feels like-" I shudder as he slowly rolls his hips. "It feels like no matter how much of you I have, it's not enough. I want all the parts." I'm flustered, and speaking through the growing pressure in my stomach is almost impossible. "It's like I want to live inside your chest; that's the only way I'll ever be close enough to you."

His lips hover over mine.

"Do you feel it?" His raspy voice moans.

"Yes," I whisper, arching my chest toward his. He doesn't mean just the physical feeling of him inside of me. He means this overwhelming closeness. The crushing weight of this.

"This is how you make me feel." He connects our bodies with long, deep strokes that bring me to the edge after only a few minutes. Tightening everywhere, my muscles start to flutter and constrict. Heat spreads through my stomach, and I can't hold back the loud, begging, stuttered cries that fall from my mouth.

"Look at me," he watches me intently as he continues his slow, torturous rhythm. This feels different from any other time we've been together. This is...love. He's speaking the words with his body.

In An'eoc there is no way to say 'I love you.' He's saying it physically, in a language that only we know.

He continues his slow rhythm, holding me tightly to him.

"Kiss me," he pleads, as he starts to lose control. He growls into my mouth as I kiss him, wet and sloppy in my delirious state.

When he stills, twitching and moaning, his forehead pressed to mine, I feel all of it. The deep warmth, the way his body trembles. But there's something else, something that I can't quite name. He whispers sweet words about devotion and fate, holding me so tightly it's almost painful.

"Nicole," his voice is so soft and broken. When I press back to look at him, he turns his face away.

"Ronan, what is it?"

"I have known more life in these months with you than ever before." He sits back and holds my face in his hands. The look from earlier is back. He looks devastated. "Thank you for finding me."

I'm starting to panic. Why does it feel like this is so much more than I'm understanding it to be?

"You would tell me if something was wrong, right?" I stare wide-eyed.

"Nothing is wrong." he runs his thumb over my lips and pulls himself away.

I want to pester him, to force him to talk, but he's already retreating.

"Clarisse and Macsen would like to use the airbridge to see the salt flats. Would you come with me?"

"Ronan, really? You want to go look at salt?"

"I would like to show you." He kisses my fingertips.

"And after, we'll talk?"

He nods before kissing me so hard my lips sting. I don't want to go look at salt flats. I want to stay in bed and hold him in my arms while he explains why he's been so distant. I want to fall asleep in his arms and wake up to still find him beside me.

I have a bad feeling about this.

Clarisse seems off. Macsen hasn't spoken a single word. Every time I look at Ronan, he's already staring at me. Not a sweet, loving stare, a stare so vulnerable and longing that it punches a hole in my chest.

"Look," he comes to stand behind me, his chest to my back. When his arms wrap around my shoulders, engulfing my body in his, I let my head lean down against his arm.

I'm not going to admit this to him, but this place is sort of amazing. Enormous slabs of salt form an almost stair-like structure up the side of a mountain. If I didn't know it was salt, I would have thought it was snow, large blocks of snow.

"You like it," he whispers behind me.

"Eh, it's alright," I bite into my lip.

His fingers nip at my waist playfully just as a slight burning sensation, a small prick of pain, spreads through my neck. Clutching my skin, I turn to face him.

"I-I think something just-" I feel woozy, my vision becoming blurry. Everything is darker. Is it night? I'm disoriented and scared. How did it get dark so fast?

His arms wrap around me tightly, holding into his warm chest.

"Don't go," I whisper as my eyelids flutter closed. I feel so heavy all of a sudden like I can't keep my eyes open. Whenever I fall asleep, he leaves, rushing off to do whatever secret thing he doesn't talk about. I hope he doesn't go tonight.

"I will wait for you forever, Nicole." His voice sounds far away.

CHAPTER 47

"Dr. Isbel? Can you hear me?"

I open my mouth to respond, but only a rough, dry cough comes out. Why can't I open my eyes?

"Ronan?" I reach my arms out, feeling for him, but my arms aren't doing what I want them to do. A sharp sting at my elbow stops my movements.

"Dr. Isbel, can you try opening your eyes?"

"Where is Ronan?" The words are lodged in my throat. Instead of my question, grunting and choking sounds come out.

"Don't try to speak, Nicole, just try to open your eyes." The soft voice says, only frustrating me further. Tell me what happened.

Were we in an accident?

Thrashing violently, I hit my head against something sharp.

"Nicole, calm down, stay still. Focus on opening your eyes. You're safe, everything is alright."

Taking a deep breath, I try to open my eyes. They feel glued together. I try to bring my hand up to peel them apart, but I still can't move my arms the way I want. They move, twitching and jerking, but I can't lift them or raise them.

A strange groan, a wailing cry, fills the air, and I start to panic. Is that Ronan? I've never been so afraid in my life. I'm completely helpless. I can't see or move.

"Dr. Isbel, I'm going to put a bit of solution on your eyes to help you open them. It will feel wet, but it's warm. Is that alright?"

I hum and wait. The warm liquid feels nice against my skin, soothing the sting. All around me, there are sounds. Beeps, so many beeps. Groans, crying, coughing, and mumbled talking. I'm surrounded by noise.

"Where is Ronan?" I try to ask again, but the words don't sound right. Something is wrong. He should be here. He wouldn't leave me if there was an accident, not unless he was seriously injured.

When I try to open my eyes, they open slowly, like there is lead in my eyelids. The lights are dim but still too bright. I can't see anything but shadows. Everything is dark and fuzzy.

"Dr. Isbel," the soft voice is beside me. I think I see her, but it's still too blurry. "My name is Dr. Lint. Can you tell me where you were born?"

"Spain, Georgia," I hear the words come out, but it doesn't sound like my voice.

"Very good. What about your birthday? Can you tell me your birthday?"

"March 24, 1956."

"That's very good. Do you know where you are, Dr. Isbel?"

"No."

"Today is June 1, 2083. You are in the laboratory at the Leven-Corp research facility."

"Wait, what?" I choke. This is a dream. It has to be a dream. I don't even have time to process this before I hear her.

"No! Where is Macsen?" Clarisse's voice comes from beside me. She sounds terrified.

"Clarisse?" I call out as forcefully as I can. My voice shakes and cracks, but it's loud.

"Nic? You're here? What the fuck?" She's uncontrollably sobbing, punching out the words between wails.

"Clarisse? Nicole?"

The voice makes both of us fall silent at once.

"Santi?"

Gasping for air, I cry so hard that no sound comes out. One of my arms is able to move enough now that I can bring it up to claw at my chest. I'm so confused, and everything hurts. Where is Ronan?

What did he do? Why are we here? Santi's alive…

More voices and sounds, beeping, crying, talking. There are people all around us. Everyone is still alive, and we're all awake.

The beeping grows louder and faster as I gulp and choke. I can't breathe. I'm dying.

"Nicole, focus on the sound of my voice. Take a deep, slow breath in through your nose. You're safe." Dr. Lint is trying to calm me down, but I can hardly hear her. "We need a sedative," she yells out, calling for help as my heart pounds so rapidly it hurts.

Another shadowy figure appears beside me, and my eyes start to drift closed. All the chaos around me starts to fade away. It's peaceful and quiet now. The soft thump of my heart echoes in my ears. "*I'll wait for you forever.*" His voice is soft, fleeting, but as soon as I hear it, I know everything will be alright somehow. As I drift away, I see his eyes, the night sky, swirling purples and blues with bursts of stars. I feel calm, my tense muscles relaxing one by one. As breath fills my lungs, I reach forward, wanting to touch his cheek or run my fingers through his hair. He's too far away, growing more distant with each passing second. He's fading away completely.

"Don't go," I whisper into the darkness, but it's too late…

"Please, the beeping is driving me nuts," I croak as my eyelids flutter open. I've been slowly waking up for what feels like an hour, and I can't take another minute of it.

"Sorry, Dr. Isbel, that's your heart rate monitor. I'll turn it down for you." When I adjust to the bright fluorescent lights, I realize I can finally see. "I'm Dr. Lint. Do you remember me from before?"

"I do."

"How are you feeling? We already drew blood and did all of those things for testing, so all you have to do is relax until you're feeling well."

I hum. "I'm disoriented and hungry, but I think I'm fine." I don't know why I'm being short with her. She didn't do anything. I'm so angry at Ronan that I could scream. Did he do this? I want to punch him and then kiss him.

"For the first forty-eight hours, we have all of you on a very specific diet. I will have them bring it in to you right away. There are also a few fellow scientists who have been very enthusiastic about seeing you. Once you're up for it, I can bring them in."

"Clarisse and Santi? Please, please let me see them!"

"They mentioned that the three of you grew very close before cryosleep. It's really good that you have a support system here to reintegrate with. You can lean into that." She smiles and hands me a folder that has at least three hundred pieces of paper in it. "This is for you to fill out over the next few days."

"Wow," I plop it down in my lap. "It's a lot."

"Yeah," she huffs a laugh. "We haven't used paper for forms or documents in years. I forgot how tedious writing can be."

"What do you use?"

"Oh," she looks like frazzled. "Everything is electric now. Computers, tablets…"

My chest burns. I wonder if it's the kind of technology that the An'eo use. I wonder if I will ever not feel like there has been a hole punched through my chest again.

"I'll bring your friends." She looks uncomfortable. It must be because tears are welling up in my eyes as a response to humans using less paper. She probably thinks I'm very odd.

Leaning back in the bed, I bite into my lip to distract myself from the painful lump in my throat. Searching my mind, I try to think of the last thing I remember. How did this happen?

Large blocks of snow scattered across a mountainside and his arms around my shoulders.

We were standing at the open door to the airbridge, looking out. He had been distant for days, then he came to our room. And…

It wasn't snowing. It was salt! We were looking at the salt flats.

Then something pinched my neck! Reaching up, I feel for a wound or a scab, anything. There's nothing but greasy residue. The realization hits me so hard that it almost knocks me out. *"I have known more life in these months with you than ever before."* He was saying goodbye.

As I feel myself spiraling out of control, the door opens. Clarisse and Santi are being wheeled into the room. The nurses take an ungodly long time setting their chairs up and locking the wheels. One of them is fussing over a pitcher of water. "Make sure you're drinking this. You are behind on your hourly intake."

We exchange awkward, forced 'hellos' until they leave.

"What the fuck is happening?" Clarisse screams as soon as the door is closed and we're alone.

"I don't know," I cover my face in my hands as tears roll down my cheeks. "I don't know, I don't know but I'm freaking out. Santi! You're alive!"

"I'm alive!" He jumps out of his chair to hug me. "Clarisse told me the whole story! I don't remember any of it!"

"I wish I didn't remember it. It was awful. I'm so happy you're alive." I fist his shirt in my hands as we hold each other.

"Did you know this was going to happen?" Clarisse's chin wobbles, but she's fighting it.

I shake my head, unable to speak the words.

"I have to-" just as she starts to speak, there is a quick tap and my door is opening again.

"Dr. Isbel, I have a tray of food. This is your water pitcher. These lines," she points out, "these indicate the hour marks. You need to make sure you're drinking this much each hour."

"I will, thank you." I grimace down at the tray of...food? What is this?

"Rest as much as you need to. Don't feel like you have to be up or moving around today. Tomorrow, we will begin the reintegration process with very short sessions with a psychologist and video modules that will introduce you to the world as it is now." She smiles, and I give her an awkward thumbs-up.

At least she leaves quickly. I'm afraid to open my mouth around anyone but Santi and Clarisse. What if I accidentally blurt out the whole thing?

"Brace yourself," Clarisse shakes her head at the tray. "Whatever is on that tray has no business calling itself food."

"Why is everything so beige?" I push the different tan squares around on my plate.

"It's supposed to be easily digested and full of nutrients. It's basically flavorless." Santi's lips tip down, and he pushes his tongue against the roof of his mouth in disgust.

I force down a few bits while they tell me what they know so far, which isn't much.

We are waking up after being in cryosleep for one hundred years. Everyone is still alive.

"Maybe it was some kind of weird shared dream?" Santi shrugs.

"No." "It was real." Clarisse and I shout in unison. I can still feel his lips on mine or the way his fingertips brushed my skin.

He is real. He exists.

There is no way I dreamed him.

"Ok," he puts his hands up. "It just doesn't make sense."

"Maybe there was a black hole or something? Or maybe this is like... an alternate universe?" Clarisse clutches her chest. Her sunken eyes are red and irritated. She's been crying for a while.

"I refuse to believe that Macsen could have known about this and not told me. I didn't even get to say goodbye!" When her voice cracks, it feels like a sucker punch to my stomach.

"I think Ronan knew." I feel hollow just saying the words.

"Why do you think that?" Santi hands both of us tissues.

"He was just really distant and sad for the last week. And he said a few things that, looking back, sort of seem like goodbyes." I sniffle. "He asked me once if I would choose him. I thought he just meant in general. It was like a hypothetical, would I choose him if I had the ability to bring everyone back? I picked him. Everything was fine until you died." I swallow down the sob building in my chest. "After you died, I think he decided to... change it. I don't know. Maybe it was all some kind of mistake. A wormhole..."

I don't even know how to articulate what I feel. Of course, I want everyone to live, but it feels like my life is over.

After Santi and Clarisse are pulled back to their rooms. I spend the next hour being poked and prodded for the next round of blood tests. They also test vision and hearing, lung function, and different motor skills.

I want them to leave. To let me wallow and cry. They keep telling me that it's normal to be emotional. Nothing about this is normal. I feel selfish and sick to my stomach. My happiness in exchange for the lives of everyone on earth? I think that's a reasonable trade, but God, my heart hurts.

"Oh, before we forget," she reaches into the small cabinet. "Here are your personal belongings from your pod locker." She hands me the sealed bag with my backpack in it. "You should take a shower if you're feeling up to it. The bathroom is equipped with a bench in the shower in case you're not ready to stand for more than a few minutes at a time."

She shows me the call button in case I need help and harps on my water intake again before finally leaving.

When I'm alone, I rip the plastic. I want to look at my parents' smiling faces. That will bring me a small piece of comfort.

Pulling the bag out, I wince at how weak my arms feel. I can barely manage a small, nearly empty bag.

Opening the front pocket, I pull out my parents' picture, already smiling before I even get a look at it. "Hey, mom and dad. It's good to see you. If you're out there in the cosmos, if you're looking down, check in on him." I hug the picture to my chest as I bring my knees up, wrapping my arms around myself to weep for everything that I'll never have again.

I wonder if he's alright. Where is he? Somewhere in the sky, far away from me, he's out there.

After crying until I feel no energy left in my body, I put the picture back. Something else catches my eye. A thin, folded piece of paper that I don't recognize.

Pulling it out, my chest heaves.

When I unfold the paper, I find words written across the back that make my stomach flop.

"You have to sacrifice for the ones you love. Humans deserve a second chance."

With shaking fingers, I flip the paper over. It's the picture I took that night on the ridge. An'eo hanging above us in the blue and purple night sky. I clutch the paper in my trembling hands.

Clicking heels and low murmuring conversations in the hallway outside fill me with paranoia. Folding the paper into a tiny square, I slip it into the card organizer in the pocket of my backpack.

Slipping the backpack under my pillow, I take a quick shower.

Has it been hundreds of years since I touched him? It feels like it was just a few hours ago. Everything hurts: my skin, my hair, my teeth. The spray of the water is like sharp, stinging pellets that hit my skin.

I won't even try to force myself to enjoy this.

After getting dressed, I snuggle into my bed, hugging my backpack close. The picture that I took with the camera he made that has his handwriting on the back is inside.

A loud thud wakes me as I jolt straight up in the bed. Looking around my empty room, I realize that it was my backpack falling out of my arms onto the floor.

Pulling it up with a groan, I plop it down in my lap. It's much heavier than I remember. I know I'm weak right now, but this is ridiculous. Unzipping the large pocket, I pull a small black box out of the bottom. It feels strange in my hands. It's heavy and hard, but also rubbery.

When I pull it open, I drop it on the mattress with a shocked squeak and cover it with my pillow.

"Oh my god, oh my god..." I jump out of bed and pace around the room.

A port key.

What the fuck?

Grabbing my backpack, I search for anything else. This must come with instructions. It's not possible he gave me this thing without a manual.

He told me how to use it, but can I just do it anywhere? Anytime? Do I need to have a space suit? What is actually going to happen to my body? Is this a 'beam me up, Mr. Scott' type situation?

A bubbling, tingly feeling fills my chest. Hope and anticipation. It's not the end. I can go to him.

"I'll wait for you forever." That's what he said.

Opening my door, I look around suspiciously for anyone. The dark hallway is quiet and empty.

Sneaking on tiptoes, I search for room 416, or was it 614? Shit.

I come to 614 and freeze. If I knock, and it's not her, I need to be prepared.

Taking a deep breath, I tap lightly on the door.

After a moment, I hear shuffling inside before the door opens, revealing a tear-stained, red-eyed Clarisse.

"Nicole?" She wipes her eyes and moves out of the way so I can enter.

"I have to show you something."

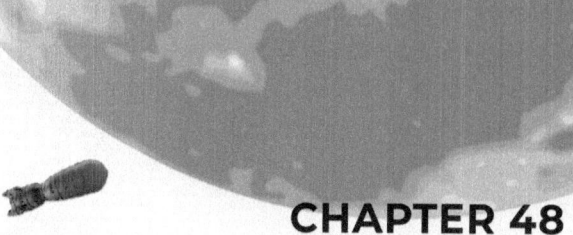

CHAPTER 48

We aren't allowed to leave the LevenCorp compound for thirty days following reanimation. Every day for fourteen days, I've had to walk around this place like everything is fine. I have to pretend that I don't have a piece of alien technology that the government of every nation would do just about anything for.

Yesterday, we had to sit through a three-hour video presentation that showed us major, newsworthy events from around the world. I held my breath as they started talking about the near meteoric collision of 2061. Clarisse's fingernails bit into my hand so tightly she almost broke the skin.

"On August 30 of 2061, researchers at NASA received images from a satellite in orbit near Mars showing an explosion. A piece of the planet, measuring an estimated ninety km, was on course to impact Earth. Instead, it was sucked back into the orbit of Mars. The impact would have been catastrophic, exterminating all life on Earth."

Everyone in the room is shocked and emotional to hear about how close scientists thought Earth was to total loss of life.

They really have no idea.

We're finally allowed to walk the grounds outside, so the three of us have spent most of our time staring up at the sky.

Everything looks normal. An'eo is gone. It's strange how quickly something abnormal can become normal. I lived twenty-seven years with nothing above me but the sky. In a few short months, An'eo hanging overhead became normal. The purple night sky was never not spectacular, but it became routine.

Looking up hurts now. I know he's out there somewhere, and I'm going to find him again.

"Are you really going to leave?"

The three of us lie in the grass, staring up at the darkening sky as the sun sets.

"Yes."

He asks me every day. Not in a judgmental way. It's like he's checking in, giving me space to change my mind.

After he died, I freaked out. Ronan did this for me. Somehow, he did all of this to give humans a second chance, a do-over. I'm not going to change my mind. I'm going back to him. Maybe it's having your cake and eating it too, but I want everything. I can't express how grateful I am that humanity has been given another chance at life. But I want him. He left me the port key because he wants me, too.

"When are you leaving?"

"As soon as possible. I know you don't understand, but every day without him feels longer than the last. I just-"

"I don't understand, but," he hesitates, "I guess I do, too. You love him."

"I want to come with you," Clarisse suddenly says. She's been silent all day. When we ask, she just nods that she's fine.

My face cracks into a huge smile before I can stop it. I knew something was wrong with her. I was silently praying it was nothing serious.

"I've been thinking about it all day. It might be a terrible idea. Macsen didn't leave me any signs that he wants me there, but I'm going to try, anyway. I have to. If I don't try, I know I'll regret it forever."

"I think you're both crazy, but…" he sighs. "I'll never say a word."

I grab both of their hands and squeeze.

After the sun sets completely, we start to walk back toward the housing unit.

"Can you do it inside? Should you be out in a field or something?" For someone who thinks this is a crazy idea, he's been really helpful in ironing out the details.

"I don't know. I wish I had asked more questions when he showed me how to use it. I think we should do it outside. We were outside when he showed it to me."

As we reach the door, we're met by Dr. Lunt and Dr. Katz, the lead lab technician.

"Dr. Isbel, can we see you for a moment?"

"Sure."

Clarisse and Santi stand and follow us into the building, joining me in the awkward silence. Once they split from us, the doctors turn to me.

"There is an anomaly in your blood work. We would like to draw again and retest."

Fuck.

"Sure, yeah. "Is something wrong?" I try to appear the right amount of nervous. Nervous like your bloodwork is abnormal. Not nervous like you know your bloodwork is abnormal because you're Sa'nu to an alien, and when your souls bound, it also modified your blood…

How did I not think of this before? He said that your blood ties together. I never put it together that mine might be different.

"Yes, we believe the anticoagulants or preservatives in your test collection vials must have been contaminated. We've run several different panels since waking you. Some of your levels are not registering correctly. We just want to rerun them and check. It has to be a malfunction of the computer or the anticoagulants in the vials. Don't worry."

"Oh, ok," I try to smile, relieved, but I don't think it looks that way.

"Are you alright?"

"Yeah, I'm just a bit light-headed. I was on my way to grab a quick snack and some orange juice when you stopped me."

"This doesn't need to be a fasted blood draw. I don't want you to feel worse. Go ahead and grab a snack and come back in about an hour."

"Thank you, Dr. Lint." Now, I am smiling with relief.

I'm trying to walk casually, but it's coming out as more of an awkward walk-jog combo. Santi and Clarisse are wide-eyed as I burst through the door, closing it quickly and leaning against it.

"Mayday, Mayday, Mayday! We've got a huge problem. I need to leave... now."

"What?" Santi is instantly tense.

"I'm ready, let's go." Clarisse pulls a backpack out from under her bed.

My panic is temporarily forgotten as I stare at her.

"What?" she shrugs. "I'm ready."

"My blood work is fishy. They are going to lock me in a lab and do science experiments on me." My hysteria comes back in full force as I start to hyperventilate.

"Ok, what if you go somewhere on the compound that isn't very busy?"

"I have no idea how this works. He said a light comes out of it. What if it's like the bat signal and everyone sees it? What if we have to stand in it for ten minutes before anything happens? We have to leave."

"Ok," he nods and rubs his chin.

"Ok?" I'm frantically pacing back and forth in front of them.

"Go get your stuff. Meet us at the back door, the one that all the employees use for smoke breaks."

"What if there are people back there?"

"It's after hours. This isn't a prison; we aren't being heavily guarded. I have an idea."

"I'll meet you there in two minutes!" I run out of the room.

Quickly checking to make sure I have all of my most precious belongings, I throw the backpack over my shoulder and rush out the door.

"This," he points to the small, dimly lit service road. "This is only used for deliveries. The gate at the end of the road might be unmanned right now. We'll see. When we get there, if there is a guard, I have a plan."

The three of us crouch down and run across the delivery bay toward the way out.

"What if they question you?" Clarisse whispers.

He chuckles and speaks at a normal volume. "I'm sure they will, but what are they going to do, torture me? Even if I say aliens abducted you, they'll never believe me."

"I guess that's true."

As we approach the gate, we run along the road, hidden among the trees. There is a small light on in the guard kiosk.

"Alright, it looks like there is a guard." He takes a long, slow breath. "I'll distract them. You run toward the gate. Stay hidden."

For a moment, no one moves. We all just stare at each other. This is it. Santi pulls both of us into a crushing hug, squeezing us in his arms. Tears blur my vision as Clarisse sniffles into his chest. I don't know what to say, no words will come. We lived through something profound and life-changing together. Even if I never see him again, there will always be a place in my heart for him.

He nods, understanding the unspoken plea in my eyes. The appreciation, the love even, that I feel for the last human man on Earth.

"If you ever find yourselves on Earth again, look me up," he smiles genuinely before running into the middle of the road, yelling loudly for help.

Holding hands, we duck down low and run behind the cover

of the trees toward the gate. The guard runs out, shining a flashlight down the road toward Santi.

"Where am I? Please, help me! I don't know where I am!" Santi yells loudly. He sounds afraid and disoriented. The guard calls for help and rushes toward Santi, who collapses on the ground.

At the gate, a large metal plate is standing up, blocking any vehicles from driving in. We can climb it fairly easily and just like that, we're out.

"Now what?" Clarisse asks once we stop running.

"Now, we go to the storage lot. They promised that everything we kept there was stored safely. Let's go see if they were telling the truth." I shrug. This is the worst planned escape to an alien planet ever.

The storage facility was less than two miles from the research compound, but it feels like we've been walking forever. Every other step, we look back over our shoulders, sure that someone is following us. Coming to drag us back.

"Isn't it weird how it feels like I dropped my car here yesterday? So much has happened. It's been one hundred years; we lived a complete life for months in a different world, but I remember it all. It's like the memories run side by side."

"Hopefully, the car still runs like it was dropped off here yesterday," she looks nervously behind her again.

The road opens into an intersection with the storage facility just across the street. Large overhead lights illuminate a huge lot. My storage unit is in there, number 1592.

The fence that used to surround the lot is gone. It's clean and well-lit, but otherwise, it looks abandoned.

"They said mechanics connected new batteries and replaced the belts in the cars. It was part of our contract. Upon waking, any vehicles left in storage would be serviced. I hope they did it." Everything hinges on this. If they didn't take care of my car, we're stuck here.

Walking through the rows of storage garages, we finally

make it to mine. My fingers shake as I put the key into the lock and turn. The heavy metal door slides up, revealing my car under a dusty tarp.

"Fuck. That's not a very promising sign."

Pulling the tarp away and swatting away the dust, we open the hood and stare down at the empty space where a battery should be.

"Well, shit." Clarisse turns around and leans against the car, rubbing her face.

"Ok, this is fine. Let's think."

After several minutes of silence, I close the hood. I wanted to drive out to where my parents are buried. I wanted to say goodbye to them before leaving. I've been clinging to the idea that it was the perfect place, the only place.

"I need to be more flexible." I sigh and open my backpack. "The lights here are bright. If this port key shines brightly, it probably won't be noticeable here. We're behind rows of other units, hidden from the road. Here is as good a place as any, don't you think?"

She smiles. "I think so."

Closing my eyes, I take a slow breath. Setting the small silver disc on the ground, we make nervous eye contact. Holding tight to the straps of my backpack, I look up at the midnight blue sky. He's out there, waiting.

As soon as I press my finger into the indentation, a dim, white light glows around us. Stepping forward, we stand in the center of the warm circle. Everything feels soft. My skin tingles, and a sleepy feeling washes over me. It feels like I'm floating, flying, I'm weightless.

When my eyes flutter open, I'm surrounded by four silver An'eo. The lasers from the weapons they've pointed at us hover over my chest.

NOTE FROM THE AUTHOR

Dear Reader,

I wanted to take this opportunity to thank you. Writing books is my dream, and knowing that you've taken the time to read them means everything to me. I can't express enough how grateful I am for your support. If you enjoyed the story, it would mean the world if you left a review. Your thoughts help other readers discover the book. Even a few words make a huge difference! If you're not able to, that's okay—I'm just happy you're here. Thank you for being a part of this journey with me. I appreciate you more than you know.

With gratitude,

Myranda

ABOUT THE AUTHOR

A bonafide motha' to five kids under the age of eight, Myranda requires no fewer than 2 cups of black coffee (2 sugars) each day to support her habits and has finally built up the courage to publish her work. She enjoys noise-cancelling headphones and long waits in school pick-up lines and can change a diaper one-handed while blindfolded.

ALSO BY MYRANDA RAE

Contemporary

When I Whisper His Name - A Big Brother's Best Friend Romance

Unplanned - A one-night stand turns into an office romance

Lewd & Lascivious - Lawyers, office politics, and a book boyfriend to die for.

The Void He Fills - An artist and her physical therapist do more than heal her body.

Pink - A workplace romance with a twist.

What's Done in the Dark - The Ruler of The Underworld finds true love in the Hades & Persephone retelling.

Paranormal/Shifter

Alphas, Kings & Playthings - She has trained for years to be the Alpha Kings breeder. But then she meets his brother…

Hardest to Love - A vampire prince falls for a human woman, and it's happily ever after—for a while.

Beast - The hellhound drags a fairy down to The Underworld.